CW00739285

DEATH ON THE HEATH

DEATH ON THE HEATH

Louise Brindley

To Greta, with love and best
wishes, from Louise. (Knowing
you prefer Crime fiction rather
than Soppy romance.)

This first world edition published in Great Britain 2003 by
SEVERN HOUSE PUBLISHERS LTD of
9–15 High Street, Sutton, Surrey SM1 1DF.
This first world edition published in the USA 2003 by
SEVERN HOUSE PUBLISHERS INC of
595 Madison Avenue, New York, N.Y. 10022.

British Library Cataloguing in Publication Data

Brindley, Louise
    Death on the Heath
    1. Women authors, English - Fiction
    2. Serial murder investigation - England - London - Fiction
    3. Detective and mystery stories
    I. Title
    823. 9'14 [F]

    ISBN 0-7278-6016-X

Typeset by Palimpsest Book Production Ltd.,
Polmont, Stirlingshire, Scotland.
Printed and bound in Great Britain by
MPG Books Ltd., Bodmin, Cornwall.

For Ollie, Jim and David Selby.
My Family. Bless Them.

One

G erry Mudd, better known to her legion of fans as the crime novelist Geraldine Frayling, had insisted on driving Bill Bentine to Heathrow, to make certain he got there in one piece.

Assuming a cramped position in the passenger seat of her Mini, not quite certain where to put his legs, the kneecaps of which seemed perilously close to his chin, Bill closed his eyes whenever his intrepid chauffeuse approached a roundabout, road junction or a set of traffic lights, thinking longingly of his roomy Golf hatchback in the garage of Gerry's house in Hampstead, hoping and praying he'd live to see it again on his return from America.

With a sideways glance at her companion, 'What's up, Bill?' Gerry asked concernedly. 'Didn't you sleep well? You've scarcely opened your eyes since we set off.'

Despite their recent engagement, she and Bill weren't sleeping together. Self-confidence had never been Gerry's strong suit, due to her weight problem. Still a stone and a bit over the odds, she had jibbed at the thought of getting into bed with him looking like a beached whale which a group of animal activists, given the chance, might well attempt to roll back into the sea.

The thought occurred that during his month-long trip to America, she would stick to a low-calorie diet, however boring, and take up jogging as a form of exercise, so that on his return home, she might well have shed a few pounds of her excess baggage. She did so want to look slim and svelte on their wedding day come September, eight months hence. Not as an elderly matron with a toy-boy in tow, but as a fitting bride for a lithe and lean groom bearing a strong resemblance to Robert Redford.

1

At Heathrow, both shaken and stirred, Bill said urgently, 'Promise me you'll keep out of trouble while I'm away.'

'What kind of trouble?' Gerry enquired mildly.

'Well, *you* know! Ferreting about, poking your nose into other folk's business, dodging deranged serial killers!'

'Ferreting about? Well I like that!' Gerry said indignantly. 'There was I, risking life and limb to bring Christian Sommer and his accomplices to justice, and *you* call it "ferreting about". Furthermore, I wouldn't have poked my nose into their business if they hadn't poked theirs into mine to begin with!'

'I know, love, and I'm sorry. It's just that my blood runs cold when I think how close I came to losing you. After all, four attempts on your life took some swallowing.'

'So did a couple of feather pillows held over my face, come to think of it. Not to mention being damn near barbecued in my bed, and being half strangled to death by Anita Temple that night I hefted a Jacobean armchair through the window of Millie Carslake's antiques shop, remember?'

'Remember? How could I ever forget?' Bill shuddered slightly. 'The reason why I'm begging you to steer clear of trouble while I'm away.'

'Not to worry, Bill, I'll be as good as gold, and that's a promise.' Her face puckered suddenly in view of their imminent separation. His flight had already been announced. Any minute now he'd be on his way to New York. She said, 'I'll miss you like crazy. You will take good care of yourself? Have you packed plenty of vests, by the way?'

'Vests?' Bill looked startled. 'I don't wear – vests.'

'You don't? Well how was I supposed to know?'

Hauling her into his arms to kiss her goodbye, 'You might have done if you'd played your cards right,' he reminded her teasingly. And then he was gone, a tall figure in a trench coat, carrying an overnight bag, one of a throng of fellow passengers jostling towards an aircraft bound for the Big Apple.

At home, loneliness struck Gerry amidships. The house felt empty without Bill, her agent, business manager and husband to be, on his way to America to sell rights in her current Virginia Vale thriller, *The Blasted Heath*. How she would manage to survive without his comforting presence in her life for a whole month, she hadn't a clue.

Throughout the traumatic events of the so-called 'Antiques Murders' of last autumn, he had become her shield and defender, her 'guardian angel', finally her saviour, without whom she might well have ended up dead in her hospital bed, by means of suffocation – a pillow held over her face by a woman she had believed to be a friend, not a deadly enemy.

Sensing danger, Bill had rushed into the room, in the nick of time, to wrest the pillow from the hands of the would-be murderess and held her wrists in a vice-like grip until the police burst in to exchange Bill's hold on the woman's wrists for a set of handcuffs.

Even so, when on Christmas Eve, he had paid her the supreme compliment of asking Gerry to marry him, and she had accepted his proposal, a niggling seed of doubt had remained that she was not really his type at all. Bill, she knew, or thought she knew, had a penchant for slender women who looked good in bikinis. So why choose her? Plump, to put it mildly.

Right, she thought, the sooner she started jogging, the better, not to mention clearing her refrigerator of all the fattening food she loved best – sausages, bacon, ice-cream and Black Forest gateaux – in favour of fish, fruit and vegetables. *Yuck!* Moreover, she hadn't an item of jogging gear in her wardrobe, which meant a trip to Hampstead Village to purchase a track-suit and trainers, plus grub relevant to the new-look Gerry Mudd.

Up early next morning, following a breakfast of muesli, skimmed milk, raisins and a banana, and wearing her new jogging gear, she shuffled self-consciously down the road from her Victorian villa which she had nicknamed 'The Eyrie', then uphill to Hampstead Heath, puffing and panting all the way.

As she got into her stride, or so she imagined, the last thing she needed was the appearance of a distraught young woman, running towards her, waving her arms, and babbling incoherently about a missing dog and a man over yonder in the bushes of a nearby spinney.

Gerry had heard of kidnapping, but *'dognapping'*? Well, one lived and learned. Grinding to a halt, she said breathlessly,

3

'Not to worry, they can't have gone far. Have you tried whistling?'

'Huh?' The girl stared at her bemusedly. 'The dog isn't missing, it's the other way round! Well don't just stand there! Come and see for yourself!'

This shouldn't happen to a dog, Gerry thought. But it *had* happened to a dog – a lurcher who, nosing round in the spinney, had come across the body of a man in a shallow grave covered with a scattering of damp earth and rotting leaves.

He was possibly a tramp by the look of his clothing – ragged trousers bound at the ankles with twine; ex-army boots and greatcoat, as if the poor devil, seeking refuge from the bitter winds scourging Hampstead Heath, had settled down to sleep in a roughly hollowed-out cradle of earth, never to see the dawn of a new day.

The body must have been there for some time, Gerry reckoned, by its advanced state of decay. Thankfully the face, half covered by a balaclava helmet, was scarcely visible, apart from the empty eye-sockets and the remains of his nose. At least the unknown man had one devout mourner at his graveside, the lurcher who, lifting its muzzle, gave vent to a piercing howl of misery and despair.

'Oh God, what on earth shall we do?' The girl was shivering violently, wringing her hands, teeth chattering.

Taking command of the situation, 'We must report this to the police right away,' Gerry said firmly, feeling in her pocket for the mobile phone Bill had given her as a going-away present, for use in an emergency, wishing to heaven she'd stayed home to cook herself a full English breakfast, and to hell with the calories. Now here she was, faced yet again with police involvement in her personal life, as she had been last summer when the discovery of her gardener's body, in her tool-shed, had triggered the series of brutal murders linked to that of her alcoholic handyman, Liam McEvoy.

'The *police*?' the girl said huskily. 'Couldn't we just go away? Pretend this never happened?'

'Afraid not.' Gerry regarded the girl doubtfully. 'Why? Unless you've got something to hide?'

'No, I swear I haven't! It's just that . . . the truth is, I'm scared stiff of losing my job. You see, the dog isn't mine.

4

It belongs to my employers, and I was told not to let it off its lead. They'd sack me on the spot if they knew I'd disobeyed their orders. Besides, they are well known people who wouldn't want to get involved in a police inquiry.'

'Oh, come on,' Gerry said impatiently, 'letting a dog off its lead is scarcely a sacking matter, and I can't see why they should become involved in the police inquiry. Who are they, anyway?'

'Their name's Lazlo,' the girl said miserably, close to tears.

'You mean Elliot Lazlo and his wife?' Gerry frowned. She had heard of them, of course. Hadn't everyone in this neck of the woods? He a renowned biographer, his wife, Dorothea, a talented artist whose exquisite paintings sold for vast sums of money at Sotheby's or Christie's, so that owning a Dorothea Lazlo painting was tantamount to owning a winning ticket in a roll-over lottery.

Thrown off her stride momentarily, 'Hang on just a sec,' Gerry demurred, 'are you telling me that Dorothea Lazlo is still alive and kicking? I thought she had died some time ago. I read somewhere that she was seriously ill in St Benedict's Hospital, not expected to live, having received the Last Rites from a Roman Catholic archbishop, no less.' Gerry sighed deeply, 'Well, going to "head office" obviously paid off in her case.'

Curiosity getting the better of her, 'What's your name, by the way, and how come you came to work for the Lazlos in the first place?' Gerry asked the girl responsible for dragging her into this mess.

'My name's Annie Scott. I answered an ad for a home help cum dogsbody, and I got the job.'

Intrigued, 'And what are dogsbodys supposed to do – apart from walking the dog?'

'A bit of everything. I help out in the kitchen, do the washing-up, peel potatoes, run errands, make beds, light fires, dust and polish: set the mistress's trays ready to take up to her room. You name it. Not that I mind. I have a nice room of my own, and the pay's good.'

'I see. So Mrs Lazlo is bedfast, I take it?' Gerry frowned sympathetically, remembering some of the woman's pictures she had once seen in an art gallery window. Exquisite paintings. How cruel that illness had robbed so talented an artist of her mobility.

Annie appeared more agitated than before. 'The mistress ain't bedfast,' she said sharply, 'if it's any of your business. She just likes her breakfast in bed. Well, are you going to phone the police or not? It's freezing cold standing here, an' *I* ain't forgotten that dead bloke in there, if *you* have!'

Casting a fearful glance towards the spinney, she added, 'All well an' good for the likes of you, with nowt better to do. A lady of leisure, I daresay, but I *need* my job, I really do, an' I should've been back half an hour ago.'

'Sorry,' Gerry said contritely, tapping in 999 on her mobile. 'Right, well that's taken care of. The police will be here soon. Now I'll ring the Lazlos. Just give me their number and I'll explain that you've been unavoidably detained, unless you'd care to ring them yourself, that is?'

'No, I'd rather you did,' Annie demurred. 'The master ain't always in the best of tempers at this time in the morning. Besides, it's *your* phone!'

'I see. On a short fuse, is he?' Gerry remarked, prodding the Lazlos' number. 'I wonder why?'

Annie said lamely, 'It's just that he has a lot on his plate at the moment, with a book to finish to a deadline, and one thing and another. What I mean to say is, he can't always get on with his work when madam's in one of her airy-fairy moods, wanting him to be with her all the time.'

Gerry held the phone away at the sound of a harsh male voice in her earhole. The voice said, 'Who is this? What do you want at this hour of the morning?'

Stifling a strong impulse to say, 'Do you know your house is on fire?', instead Gerry responded charmingly, 'Mr Lazlo? Sorry to disturb you, but something unpleasant has occurred involving a Miss Annie Scott.'

'What the hell are you on about?' The voice on the line was far from charming. 'How did you get hold of this number anyway? It's ex-directory.'

'Annie gave it to me,' Gerry explained cautiously.

'Then she had no damned business! Where is the wretched girl anyway?'

'Annie's on Hampstead Heath,' Gerry replied coolly, 'awaiting the arrival of the police in connection with a body she discovered whilst exercising your dog. Needless to say, the "wretched girl" is in a state of shock, so is the dog. As for your wife's breakfast tray, you'd best take it up to her yourself, hadn't you? Well, goodbye Mr Lazlo. I can't say it has been a pleasure talking to you, because it hasn't!'

'No, don't hang up! A body you say? But that's incredible!'

'Oh, I don't know. There's a lot of them about, if you know where to look. I came across three of them recently as a matter of fact. One in my garden shed, another on a mortuary slab, the third in a smugglers' cave in Robin Hood's Bay. Easy peasy, no problem. I have a talent in that direction.'

'This is no laughing matter,' Lazlo said severely. 'Just who are you, anyway? If this is some kind of hoax call . . .'

'Who's laughing? I'm not, I assure you, and this is no hoax, believe me!'

Lazlo did believe her. He said, less abrasively, 'I'm sorry. Please tell me more about the – body. Is it that of a man or a woman?'

'A man,' Gerry said shortly. 'A tramp, judging by his clothing.'

'Any suspicion of – foul play?' Lazlo asked uneasily.

'That's not for me to say,' Gerry said piously. 'That's up to the police pathologist to decide, though I daresay it won't take him long to suss out the bullet hole in the poor bloke's greatcoat.'

'You mean to tell me the man was – murdered?'

'No, I don't think so,' Gerry supplied cheerfully. 'My belief is that he was already dead, from exposure, before someone fired a bullet into his heart to make certain he was was dead. A matter of deduction really. You see, had he been shot before he died, there'd have been a lot of blood on the greatcoat he was wearing. There wasn't. You see, Mr Lazlo, dead men don't bleed!'

She added pleasantly, 'Sorry, gotta go now. The police have just arrived.'

Here I go again, she thought, up to my neck in trouble once more despite Bill's warning to steer clear of it.

Thankfully, this time she would not be faced with her old protagonist, Detective Inspector Clooney, who had quit the Force last Christmas. At least she thought he had done so. Now here he was, coming towards her as large as life and twice as ugly.

'Oh no,' she wailed, 'not you again? What on earth are you doing here? I thought you'd retired.' Tact had never been Gerry's strong point.

Clooney smiled grimly. 'I could ask you the same question. Rather odd, isn't it, this penchant of yours for finding dead bodies in unlikely places?'

'I didn't find it, the dog did,' she responded sharply. 'I just happened to be in the wrong place at the wrong time, as usual. I was jogging along the path, minding my own business, when the girl over yonder hurried towards me, waving her arms and babbling about her dog having gone missing. Well, what was I supposed to do, keep on jogging?'

'I see. So just how and when did the body enter into it?'

'When the dog discovered it in the spinney,' Gerry explained.

'Then what?' Clooney demanded.

'Well, the girl, Annie Scott's her name, dragged me into the spinney for a look-see. The dog was sitting near the grave, howling its head off. Obviously the man was as dead as mutton, so I phoned for the police. Ask Annie, if you don't believe me.'

'Oh, I *shall*,' Clooney assured her unpleasantly. 'I shall require detailed statements from the pair of you when the SOC officers have completed their initial investigations into the manner of death of the deceased, whether by natural causes or foul play. Hopefully the former. If not, need I remind you, Miss Frayling, of the questioning necessary to arrive at the truth of the matter?'

'No, I guess not,' Gerry acceded miserably, remembering the grillings she'd received from DI Clooney in connection with the 'Antiques Murders' of last year, when he'd tried his damnedest to prove her guilty of a series of crimes she hadn't committed. Of which, in the long run, she had proved to be entirely innocent, thanks to Bill Bentine.

She said shakily, wishing that Bill, her guardian angel, was here with her right now, 'See here, Inspector Clooney, my belief is that the poor devil, in that grave over yonder, died of exposure long before someone who wanted him dead fired a bullet into his heart. And if you think that "someone" was me, you need your brains testing! After all, why should I? I'd never clapped eyes on the man before.'

Prepared to ignore Gerry's remark concerning his cranial matter for the time being, Clooney could not so easily dismiss her reference to a bullet hole in the dead man's heart.

He said pompously, 'That is up to the pathologist, not you to decide,' wishing to high heaven that he had not been prevailed upon to postpone his retirement until a new DCI had been appointed to take charge of the Hampstead Police Station. Had he realized for one moment that, early in the new year, he'd be called upon to face Gerry Mudd once more, he'd have booked himself a passage aboard a slow boat to China, Vladivostock or Timbuktu. Anywhere in the world, to be rid of her.

'Now,' he continued loftily, 'I'd best have a word with Miss Scott. A friend of yours, I surmise?'

'Well no, not really. I'd never clapped eyes on her either, until an hour ago,' Gerry supplied uneasily, wishing she'd kept her mouth shut about the bullet hole in the cadaver's greatcoat.

'Then how come you knew her name?' Clooney persisted.

'Because I asked her. As simple as that,' Gerry said wearily, sick and tired of the questioning, with a pit of hunger in her stomach which only a full English breakfast, sausages, eggs and bacon, toast and marmalade could fill. 'So why not wheel the pair of us down to the local nick for further questioning? Anything rather than having us stand out here in the cold morning air wittering on about some poor dead sod who neither of us knew from Adam? At least we'd be warm in the nick!'

'How well you read my mind, Miss Frayling,' Clooney said sourly, snapping his fingers at a police-car driver, to whom he gave implicit instructions to drive Gerry, Annie, and the dog to Hampstead Police Station, without further delay.

Two

'Look, Annie,' Gerry said kindly to the trembling girl beside her on their way to the cop-shop, 'no need to worry unduly. Just answer the questions put to you plainly and truthfully. I'll do the same. It shouldn't take long. An hour or so at the most, then I can get back to my jogging, you to your dogsbodying. OK?'

'But what if . . . ?' The girl's face crumpled, tears rained down her cheeks.

'If – *what*?' Gerry looked startled. 'No, don't tell me. I'd rather not know!' Was it remotely possible, she wondered, that Annie knew the identity of the dead man? If so, poor Annie might well be in serious trouble, with far more to lose than her job.

Knowing Inspector Clooney as well as she did – from bitter experience of his ruthless questioning technique, which had led her to believe, at times, during the 'Antiques Murder' enquiries that, however innocent, she might well end up in a women's prison, picking oakum, or whatever women prisoners were supposed to do to while away the time – she felt that Annie could be held for further questioning if Clooney suspected her of withholding information.

She said, sotto voce, 'Do try and pull yourself together.' About to add, 'Otherwise old Clooney'll have your guts for garters', better not, Gerry thought. The state the girl was in, trembling and crying, one harsh word from DI Clooney and she'd probably confess to having strangled the deceased with her bare hands. The implacable detective inspector had that effect on women, Gerry knew to her cost, remembering the times she'd felt like confessing to the 'Antiques Murders' to be rid of his relentless interrogation.

Thankfully, she'd been strong-willed enough to stand up to

him, to fight him every inch of the way, able to provide proofs of her innocence. But what of poor Annie Scott, who, Gerry now felt reasonably certain, knew more about the body in the spinney than she had initially let on? Oh God, she thought, entering the portals of the Hampstead Police Station with Annie beside her, clinging on to her arm for support, what a diabolical situation to be landed in, through no fault of her own. Whatever would Bill say, when he found out?

Clooney leaned forward, brow furrowed, to interrogate Annie. 'Tell me, Miss Scott, is it your custom to exercise your dog on Hampstead Heath first thing in the morning?'

Annie looked stricken. 'Yes. No,' she faltered, as if mesmerized by the DI's eyes boring relentlessly into hers.

'Oh come now, Miss Scott. It's a simple enough question. Is your answer yes, or no?'

'Yes, I do walk the dog on Hampstead Heath first thing in the morning, 'cept on my day off. But the dog ain't mine, it belongs to my employers.'

'I see. And the name of your employers?'

'I'd rather not say, sir.' Annie swallowed hard. 'You see they're well known people who wouldn't want to be mixed up in a – a murder!'

'Murder?' Clooney smiled grimly. 'So you obviously believe that the body in the spinney was that of a murder victim? What led you to that conclusion? Possibly you had seen him somewhere before? The truth now, Miss Scott. Had you seen him somewhere before? If so, *where* exactly?'

Out of her depth, clutching at straws, 'I don't know for certain, all I know is that a tramp came to my employers' house last Christmas Eve, seeking shelter. A rough looking bloke wearing an army greatcoat and a balaclava helmet. I only caught a glimpse of him on the back doorstep, being busy at the time helping Cook in the kitchen, the house being full of visitors. With everything in an uproar, food to prepare, beds to be made up, I scarcely knew if I was on my head or my heels, and that's a fact!' Tears trickled down Annie's cheeks. 'I'm telling you the truth! That's all I know, and you'd better believe it!'

But Clooney wasn't through with her yet. Far from. He said

11

coldly, dispassionately, 'Now I want to know the name of your employers, their address and so forth. Furthermore, I shall require a list of those present at that Christmas house party of theirs, and exactly what became of that so-called tramp who appeared on their doorstep on Christmas Eve.'

Backed into a corner by Clooney's persistence regarding the name of her employers, Annie uttered their names reluctantly, deeply regretting the circumstances which, inevitably, would lead to the loss of a job she had liked enormously, when they, Elliot and Dorothea Lazlo, discovered that she, Annie Scott, a mere servant, had, albeit unwillingly, drawn them into an unsavoury murder inquiry.

'Do come in, Inspector.' Elliot Lazlo, tall, wearing horn-rimmed glasses, casually yet elegantly dressed, with thick, slightly greying hair brushed back from his forehead, smiled thinly as he allowed the policeman entry into the hall of Bagdale Manor. 'A curious business this, and I fail to see what light I can possibly throw on it.' He shrugged slightly. 'Even so, you'd best come through to my study. Needless to say, I'll do everything possible to aid your enquiries.'

So saying, he led the way to his private sanctum, a panelled apartment on the ground floor, book-lined, richly carpeted and furnished with deep leather armchairs, a massive mahogany desk on which sat a word processor, stacks of leather-bound folders, several silver-framed photographs, a crystal vase containing a single white rose, and numerous earthenware pots in which were arrayed common-or-garden biros, pencils, coloured highlighters and bottles of liquid paper.

A log fire burned brightly in the hearth of a marble fireplace, above which hung the portrait of a remarkably beautiful woman. 'My wife,' Lazlo said, indicating the painting with a gesture of his right hand. 'Dorothea Lazlo. Possibly you've heard of her?' Not awaiting Clooney's reply, Lazlo continued, 'The poor darling hasn't been at all well recently, the reason why I don't want her drawn into – all this – unpleasantness. You take my meaning, Inspector? Now, do sit down. Make yourself comfortable, and fire away with your questions. A drink, by the way? Whisky and soda?'

'Not on duty, sir,' Clooney said decisively, unearthing his notebook, seated on the edge of his leather armchair, determined not to get too comfortable in this richly furnished room, faced with a charismatic customer like Elliot Lazlo to whom he had taken an instantaneous dislike from the moment he'd clapped eyes on him, just as Lazlo, Clooney suspected, had taken an instant dislike to himself.

He said, 'I understand from Miss Annie Scott's statement, made earlier today at the Hampstead Police Station, that a tramp, resembling the dead man discovered in a shallow grave in the early hours of this morning, had called here, on Christmas Eve, seeking shelter. Tell me, Mr Lazlo, did you come into contact with such a person?'

Wrinkling his forehead, 'Christmas Eve, you say?' Lazlo prevaricated. 'Why, I scarcely remember. The house was in turmoil, as you can imagine, with guests arriving at frequent intervals all afternoon, in need of refreshment, hot baths before dinner. The servants buzzing about like blue-arsed flies; Cook in the kitchen basting the ducks, I shouldn't wonder: Annie Scott preparing the vegetables. How the hell should I know?'

Consulting his notebook, 'According to Miss Scott's statement,' Clooney reminded him, 'when what she described as a tramp appeared on the kitchen doorstep and wouldn't go away, sensing trouble, she sought your advice on the matter, whereupon you came downstairs to the kitchen to have a word with the man. Now do you recall?'

Lazlo's frown deepened perceptibly, then, as if lightning had struck, 'Oh yes, of course. Now I remember! I told the poor fellow to seek shelter at the Salvation Army refuge in Outgang Lane, gave him a tenner, wished him luck, and that was it! He went away as good as gold!'

'What was he wearing at the time?' Clooney asked remorselessly.

'Good God, man, I scarcely noticed! Why? Is it important?' Lazlo was angry now, deeply resentful of the DI's questions. Rising to his feet, he snapped, 'I'd like you to leave now, Inspector Clooney. I have nothing further to say to you!'

Clooney said imperturbably, 'Sit down, Mr Lazlo, unless you would rather accompany me to the Police Station for further questioning. The choice is yours entirely. I couldn't care less one way or the other. Here or there, it's all the same to me. Just as long as I'm in charge of this investigation, and I *am* in charge of it, Mr Lazlo, believe me, I shall want to know every detail relevant to the death of a murder victim discovered on Hampstead Heath in the early hours of this morning by a servant in your employ. Do I make myself clear?'

Lazlo sat down abruptly.

When Bill phoned to announce his safe arrival in the Big Apple, 'What's your hotel like?' Gerry asked brightly.

'Big, noisy, overheated, but the grub's OK,' he replied. 'T-bone steaks, fries, butterscotch pies, pancakes with maple syrup, honey-roast ham, fried eggs, sunny side up . . .'

Gerry groaned. 'No need to rub it in!'

'Why?' Bill laughed. 'Short of vittals, are you? I could send you a food parcel if you like.' Then, more seriously, 'Gerry, are you all right? Come on, you can tell me!'

'You won't be angry with me? Promise? You see, it wasn't my fault. If Annie hadn't flagged me down, and if the dog hadn't started nosing round in the spinney, the body wouldn't have come to light, neither would Clooney, and we, Annie and I, wouldn't have ended up making statements. Oh, if only I'd kept on jogging!'

'Hey, hang on, you've lost me! Who's Annie, for Pete's sake?' Bill wanted to know. 'What dog, what body?'

'Annie? Oh, she's the Lazlos' dogsbody. You've heard of the Lazlos? They live in that posh house in Well Walk, Bagshot Manor or some such, the one with that walled garden. What I'd give to take a peek at it from the inside. Hmm, suppose I could borrow a ladder from Dickens at the garage. What do you think?'

'That you'd better start at the beginning! Anyway, I thought the garage man's name was Charlie. And how did Clooney get in on the act?'

'Because I rang the police on my mobile. Well, I *had* to! You see, there was this body in the spinney, and we couldn't just let him stay there, could we? Poor Annie was dreadfully upset, scared of losing her job if the Lazlos found out she'd let the dog off its lead. But they were bound to find out sooner or later. It was all pretty scary, with Annie bawling

14

her eyes out, the dog howling like a banshee, and the dead bloke with half his face missing and a bullet hole in his greatcoat.'

'I thought Clooney had retired last Christmas?' Bill said bemusedly, trying to make sense of the plot so far; failing utterly to do so in any detail from Gerry's garbled account of it.

'So did I. But apparently not. There he was, as large as life and just as nasty. My heart sank to my trainers when I saw him getting out of the police car.' She paused briefly, recalling the incident. 'He wasn't best pleased to see me again, neither, I can tell you!'

'I'll bet he wasn't,' Bill responded faintly. 'Then what happened?'

'A visit to the cop-shop, that's what! Oh Gawd, Bill, I wish I'd kept quiet about that bullet hole in the dead bloke's greatcoat. Me and my big mouth! When will I ever learn?'

'So where are you now?' Bill asked, heart in mouth, imagining his bride to be banged up in a cell at the Hampstead Police Station.

'At home, of course. Where else?'

Where else indeed? Bill thought, allowing his imagination to run away with him. Knowing Gerry, she might be anywhere. Scaling a ladder, for instance, in the dead of night, for a look-see into the Lazlos' walled garden, aided and abetted by Charles Dickens.

Elliot Lazlo had reluctantly agreed to a visit to the Hampstead mortuary to view the remains of the murder victim discovered on the Heath earlier that day.

'Really, Inspector Clooney, is this strictly necessary?' he'd protested initially. 'After all, a man in my position. A well-known biographer with a string of highly regarded publications to my name: *The Life of Alfred, Lord Tennyson*; *Gordon of Khartoum*; *The Real Life Adventures of Robert Louis Stevenson* for instance. Hardly likely, wouldn't you say, Inspector, that I'd be likely to identify the body of a man glimpsed briefly last Christmas Eve?' He paused momentarily. 'Even if I did, how would my identification of a – tramp – assist your enquiries into the death of the poor devil? Unless, of course, you believe me capable of firing a bullet into the heart of a man already dead from exposure?'

'Interesting you should say that,' Clooney smiled grimly. 'The cause of death has not so far been established, and no one except myself, the Scenes of Crime officers, the pathologist, presumably Miss Scott and a woman called Frayling, to the best of my knowledge and belief, know about that bullet hole. Perhaps you would explain how you knew about it? Do you possess a firearm, by the way?'

'No, certainly not, and I was told about the bullet hole by a woman who rang up early this morning on Miss Scott's behalf. The Frayling woman, I imagine. She didn't give her name. Frankly, Inspector, she put my back up. I resented her manner intensely.'

Clooney knew the feeling. He said coolly, 'Now, sir, I'm ready if you are. My car's outside. This shouldn't take long. I shall, of course, require a statement from you after you've viewed the body. Unpleasant, I know, but normal procedure, I assure you, in the initial stages of a murder inquiry.'

'But surely, if the man died of exposure?' Lazlo protested, preceding Clooney to the police car parked outside the front entrance of Bagdale Manor.

Alone in the Eyrie, upstairs in her attic studio, feeling nervous and ill-at-ease, pondering the events of the day, Gerry thought about Annie Scott: wondering if she was, even now, packing her belongings prior to moving on to fresh fields and pastures new, having been given the bullet by her employers. Dare she risk a phonecall to Bagshot Manor, Upshot Hall or whatever its name was? Well, why not?

Truth to tell, she felt responsible for the poor kid, quite motherly towards her as a matter of fact. Taking that risk, Gerry prodded the number Annie had given her that morning, which she had scribbled on the back of her hand.

A woman's voice answered, 'Bagdale Manor. Mrs Brook, the housekeeper, speaking. How may I help you?'

'I'd like a word with Miss Scott,' Gerry said, putting on her posh voice.

'Miss Scott?' The housekeeper sounded pained. 'I'm afraid

16

that's not possible, madam. Miss Scott is no longer with us. She left here shortly after lunch.'

'Did she say where she was going?' Gerry asked, letting her posh accent slip a little. Not that she cared tuppence about her accent. All she cared about was Annie's present whereabouts.

'I haven't the faintest idea,' Mrs Brook said off-handedly. 'She simply packed her belongings and went off without a word. The last I saw of her, she was standing at a bus-stop near the corner of Well Walk. Which bus she caught, I don't know. Nor, to be entirely honest, did I care one way or the other.'

'I see. A case of I'm all right, Jack?' By this time, Gerry's posh accent had slipped entirely; her Cockney accent came shining through. 'So you couldn't have cared less about a poor little lass losing her job: hadn't a kind word to say to her? That figures! Well, just wait till your turn comes to be turned out of house and home, which it will, as sure as eggs, the moment you put a foot wrong with your employers. Could be tomorrow or the day after! I just hope when you're standing at a bus-stop, not knowing which way to turn, that no one will utter a kind word to you neither!'

So saying, Gerry cut off the conversation abruptly. Sick at heart, she thought of poor Annie, so cruelly sacked for – what? Letting a dog off its lead? Missing a morning's work through no fault of her own? Or was there more to it than that? Because she had recognized the corpse in his shallow grave as a man who had turned up, last Christmas Eve, on the Lazlos' back doorstep, seeking shelter?

Another thought occurred. The dog! The Lazlos' lurcher, squatted beside the dead man's scooped-out cradle of earth, muzzle lifted, howling its misery and grief to the thin, cold air of a bitter January morning. Could the dog have known the dead man? Gerry wondered.

But where was Annie? She must find Annie. But where to look for her? She might be anywhere. In the heart of London, most likely, in need of a good hot meal, a bed for the night, a shoulder to cry on.

Suddenly, the doorbell rang. Hastening downstairs to answer the summons, Gerry flung open the door to find Annie there

17

on the doorstep, a forlorn figure clutching a suitcase and an assortment of carrier bags.

'Oh, my dear. Come in,' Gerry said warmly. 'Come through to the kitchen, I'll make you something to eat. Bacon and eggs OK? Just leave your things in the hall, we'll take them up to your room later, when you've had something to eat. I'll just nip upstairs and switch on the electric blanket. There's plenty of hot water so you can have a bath before bedtime. Be back in a sec. No need to cry, love. You're safe now. You can stay for as long as you like. How did you find me, by the way?'

'I looked you up in the phone book,' Annie said simply. 'I had nowhere else to go, you see? But I'll not stop long. I'll not be a nuisance. It's just that you were kind to me this morning, an' I thought . . .'

'You thought right,' Gerry said briskly, hurrying upstairs to switch on the electric blanket, after which, returning to the kitchen, she set about cooking eggs and bacon, sausages and mushrooms for the pair of them – and to hell with the calories.

When they had finished tucking in, Gerry took Annie through to the sitting room, drew the velvet curtains against the night, switched on the electric fire, and settled Annie in an armchair near the hearth. 'Feeling better now?' she asked.

'Much better,' Annie replied gratefully. 'You have a lovely house, Miss Frayling.'

'Yes, it is rather swish, isn't it? Call me Gerry, by the way, everyone else does. Well, almost everyone.'

'You're quite famous, aren't you?' Annie ventured shyly.

'Am I? I hadn't noticed.'

'Like Mr Lazlo. Only he writes stuffy books, not thrillers.'

'Tell me, Annie. Why did he sack you? Did he give you a reason? More importantly, did he give you a month's wages in lieu of notice? Did he give you a reference?'

'No. All he gave me was a good telling off for blabbing to the police, what he called disloyalty. He was so angry I thought he was going to hit me. I told him it wasn't my fault but he wouldn't listen. He wanted to know what I'd told the police.'

'And what had you told them?' Gerry asked the question gently. The girl had had a rough time that day. No use upsetting her further, giving her the 'third degree' as old Clooney had done.

'I told them a tramp had come to the kitchen door on Christmas Eve, and I'd fetched him – Mr Lazlo – to see the man.'

'The man we found in the spinney?'

'I think so, by his clothes. I couldn't tell by his face.' Annie shivered recalling that face, or what used to be a face. 'I also mentioned the house was in a bit of an uproar at the time, being Christmas Eve, with guests arriving, wanting this, that and t'other, the housekeeper and Cook not in the best of tempers, and Bruno making a nuisance of himself.'

'Bruno?' Gerry frowned, imagining a young footman, under the influence of drink, staggering about in the hall.

'Bruno, the dog,' Annie explained. 'He'd been acting strange all day. The master was furious about the dog being in the kitchen. "Get that damned animal out of here at once," he told me. "Take him out to his kennel and fasten him up," which I did, right smartish I can tell you, though I had a job to get him past the bloke on the doorstep.'

'So you didn't hear the conversation between Lazlo and the tramp?' Gerry asked, frowning.

'No, I didn't. Truth to tell, I was glad to be outside in the garden, things being so awkward indoors. When I returned, the tramp had gone away and the master had gone back upstairs.' Her lips trembled. 'I felt sorry for Bruno being outdoors in the cold. It didn't seem fair. The poor thing was shivering and whining. But I nipped out later and brought him in, sneaked him upstairs to my room, settled him down in front of the fire and gave him something to eat, just a few scraps of duck and such left over from dinner.'

'That was kind of you, Annie. Brave, too, taking matters into your own hands, risking the sack if the boss-man had found out.'

'I know, and I didn't care,' Annie said defiantly. 'Not at the time. I figured they'd be hard-pressed to do without me with a houseful of people to see to, fires to be lit, beds to make, piles of washing-up to be done, veggies to prepare. Cook was fair run off her feet, so was I.'

'How many people?' Gerry asked. 'House guests, I mean.'

'Oh, let me think. Well, there was Bretton Sandys, Mrs Lazlo's son by a former marriage, his wife, Carla – a right little madam. Alex French, Bretton's boyfriend, I shouldn't wonder – a right cocky devil. There was Mrs Coverdale, Mr Lazlo's sister, and her daughter, Pippa, Dr Edmund Sloane, Mrs Lazlo's personal physician – a dyed-in-the-wool bachelor but a real gent, and a couple called Dumas, Mr Lazlo's literary agent and his wife – very high and mighty. Eight in all for breakfast, lunch, tea and dinner. No wonder Cook was doing her nut with all that grub to see to: full English breakfasts, buffet lunches with all kinds of fakey food on the menu, fiddly things like volly-vaunts, sausages on sticks, poached salmon an' salads, not to mention all them scones, cakes and sandwiches for afternoon tea: egg and cress an' cucumber with the crusts cut off. Greedy pigs! Followed by a four-course dinner; roast duck and all the trimmings on Christmas Eve, roast turkey on Christmas Day, roast beef and Yorkshire puddings on Boxing Day. Thankfully, they all cleared off after breakfast the following day, and weren't we glad to see the back of them!'

'I'll bet you were,' Gerry sympathized. 'Just one thing puzzles me. You seemed nervous about losing your job this morning, remember? Yet you didn't give two hoots on Christmas Eve. Why the change of heart?'

''Cos I'd had time to think, that's why. Jobs ain't all that easy to come by at this time of year. Like I said before, I had a nice room and the pay wasn't bad. What's wrong with that?'

'Where are you from, Annie?' Gerry asked cautiously, not wanting to pry too deeply into the girl's personal affairs, having detected a note of hostility in her last reply.

'York,' Annie said briefly. 'Leastways that's where my parents live now. My Dad's a railwayman, a signalman by profession. We moved from Darlington to York when I was fifteen, when Dad was offered a better-paid job.'

'How old are you now, Annie? Nineteen? Twenty?'

'Eighteen and a bit,' Annie admitted defensively. 'And if you're wondering what I'm doing here in London, I just wanted to go it alone for once in my life. Find myself a decent job, stand on my own two feet. Ma and Da nearly threw a fit when I answered that advert for a – dogsbody. Not that the advert said that exactly. It said, "Wanted. a bright, willing, intelligent young lady for an interesting position in a manor house in Hampstead. Excellent pay and accommodation. Please reply, in writing, to . . ." Well, there you have it in a nutshell. I wrote a letter to Elliot Lazlo, Bagdale Manor, Hampstead, got the job, and here I am!' Again came that note of hostility in Annie's voice.

Gerry said kindly, 'You're tired, Annie, so am I. It's been a long day. Your bed should be nice and warm now. Come, I'll show you up to your room, and I'm so pleased you're here, love, that you came to me for help.'

'I had nowhere else to go,' Annie uttered forlornly, tired out by the exigencies of the past few hours of her tender young life, recalling painful memories of that dead man she'd discovered in the early hours of the morning, her interrogation at the Hampstead Police Station, the subsequent loss of her job, her home, her livelihood. Above all, the loss of her beloved Bruno, an animal she loved and cared for deeply, which she may never see again in her present circumstances.

'Go to bed now, and sleep you well,' Gerry said, kissing her goodnight. 'Not to worry. We'll think of something. And you are welcome to stay here for as long as you like.' A thought occurred. 'Friends of mine, Maggie and Barney Bowler, who own a hamburger joint in the Old Kent Road, are probably in need of help right now, I'll give them a ring first thing in the morning. Not exactly Bagdale Manor, but Maggie and Barney are the salt of the earth, and they'd take care of you just fine, if it's a job you're wanting!' Understanding poor Annie's need of independence, not charity.

'Thanks, Miss Frayling,' Annie murmured wearily, entering her bedroom and closing the door behind her.

Up bright and early next morning, on her way to the kitchen to cook breakfast for two, passing Annie's bedroom door, she knocked and sang out, 'Breakfast in twenty minutes. Don't bother to dress. Come as you are. Dressing gown and slippers perfectly acceptable!'

There was no reply. Gerry knocked again, filled this time with a curious sense of foreboding. On an impulse, opening the door of Annie's room, she saw, to her dismay, that the bed had not been slept in, that the room was empty of Annie's belongings, that the girl had simply disappeared into the wild blue yonder. But *why*? And where was she now?

Questions to which, Gerry realized, there was no immediate answer.

Three

H aving failed to identify the deceased, or his clothing, and having made a statement to that effect, Lazlo was allowed home, complaining bitterly at what he termed 'police ineptitude and high-handedness' in treating him as a criminal, not as a respected member of the Hampstead community.

Reading through the statement following Lazlo's departure, it was easy to tell the fellow was a wordsmith, Clooney reckoned. He'd requested a statement, not a bloody essay.

> I hereby categorically declare that to the best of my knowledge and belief I had no prior knowledge of the body I was today called upon to identify, a man who, supposedly, had come to my home on Christmas Eve 2001, seeking shelter. An incident which, if it happened at all, I scarcely recall, having far more important matters on my mind at the time.
>
> In any event, the face of the dead man was beyond recognition, in an advanced state of decay, and the clothing I was shown was equally unidentifiable. The entire exercise I regard as an intrusion into my privacy and a complete waste of time. I also state that never at any time in my life have I owned a firearm, abhorring, as I do, weapons of destruction of any kind whatever . . .

And so it went on, to Clooney's disgust. More a condemnation of police methods than a statement, he considered wearily. Even so, the body of a murder victim lay on a marble slab in the mortuary adjacent to the Police Station, a poor devil who had died as a result of skull fracture caused by a blow to the head from a blunt instrument of some kind, before a bullet had been fired into his heart at close range.

The obvious conclusion? Not one person, but two, had wanted him out of the way, pretty desperately by the look of it, one of whom had known for certain that he was dead, the second of whom, believing the man was merely sleeping, had pressed a revolver to the man's heart and pulled the trigger. In essence, a double murder on the same victim.

But who was that victim? So far no clues to his identity. It was up to him, Clooney realized with a sinking heart, to discover the man's identity: to bring his murderer and his would-be assassin to justice.

The thought occurred, as he went home to an empty flat, his wife having left him, that he was far too old and tired for this kind of caper. The sooner they found a younger man to replace him, the better – and yet, still in charge of the case, however difficult it may be, he would see it through to the bitter end, come hell or high water. A matter of pride, of stubborn pride in finally quitting the Met in a blaze of glory. Despite his age, still a force to be reckoned with. A kind of 21st-century Hercule Poirot.

Worried sick about Annie, Gerry spent a restless day wondering where she was: why she had decided to steal away like a thief in the night rather than accept her offer of a caravanserai, however temporary, depending on Annie's own decision whether to stay or to move on in due course. Whichever, Gerry would have helped her in every way possible to find a new job or return to her parents' home in York.

Had the girl resented her questioning of the night before to such a degree that she had felt it necessary to leave so abruptly without a word of explanation? It didn't make sense. Annie had come to her of her own free will, had turned to her as a friend in need, and she, Gerry, had felt privileged that she had done so. So why the sudden turn about? What on earth had possessed her to gather together her belongings and quit the house so silently, presumably in the early hours of the morning, and without sleep, judging by the unruffled state of the bed, the electric blanket still switched on? No sign of her having been there at all, or in the bathroom along the landing.

Later that afternoon, Gerry drove to Bagdale Manor to beard Elliot Lazlo in his lair, determined to find out if he knew

Annie's whereabouts. It was a curious house, she decided, originally a Tudor building with odd bits tacked on to it. In Tudor times, the manor would have occupied a great deal of private land, she imagined, and the length of the walled garden to the rear of the house bore witness to that, long before Hampstead Village had come into the picture. Now the original Tudor edifice appeared as an anachronism among the Victorian bay-windowed houses which had sprung up in its vicinity. It seemed out of keeping, somehow, to approach the front door by means of an iron gate and a common-or-garden path set between spotted laurel bushes. Undaunted, Gerry pushed open the gate, marched up the path and tugged the iron bell-pull.

A stout middle-aged woman answered the summons, presumably the housekeeper. Regarding Gerry, in her jogging gear, with a baleful glance at the red Mini parked in the roadway beyond the privet hedge, 'Yers,' she said, 'how may I help you?'

'I'm here to see Mr Lazlo,' Gerry replied shortly. 'My name is Frayling, and it's very important – to do with a murder inquiry and a missing person.'

'Mr Lazlo is otherwise engaged at the moment,' the woman said impassively. 'In any case, he does not receive callers without a prior appointment. My advice to you is to ring him first to make an appointment.'

'No, sorry, like I said, this is very important. I'd best come in and wait till he's disengaged, hadn't I? I shan't mind a bit. Any old chair will do till he's finished his tea, or whatever.'

'Now see here,' the housekeeper bridled, deeply affronted, 'you can't simply enter other people's property without a by your leave. One more step, and I'll phone the police!'

'Oh, yes please,' Gerry responded eagerly, 'be sure to ask for Detective Inspector Clooney. I could do with a bit of police back-up right now!'

An imperious voice rang out, 'What is it, Mrs Brook? Another damned newspaper reporter?' A tall figure emerged from Lazlo's inner sanctum. 'I thought my instructions were quite clear. Apparently they were not clear enough!'

'Whoops! Sorry Mrs Brook,' Gerry said mischievously, edging past the housekeeper, 'but I did try to warn you, remember? Put a foot wrong and you too could end up standing at a bus-stop on your way to the nearest employment agency.' She continued merrily, 'Ah, we meet at last, Mr Lazlo! Now, about Annie Scott!'

'Annie Scott?' Off guard, Lazlo's expression betrayed his inner wariness at the mention of her name. 'What about her?'

'She's gone missing,' Gerry supplied relentlessly, 'and I want to know where she is! She turned up on my doorstep last night in a sorry state, in need of a hot meal and a friend to turn to, and little wonder, since she had been dismissed, out of hand, by your good self. This morning, I discovered that her bed had not been slept in, that the poor kid had simply disappeared into the wild blue yonder. Now I want to know why: what became of her, and I'm determined to find out.'

'You'd best come through to my study,' Lazlo said briefly, 'Miss, whatever your name is.'

'Frayling, Geraldine Frayling,' Gerry reminded him. 'The person who rang you yesterday morning following the discovery of a dead body on Hampstead Heath, remember?'

'Well, yes, I do vaguely remember,' he admitted, leading the way to his sanctum. 'Even so, I fail to see what all this has to do with me!'

'Then I'll enlighten you, shall I?' Gerry said engagingly, plumping herself into a leather armchair near the roaring log fire. 'Fact Number One, an eighteen-year-old girl, lately in your employ, has disappeared in mysterious circumstances, and I want to find out what has become of her. Fact Two, that girl was unfairly dismissed in my view; had done nothing to warrant being given the boot without notice, more cruelly without a reference, so it has a great deal to do with you, don't you agree?'

'No, I do not! Even less to do with you. If you're worried about Miss Scott's whereabouts, you should have notified the police, not turned up here to make a damned nuisance of yourself.' He paused briefly. 'As an employer, it is my right to dismiss unsatisfactory servants as and when I choose. Miss Scott had been extremely rude to both myself and my wife on more than one occasion recently. Things came to a head yesterday when I learned that she had let my dog off its lead despite my explicit instructions not to do so.'

'Yeah,' Gerry remarked, 'I can see why. The dead man

in the spinney. Hard cheese the dog came across the corpus delicti, wouldn't you say? Had Annie obeyed your explicit instructions, the poor devil might still be lying there for someone else to find. Children perhaps?'

'What the hell are you implying?' Lazlo's face darkened.

'Since you ask, I'll come straight to the point. A habit of mine. Ask anyone who knows me. They'll tell you I don't waste time implying. I think you knew where the body was buried, and why. Is that plain enough?'

'But this is monstrous!' Lazlo rose quickly to his feet. 'I want you out of here right now! Understood?' Hands clenched into fists, towering over her, beside himself with anger, 'Well, you heard me! You have till the count of five. Five, four, three, two—'

'Hey, calm down,' Gerry said mildly, interrupting his counting. 'Annie said you were on a short fuse, but this is ridiculous. No wonder the poor kid was scared stiff of you. She told me she thought you were about to hit her at one point. She told me a lot of other things besides. The tramp who came to the kitchen door on Christmas Eve for instance. A curious coincidence in my opinion. A man alive and kicking one minute, as dead as mutton the next. At least within hours of his brief encounter with you, Mr Lazlo. Now, do please sit down. You're making me feel nervous towering over me with your fists showing white at the knuckles.'

'Just who the hell *are* you?' he demanded hoarsely. 'And what do you want from me? *Money*? Is that it?'

'No, far from. I have more than I know what to do with as it is, ta very much. I simply want to know what has become of Annie Scott.' She added, 'I think that you know! You're just playing hard to get!'

'Very well then, I'll tell you!' Sitting down, Lazlo ran his fingers distractedly through his mane of hair. 'Annie Scott came here in the early hours of this morning. I was asleep at the time, and then suddenly wide awake, I became aware of footsteps on the landing outside my door.'

'Go on,' Gerry murmured encouragingly, her crime writer's instinct aroused. 'Then what happened?'

'I got up, opened my bedroom door, switched on the light, and there she was. I'd caught her red-handed.'

27

'Doing *what* exactly?' Gerry asked, agog with curiosity.

'Stealing from me, if you must know. That much was evident. She couldn't deny it, she didn't even try.'

'Stealing what, for heaven's sake?'

'My dog! She had it in her arms when I saw her, attempting to smuggle it downstairs to the front door.'

'Yes, of course,' Gerry sighed deeply, 'I might have guessed. Annie thinks the world of that dog. So what did you do? Call the police, have her arrested for dognapping?'

'No, I did not! I should have done, but I didn't. I told her to keep the bloody thing if it meant so much to her. It was a damned nuisance anyway, and my wife didn't care for it. I told her to get out and stay out; advised her to go back to her parents, where she belonged. I rang for a taxi to take her to King's Cross Station. The last I saw of her, she was on the back seat of the taxi, the dog beside her. Well, there you have it in a nutshell. I imagine she'll be home and dry by now. Satisfied, are you?'

'Not entirely,' Gerry demurred. 'Not until I have her parents' address and phone number, just to make certain she arrived safely at her destination, if you wouldn't mind giving me that information.'

'If you insist,' Lazlo acceded ungraciously. Having done so, 'Now,' he said brusquely, 'shall I show you the door, or can you find your own way out?'

'OK. I get the message.'

On her way to the front door, Gerry glimpsed the figure of a tall, slender upright woman on the staircase. A remarkably beautiful woman. Dorothea Lazlo, no less, betraying no sign of old age or infirmity despite her beautifully coiffed greying hair and her recent, life-threatening illness. Longing to speak to her, better not, Gerry decided regretfully. She had already outstayed her welcome at Bagdale Manor. Welcome? Well scarcely that. But discretion was, perhaps, the better part of valour. So thinking, she beat a hasty retreat to the safety of her little red Mini.

At home, picking up the phone, she dialled the number Lazlo had given her. A woman's voice answered.

'Mrs Scott?' Gerry asked brightly. 'You don't know me, but I'm a friend of Annie. May I speak to her?'

'But Annie isn't here, she's in London. She works there. We, her father an' me, haven't seen her for ages.' A worried note crept into the woman's voice. 'What made you think she was here? She is all right, isn't she?'

'So far as I know.' Gerry spoke reassuringly. 'She stayed with me last evening. She was fine at the time.'

'Where do *you* live, then?'

'In London. Hampstead to be precise. My name is Frayling, by the way. Look, Mrs Scott, I'll give you my address and phone number. If – that is when – Annie turns up will you ask her to get in touch with me?'

'What do you mean, if and when she turns up? We're not expecting her. If there's owt wrong, I want to know about it. After all, I *am* her mother!'

Hopeless at prevarication, Gerry said unhappily, 'All I can say is, that to the best of my knowledge and belief, Annie intended catching an early morning train to York from King's Cross. The reason for my phonecall, to make certain she'd arrived safely.'

'But she *hasn't*, has she?' Mrs Scott drew a sobbing intake of breath. 'So where *is* she? What's become of her?'

'I'm sorry, I don't know. But I'll do my best to find out.' As she hung up, a trickle of fear ran down Gerry's spine. A premonition of danger of the kind she'd experienced the day she'd discovered Liam McEvoy's body in her garden shed.

Alerted by the whining of a dog in the women's cloakroom at King's Cross Station, an early morning cleaner had come across the body of a young girl jammed into a toilet compartment, the dog beside it. 'A kind of greyhound: the poor thing shivering with cold and fright,' she told the station-master when she'd reported the matter to him. 'Pitiful, it were. The poor lass kinda propped up behind the door, her face all purple an' mottled wi' her tongue stuck out, an' the dog tryin' its best to keep her warm. What's the world comin' to, I should like to know? I mean, who in their right senses would want to harm a young lass no older than me granddaughter?'

Who indeed? But someone had, Gerry thought, sick at heart when she heard reports of 'The King's Cross Murder' on the six o'clock news bulletin.

So far, the murder victim had not been identified, the newscaster intoned dispassionately, but she was of average height, slimly built, aged about nineteen, with short fair hair, wearing a tweed skirt, a red jumper and anorak, flat-heeled brown shoes and carrying a shoulderbag from which had been stolen – apparently – clues to her identity. She had, however, more than likely been the owner of a lurcher, discovered at the scene of murder, with whose lead she had been strangled.

He went on to say, fronting pictures of King's Cross Station flashed on to a screen behind his news-desk, that Detective Chief Inspector Brambell, of Scotland Yard, had issued an appeal to anyone knowing the identity of the victim to contact him or his Scotland Yard colleagues at once, on the following phone number . . .

Later, picking up the phone and dialling Scotland Yard, requesting a person-to-person call with DCI Brambell, 'It is rather important,' she told the person who answered her call. 'You see, I know the identity of the King's Cross murder victim.'

Four

'Sit down, Miss Frayling. This must have come as a nasty shock to you. Identification of a body is never easy or pleasant. We are just so grateful for your help in our enquiries. Now, before we proceed, may I offer you refreshment? Tea or coffee?'

Thinking that a slug of brandy wouldn't go amiss, Gerry settled for coffee; strong with two spoonfuls of sugar. Detective Chief Inspector Brambell was right in saying that Annie's death had come as a shock to her. She had not imagined for one moment that she would be called upon to identify her poor dead body in the Scotland Yard mortuary. She realized, however, that investigation into her murder could not proceed without proof of the victim's identity.

She had gagged momentarily in the mortuary, gazing down at Annie's bloated features. Asked if she recognized the girl on the slab, she had simply nodded and murmured, 'Yes.' Then a young WPC had led her into the main building, telling her gently not to hurry, to take her time, saying she'd done well, that lots of people, men and women, either fainted or became hysterical following a visit to the mortuary, whereupon Gerry, feeling physically sick, had made a dash for the nearest loo.

This time, at least, she was being given VIP treatment by DCI Brambell and his colleagues. A far cry from her treatment at the Hampstead Heath nick under the auspices of her bête noire, DI Clooney.

Brambell, slightly built, sixtyish, wearing grey flannel trousers, a blue shirt, bow-tie and a grey hand-knitted cardigan with bulging pockets, gave the impression of a country doctor, shrewd yet kindly. He said, when the coffee cups had been brought in and placed on his desk, 'Am I right in thinking that you are a writer of crime fiction, Miss Frayling?'

31

'Yes. Why?' About to add, 'Is it a punishable offence?' she decided not to. DI Clooney had made abundantly clear to her, on more than one occasion, his dislike of crime novelists in general, herself in particular. Apparently Brambell held no such inhibition. He said, 'My wife is a great fan of yours and your female sleuth – Virginia Vale.'

'Really?' Gerry beamed, feeling more relaxed, especially when her host offered her a chocolate digestive biscuit to accompany the coffee, adding, 'Please do help yourself. Or would you prefer something more substantial?'

'No, ta very much. You see I'm trying to lose weight,' Gerry explained, thinking, as she nibbled her chocolate biscuit, that she would give her eye teeth for a hamburger and chips – a Maggie and Barney Bowler special at their hamburger joint in the Old Kent Road. Perhaps she'd pay them a visit when DCI Brambell had completed his investigation. So far, he hadn't even started asking questions, in direct contrast to Clooney, who would, by this time, have had her hog-tied and branded as a suspect involved in the death of a girl she had scarcely known, let alone – murdered.

'Something on your mind, Miss Frayling?' Brambell asked sympathetically, in the manner of a kindly medico wanting to know where it hurt.

'No. Yes. That is, I didn't know Annie Scott very well, but when she turned to me for help, I offered her a bed for the night. Next morning, her bed hadn't been touched, let alone slept in. She'd left the house without a word: had disappeared into thin air.'

'Now why was that, do you imagine?' Brambell said mildly.

'Because she wanted something she felt was hers by right. I didn't know that at the time, but I do now.'

'I see, and what was that – something?'

'Elliot Lazlo's dog. The one found beside her body. Poor Annie thought the world of that dog. Where is it now, by the way? It won't be – put down or anything, will it? Annie would never forgive me if I let that happen! You see, when Lazlo caught her trying to steal it, he gave it to her. I know, because he told me so himself, yesterday afternoon when I went round to see him. He told me he'd rung for a taxi to take Annie to King's Cross. He said the last he'd seen of her, she was on the back seat of the taxi, the dog beside her.'

'Did he indeed?' Brambell mused thoughtfully. 'Hmm, interesting. I must have a word with Mr Lazlo. I take it you mean *the* Elliot Lazlo? The biographer?'

'The self and same. You see, Annie worked for the Lazlos as a – dogsbody. That's how we came to know each other, how we came across the body of the man in the spinney. Leastways, the dog found the body, so I rang the police on my mobile and the next thing we knew we were at the Hampstead Police Station for questioning. And my fiancé, Bill Bentine, who's in America at the moment, wasn't best pleased when I told him I was in trouble with the police again.'

'*Again*? Why, had you been in trouble with them before?'

Gerry stared at him disbelievingly. She said huskily, 'Oh, come off it, Inspector. You knew all along, didn't you? The "Antiques Murders", remember? What is this, a game of cat and mouse?'

Brambell's eyes narrowed. His entire demeanour changed suddenly from that of a friendly country doctor to that of a high-ranking Scotland Yard detective. 'No, Miss Frayling, it is not. Far from! This is a murder inquiry. Two particularly brutal murders have been committed, and it is my business to discover the person or persons responsible for those murders. Which I shall, believe me.' He smiled grimly.

'I'm sorry, Inspector. I didn't mean what I said. Speaking out of turn is a nasty habit of mine. So, apparently, is getting mixed up in – murder. But I'm sure DI Clooney has told you all about me and my big mouth?'

Brambell smiled faintly. 'For what it's worth, Miss Frayling, you are not a suspect in this case.'

'I'm not? Oh, thank God! Wait till I tell Bill, he'll be over the moon. He's got it into his head we'll be getting married in prison.'

Brambell laughed. 'You're free to leave now, Miss Frayling. Thanks again for your help. Any immediate plans?'

'Well, I wouldn't mind a bit of a break with friends of mine. I'm feeling a bit lonely at the moment. I miss Bill – and Annie.' Getting up to leave, 'You will let me know about Annie's dog, won't you?'

'Yes, of course. By the way, Annie's parents have been told of their daughter's death.' He spoke softly, compassionately. 'They will be here soon.'

'Poor things,' Gerry murmured. 'You'll have to question them, I suppose?'

'Afraid so. Possibly they may have information vital to our enquiries.'

Gerry said, frowning, 'I'd almost forgotten. The night she came to me for help, after losing her job, Annie mentioned the names of several people present at the Lazlos' house party last Christmas. She also told me that a tramp had come to the kitchen door, wanting to see Mr Lazlo.'

'And did Mr Lazlo speak to the man?' Brambell asked intently.

'Yes. Annie went in search of him, and Lazlo came down to the kitchen for a word with him. Not that Annie heard the conversation because of the dog. Lazlo told her to take it outdoors and fasten it up, which she did, against her will, I might add. Later, she smuggled it back indoors, took it up to her room and gave it something to eat, the poor thing.'

'I see. Now, about the names she mentioned. Can you remember them?'

'No, not really. Just one or two.'

'One will do, Miss Frayling,' Brambell assured her.

'Well, there was a Mr Bretton Sandys, Mrs Lazlo's son by a former marriage,' Gerry recalled, 'his wife, and a literary agent called Dumas. I remember thinking what a damn silly name for a literary agent, that he must have made it up. But then,' she sighed deeply, 'my motor mechanic is called Charles Dickens, and he sure as hell didn't make *that* up!'

Brambell escorted her to the door. He said, 'I gather that you and Detective Inspector Clooney haven't always seen eye to eye. Even so, he is a first-class man in his field, and he is still closely involved in the investigation.'

'I see.' Gerry sighed. 'We just rub each other up the wrong way somehow. I'm too outspoken, that's my trouble. He seems never to believe a word I say and here am I, too daft to be dishonest!'

She continued shakily, 'The trouble I had convincing him I was innocent of the 'Antiques Murders', you wouldn't believe.'

'But you were proved innocent in the long run,' Brambell reminded her gently, 'and the help you have given us in this investigation is greatly appreciated, believe me. Providing Miss Scott's home telephone number, for instance, enabling us to get in touch with her parents. Above all, in your identification of the deceased, without which further investigation would have been virtually impossible.'

'Thanks.' Gerry smiled gratefully at DCI Brambell. 'Now, with your permission, I would rather like to visit my friends, the Bowlers, at Barney's Hamburger Joint in the Old Kent Road.'

Brambell laughed. Liking Gerry enormously, he twinkled, 'Go ahead, Miss Frayling. Just don't forget your diet, that's all!'

'*Diet*? What – diet?' Gerry asked, tongue in cheek, on the way to her little red Mini.

Maggie and Barney welcomed Gerry with open arms. They hadn't seen her since Christmas which they had spent at the Eyrie, rejoicing in the news of Gerry and Bill's engagement, which they'd announced at breakfast on Christmas morning, when Gerry had fluttered her left hand becomingly over the plates of bacon and eggs to show off her sparkling diamond engagement ring.

'You've chosen well, lad,' Barney had said wisely, nodding like a mandarin. 'Gerry's a treasure.'

Bill laughed. 'I know. She keeps on telling me so.'

'Eh, I'm so happy I could burst,' Maggie said, promptly bursting into tears, 'to think of our Gerry getting married! Barney an' me think the world of her; allus have done, as if she were our own flesh an' blood. Like the daughter we allus wanted an' never had!' At which point Bill, with his instinctive flair for saying and doing the right thing at the right time, said expansively, 'Let's make this a champagne breakfast, shall we? There's a bottle of Bollinger in the fridge!'

'Now you're talking,' Maggie sniffed, blowing her nose and drying her eyes. 'Huh, I've never had champagne an' bacon an' eggs before.'

Bill said, 'Let's ditch the bacon and eggs, shall we, Gerry love? We'll have smoked salmon and scrambled eggs instead.

What's good enough for Prince Charles is good enough for us!'

'Eh, we'll be pi-eyed by lunchtime,' Maggie remarked happily, sipping champagne as Bill scrambled eggs in lashings of butter and cream and Gerry set out platefuls of succulent, oak-smoked Scottish salmon. Trust Bill, she thought fondly, to turn an ordinary breakfast into a 'royal' occasion. No longer just Bill, but *her* Bill – her future husband.

Future husband? The fact had scarcely registered, at first, that she and Bill Bentine were destined to become man and wife in the not too distant future. To be truthful, it still hadn't. Perhaps if they'd slept together? But Gerry, an old-fashioned girl at heart, had not wanted that. Not, at least, until she had something resembling a waistline.

Now, here she was in Maggie and Barney's hamburger joint, about to scoff a couple of hamburgers and chips. Comfort food pure and simple, she reckoned, following her visit to the Scotland Yard mortuary to identify poor Annie Scott's body.

'What's up, love?' Maggie wanted to know, watching Gerry closely as, with tear-filled eyes, Gerry pushed aside her plate of food untasted. 'Come on, you can tell me! Barney and I are your friends, remember?'

When the story was told, Maggie said concernedly, 'You'd best stay here with us for a while. Your room on the top floor is vacant. What you need right now is a good sleep, a bit of peace and quiet.'

'Thanks, Maggie, but it's too early to go to bed. Besides, I haven't any luggage with me. Not so much as a toothbrush or flannel. I really do need to go home for the time being. But I'd love to come back at the weekend, if you'll have me.'

'You're welcome here any time, you know that,' Maggie said huskily. She added astutely, 'You're missing Bill, I daresay.'

'Oh Maggie. If you only knew how much!' Gerry confessed. 'The house seems empty without him.'

'Yeah, well, I can understand that,' Maggie responded with a sigh. 'The way I'd miss Barney if he buggered off to America. But don't you tell him I said so. I'd never hear the last of it if you did!'

Gerry smiled, knowing that Maggie was trying to 'buck

her up', that she was deeply concerned about Annie Scott's murder. 'The poor kid,' she'd kept on murmuring when Gerry was telling her what had happened. 'It's a damn shame. Who could have done such a wicked thing? That photographer bloke I shouldn't wonder. Elliot what's his name?'

She'd paused, wrinkling her forehead. 'If I was you, Gerry love, I'd get on the next plane to New York, let Bill tek care of you.'

'If only I could, but I can't. Not with a murder inquiry going on, me being a material witness and all, with Scotland Yard and Inspector Clooney breathing down my neck. There's bound to be an inquest, and I'll have to give evidence. Besides, I want to find out what's happened to Annie's dog.'

And so, bidding a temporary farewell to the Bowlers, Gerry returned to the Eyrie, dreading being alone in the house, beginning to wish, for the first time ever, that she had bought a modern bungalow not a Victorian mansion. But she had fallen in love with the house at first sight, which she had bought for a song from its former owner, a renowned archaeologist, who had also been murdered, along with her gardener Liam McEvoy, and her volatile French housekeeper, Anna Gordino.

All in the past now. Even so, Gerry shivered slightly as she entered the house, wondering if, when she and Bill were married, she'd be wise to sell the Eyrie and its heavy Victorian furniture and make a fresh start elsewhere? She must ask Bill what *he* thought when he returned home from America. This was something they would need to discuss face-to-face, not during a transatlantic phonecall . . .

Deep in thought, Gerry nearly jumped out of her skin when, barely across the threshold, the hall telephone shrilled suddenly into the silence.

Picking up the receiver, 'Hello?' she said nervously. 'Who's there?'

A woman's voice answered. Speaking softly, shakily, the voice said, 'My name's June Scott. Annie's mother. You gave me your phone number, remember?'

'Yes, of course.' Scarcely knowing what to say to the poor woman that wouldn't sound trite in the present cir-cumstances, Gerry said warmly, sympathetically, 'I gathered from Detective Inspector Brambell that you and your husband were on your way to London. Where are you now, by the way?'

'At a bed and breakfast hotel near King's Cross Station,' the woman replied, close to tears.

'How long for?' Gerry asked gently.

'We, that is her father an' me, aren't quite sure at the moment,' June Scott admitted bemusedly, 'it all seems so unreal, somehow, being here at all, I mean, with our little girl's funeral arrangements to see to and – oh, I'm sorry. Not making much sense, am I?' The woman's voice broke suddenly.

'You are to me,' Gerry answered levelly. 'Now, Mrs Scott, here's what I want you to do. Cancel your bed and breakfast accommodation, and come to stay here with me! I have room and to spare. Take a taxi. I'll give you my address. No need to talk if you don't feel like it. Come to think of it, I don't feel much like talking, myself, at the moment. But I can at least offer you privacy, a good hot meal – if you don't mind eating in the kitchen, that is. So please, do say you'll come?'

A slight pause occurred, then, 'Yes, Miss Frayling,' June replied. 'I've had a word with my husband, and he agrees to our staying with you for the time being, if you're sure we won't be too much trouble.'

'No trouble at all, I assure you,' Gerry said, hanging up the receiver, prior to rushing upstairs to switch on the electric blanket of the double bed occupied by Maggie and Barney, last Christmas, then hurrying downstairs to the kitchen to prepare a hearty supper for Annie's parents. Nothing too fancy, but sustaining; reconstituted Knorr Swiss asparagus soup, grilled lamb chops with mashed potatoes, gravy, and defrosted peas and cauliflower florets, avec mint jelly, followed by a deep-dish apple pie, thick Jersey cream, coffee and After Eight mints. Little of which she could partake of herself, Gerry realized, if she wished to emerge, slim and svelte, on her wedding day – come September, wearing a slim-fitting gown of oyster satin, not a kind of circus tent to minimize her avoirdupois.

When the doorbell rang an hour later, Gerry, wearing a long black jersey-wool skirt, a purple wool sweater and matching

cardigan, welcomed into her home Annie's parents, June and
Arthur Scott. Hands outstretched to greet them, 'I'm so glad
you're here,' she said quietly. 'Do please come in, and make
yourselves at home.'

'We're not in need of bloody charity, think on,' Arthur Scott
uttered sharply.

'Oh, I am pleased,' Gerry said brightly, 'I'd hate you to
think I was running an almshouse.'

'Take no notice. He's upset,' his wife said apologetically.

'So am I,' Gerry said levelly. 'I scarcely knew Annie, but
I liked her and I'm sorry about what happened. I did my best
to help her, now I'm doing the same for you. Charity doesn't
enter into it, just common humanity. All right, Mr Scott?'
Gerry, a strong believer in speaking her mind and clearing
the air, continued pleasantly, 'Now, come in, I'll show you
your room. Come down when you're ready. Meanwhile, I'll
pop the kettle on for a cuppa. I daresay you could do with one.
I know I could.'

Getting out the cups and saucers, Gerry wondered if Arthur
Scott's attitude problem had a bearing on his daughter's
decision to leave home when she did. Some men were bullies
from birth – her own father, Fred Mudd, included, though
unlike June Scott, her mother had given Pa as good as he
sent. Thankfully, since their divorce and re-marriages, Gerry
saw little or nothing of either of them nowadays, which suited
her fine. Maggie and Barney Bowler meant far more to her
than her own parents ever had.

When the Scotts appeared in the kitchen, Gerry made and
poured out the tea, pleased to note that Arthur seemed more
subdued after a wash and brush up. Well, better that than a
wash and dust-up.

June said, 'You have a lovely home, Miss Frayling. It's very
big, isn't it? Aren't you nervous, living alone I mean?'

'Not really. I'm used to it. In any case, I'm not always
alone.'

Embroidering the truth a little to disabuse Arthur of the
notion that here was a lonely lady unable to fend for herself,
a candidate for bullying, she continued mistily, 'My fiancé's
away at the moment, but he'll be home soon, and my adoptive
parents are forever popping round for a chat. They're show-biz

folk, you see? Barney's a boxer, his wife's a champion lady mud-wrestler.' This was true, in essence. She simply neglected to add the word 'ex'.

'Besides which, my closest friend is a well known female detective,' meaning her fictitious supersleuth Virginia Vale. Again, true in essence, inasmuch as Virginia was her alter ego, and one could scarcely come closer to anyone than that.

'Also, the police are very good at keeping an eye on me.' Suddenly deeply ashamed of herself, realizing that she could probably floor Arthur without help if the need arose, she said, 'I'm sorry, I tend to get carried away at times,' feeling intense pity for poor Mrs Scott, saddled with a brute of a husband and grieving for a daughter she would never see alive again.

'If you've finished your tea,' she said gently, 'why not come through to the drawing room whilst I see to supper? Or I could bring it upstairs if you'd sooner go to bed.'

'I ain't all that hungry,' June confessed, her face a mask of pain, 'an' I doubt I'll get much sleep, things being as they are.'

Taking control of the situation, realizing that the poor woman was nearing the end of her tether, 'Come with me, Mrs Scott,' Gerry said tenderly. 'I'll take you up to your room, tuck you up in bed, give you a couple of aspirin. I daresay you'll drop off before you know it. You're plumb worn out!'

'What about Arthur?' June demurred anxiously, on her way upstairs.

'Not to worry. He'll be fine, just fine!' Glancing over the banister at him, 'Won't you, Mr Scott?' Daring him to say otherwise by a certain look in her eye. 'I'll give him a nice hot meal, and there's beer in the fridge, a bottle of whisky in the drawing room.' Gerry's plans included putting him into what she now thought of as Annie's room, to sleep, but he'd find out about that later, when he was full of food and booze.

When Bill rang later, 'Sorry, love, I can't talk right now,' Gerry hissed into the receiver.

'Why not? What's up? Not more trouble?'

'The worst kind. There's been another murder. The victim's mother's asleep upstairs. I gave her sleeping pills, not aspirin. Her husband's spark out in the drawing room, as "nissed as a pewt", and I want him to stay that way, otherwise he may turn nasty. You do see the fix I'm in, don't you? Thanks, love, I knew you would! Night darling, and God bless!'

Five

After breakfast the following morning, Arthur Scott, who had polished off six tins of beer and a bottle of Scotch after his supper the night before, said he fancied a walk in the fresh air to clear his head.

At the front door, pointing him in the direction of Hampstead Heath, watching him lurch unsteadily down her garden path, wondering how he'd react to an itemized bill for bed, board and booze on the termination of his visit, Gerry turned her attention to Mrs Scott, who was in the kitchen drinking tea and nibbling toast and, not unsurprisingly, had enjoyed a good night's sleep – said she was feeling much better as a result. Thank God for Nytol, Gerry thought fervently, handing her a jar of organic honey to spread on her toast.

'I never even heard Arthur come to bed,' she said innocently. Gerry thought it expedient not to mention that Arthur had spent the night on her drawing-room sofa.

She said, 'Forgive my asking, but what are your plans for today? Do the police know you're here?'

'No. I never thought to tell them. Why? Should I have done? Sorry, but Arthur an' me weren't thinking too clearly last night.'

'Not to worry. I'll give them a ring, right away,' Gerry said brightly, heading towards the hall telephone, calling over her shoulder, 'Do try that honey, by the way. It will do you good.'

Returning to the kitchen, 'Well, that's taken care of. Inspector Brambell sent his best wishes, by the way, and he's sending a car to pick you up at midday, if that's all right.'

'It'll have to be, won't it?' June responded bleakly. 'They'll be wanting to know about the – funeral, I expect. Poor Annie's funeral. Only I can't believe she's dead! I really *can't*! I mean, who could have done such a wicked thing as to strangle a bonny young lass who hadn't an enemy in the world?'

Staring up at Gerry, 'Do *you* know? Why did Annie come here the night she died? I don't understand! But I need to *know*! What did you talk about? What did she say to you? Inspector Brambell said she was supposed to stay the night. So why didn't she?'

'Because of the dog,' Gerry replied quietly, sitting down opposite Mrs Scott. 'Because that dog meant the world to her, and she wasn't about to leave London without it.'

June burst forth, 'You mean to tell me that a damned dog cost my girl her life?' Groping desperately for a ray of light in her present darkness of spirit, to latch on to, she continued hoarsely, 'Arthur and me didn't even know that Annie had been sacked from her job until Inspector Brambell told us, and nowt at all about her involvement in a police inquiry into the discovery of a body on Hampstead Heath. A tramp, by all accounts. As if Annie was somehow connected with him. As if she could have been! Not our Annie! Not our girl!'

Gerry said gently, patiently, 'Unknowingly, of course, she was unlucky enough to have caught sight of that tramp before his death: had witnessed a meeting, had, perhaps, overheard a conversation she wasn't meant to hear. I'm sorry, Mrs Scott, that's all I can tell you, except that I was with Annie, on Hampstead Heath, just after the dog came across the body of the tramp.' She paused. 'The man had been brutally murdered, just as poor Annie was murdered. Don't ask me why! I simply don't know! I only wish to God I did!'

'I'm sorry, Miss Frayling,' June uttered brokenly, 'you were kind to Annie, just as you've been kind to Arthur and me, and we're grateful for that, believe me, even though he said what he did about not wanting – charity. His tongue gets the better of him, at times, that's all, especially when he's upset!'

'Does he often get upset?' Gerry asked. 'Was he upset when Annie left home?'

'Of course he was. We both were. We tried to talk her out of it, but Annie had a mind of her own. She'd left school at sixteen, had taken a job as a shop assistant, but she wanted to what she called "better herself". I rue the day she saw that advert in our local paper. Truth to tell, I never thought she'd get it, but she was short-listed, an' next thing we knew she went off to London for an interview. Mrs Lazlo had written to her enclosing a return ticket to York, a photograph of the house and a kind of summary of her duties should her interview prove successful.'

'Mrs Lazlo, you say?' Gerry frowned slightly. 'You're sure Mrs Lazlo sent that letter?'

'Oh yes, perfectly sure. Why?'

'No particular reason. It just seems a bit odd, that's all. I understood that hiring and firing servants was Mr Lazlo's province, not his wife's. In fact he told me so himself.' She smiled. 'Don't worry, it isn't important.'

Even so, Gerry couldn't help wondering why the subterfuge? Why the photograph of the house, the summary of duties in the event of Annie landing the job, as if it had been pre-determined that she should? But that was ridiculous – wasn't it? A case of her writer's imagination working overtime? Perhaps, but why that advert in a York newspaper when London was teeming with young unemployed girls in need of a job? Why a return railway ticket from York when, in the event of Londoners being called for interview, bus fares would have sufficed?

But no, it had to be someone living in York, Gerry figured. Not necessarily Annie but a girl within striking distance of London, with a regular connecting rail link between the two cities. But *why*? For what possible reason – unless the murder of an innocent young girl had been planned well in advance as an alibi – for what? More importantly, by whom? Presumably a deranged serial killer with another murder in mind.

'Are you all right, Miss Frayling?' Mrs Scott asked anxiously, breaking Gerry's train of thought.

'Yes, I'm fine,' Gerry replied, keeping her thoughts to herself, 'just a bit tired, that's all. At a bit of a loose end.' She smiled, 'Please, would you mind calling me Gerry? Miss Frayling sounds so formal, and I'm far from being a formal kind of person.'

'You're a very nice person,' June said mistily. 'What I mean is, inviting us here to stay with you, making Arthur an' me feel so welcome, the way you did poor Annie.' She added wistfully, 'Would you mind very much showing me her room? I know she didn't sleep in it, but . . .'

'No need to explain,' Gerry said gently. 'It's the first room on the landing, next to yours. Take your time. I'll stay down here, start the washing-up, draw back the drawing-room curtains, do a bit of clearing up: write a shopping list. Make like a housewife.' Thinking that, with a modicum of luck, she'd have time to winkle Arthur's empties to her wheelie-bin, unnoticed. As for her shopping list, she must remember to add to it bread, butter, and booze. Above all booze, as a means of keeping Arthur under control.

When June came downstairs from her silent communion with Annie, Gerry had finished the washing-up, cleared away the empties from the drawing room, and was sitting at the kitchen table adding items to her shopping list, such as milk and tea-bags, fresh fruit and vegetables, cheese, meat, biscuits and toilet rolls, deriving a fiendish delight in imagining Arthur's face if she did, wickedly, decide to slip him a bill for his board and lodging. Serve him damn well right if she did.

She wouldn't, of course, for June's sake. Poor June, a once pretty woman, she imagined, now bowed down by the tragedy of her daughter's death. Also, more than likely, by her rough diamond of a husband, the kind of man, Gerry suspected, who, coming home from work, would expect to find his food on the table, and plenty of it. He'd polished off everything Gerry had set before him last night, soup, three lamb chops, mashed potatoes, veggies and pudding, belching windily afterwards, which she'd taken as a sign that he was filled, fed to capacity. In short, well fed up, as Gerry herself had been by his greed and total lack of finesse.

No wonder Annie had wanted to leave home, just as *she* had done when her own father had appeared, at table, wearing his cap, which he also wore day long about the house, to her mother's intense annoyance, hence the countless rows that had erupted between them, ending in battles accompanied by flying crockery when her ma's dander was up. Annie must have jumped at the chance of a job in a posh house in Hampstead, a room of her own, far away from her overbearing father and her downtrodden mother.

June Scott said hesitantly, 'I just wondered, Miss Frayling – Gerry – if you would mind going with us to Scotland Yard, this afternoon? A bit of a cheek, I know, but well, to be honest, I

45

could do with a bit of moral support, an' Arthur's not much use in that department.'

'Of course I'll go with you,' Gerry responded cheerfully, making up her mind to have a quiet word with Inspector Brambell about the letter Annie had received from Mrs Lazlo and her own, possibly erroneous conclusions that Annie had been a pre-determined murder victim to cover the tracks of a deranged serial killer in need of an irrefutable alibi to prove he was elsewhere when Annie was murdered at King's Cross Station.

Meanwhile, Gerry suggested a shopping trip to Hampstead Village to purchase the items on her shopping list, reminding June that it would do her the world of good to get out of the house for a while, to choose what she wanted for supper, because she really must try to eat something to keep body and soul together.

In the event, wandering round the village supermarket, June said she thought she could manage a bit of roast ham and salad for her supper, with Heinz salad cream, not mayonnaise. She didn't care for mayonnaise, neither did Arthur, who preferred Heinz tomato sauce with his food. Lots and lots of tomato sauce. And so, Gerry obediently purchased a quarter of roast ham, a bottle of Heinz salad cream and two bottles of tomato sauce, in addition to the bread, milk, tea bags, the six-pack of beer and the litre bottle of Scotch whisky already ensconced in her shopping trolley, not to mention a ready-cooked chicken, two fillets of rump steak, a half stone of potatoes, a bag of mixed salad leaves, a pound of tomatoes, a cucumber, a pound and a half of mushrooms, two sticky toffee puddings, a carton of custard, six chocolate éclairs, and a box of Nytol sleeping pills, the bill for which purchases amounted to tuppence short of forty quid. Well, Gerry thought, gritting her teeth as she proffered her credit card, at least June had enjoyed her outing to the supermarket. But what about loo-rolls? What on earth had possessed her to forget so important an addition to her shopping trolley, Gerry berated herself sharply. But not to worry, there was a chemist's shop next door to the supermarket, from which she eventually emerged lugging a dozen rolls of Andrex.

In the passenger seat of the Mini, June said anxiously,

'Time's getting on. Almost half past eleven already. What if Arthur isn't back in time for the car to Scotland Yard? He's been gone ages! What if he's met with an accident? Oh, Gerry, what do you suppose has become of him?'

With a modicum of good luck, Gerry thought maliciously, a broken leg, better still, two broken legs, a fractured collar-bone, several busted ribs and concussion. But no such luck. There he was, as large as life, apparently undamaged, on the doorstep of 'The Eyrie', awaiting their arrival, complaining bitterly that he was 'cod frozen' at being kept waiting so long, and wanting to know where the hell they had been, to which tirade Gerry replied charmingly that she hadn't realized he'd be so anxious to gain admittance to her 'almshouse'. But, since he was here, he'd best make himself useful in carrying the bags of shopping indoors, thrusting them at him, one by one, from the boot of her Mini, calling out to him, 'Here, catch!' and 'Whoops, sorry,' when the bag containing the booze landed squarely on the great toe of his left foot. Then, 'Well, that's the lot! Now, how about a nice cup of hot Bovril before we set off for Scotland Yard?'

Excusing herself, Gerry absented herself from Inspector Brambell's office during discussion of Annie's funeral, which she felt to be a private matter, in which she as a non-family member could not possibly participate. 'I'll wait in the corridor,' she said, with an encouraging smile at June. Brambell nodded his approval of Gerry's sensitivity. A nice woman, he thought, despite DI Clooney's oft-repeated condemnation of her as a 'pushy' individual. Brambell wondered, not for the first time, if he should dismiss Clooney from this particular investigation, well aware of the older man's proclivity to put people's backs up, as he had done Geraldine Frayling's. On the other hand, the old boy was overdue for retirement, and to dismiss a senior officer without justifiable cause would come as a grave discourtesy towards a colleague presently awaiting a replacement DCI to assume the responsibility of the Hampstead Police Station.

Brambell had, at least, the reins of the King's Cross Murder investigation in his own hands, not that he was making much progress at the moment. The whole sorry affair being linked with events at Hampstead where Annie had spent the past months of her life working for the Lazlos.

Brambell cursed his luck that Clooney, not he, had interviewed Elliot Lazlo: had elicited from him a statement which said virtually nothing of importance, beyond a categorical denial of any involvement whatever in the death of the tramp on Hampstead Heath. But the man *must* be involved. Possibly a visit to Scotland Yard would loosen his tongue?

Geraldine Frayling had, at least, given him the names of four people present at the Lazlos' Christmas house party; those of Bretton Sandys, his wife, and the Dumases, those aptly named literary agents, due for interview once their whereabouts had been discovered. Unsurprisingly, Annie's parents had been unable to supply information relevant to their daughter's demise. To the contrary, he had become bogged down by matters pertaining to the poor girl's funeral: the arrangements necessary to the release of her body for burial in York.

The arrangements concluded to the Scotts' satisfaction, seated at his desk, head in hands, when they had left his office, hearing a knock on the door, straightening his shoulders, 'Come in,' he called out, hoping for a pot of tea and a plate of biscuits, though he hadn't, so far as he could recall, had any lunch yet. No wonder, the hands of his office clock stood at twenty minutes past one, which meant, God damn it, that the canteen's specialité de la maison, steak pie, mashed potatoes and peas, would have disappeared long ago, in which case he'd have to settle for sausages, chips and baked beans.

Gerry came into his office. 'I'm sorry to disturb you,' she apologized, 'but, putting two and two together, I believe that Annie Scott's murder was planned well in advance, that her job with the Lazlos was pre-arranged by her killer. Why else would he have placed an advert in a York paper? Why send her a return rail ticket to York, when one advert in the London papers would have sufficed? Why send her a photograph of Bagdale Manor and a list of her duties should her London interview prove successful? Why should Dorothea Lazlo have sent that letter? Because she *didn't*, that's why! At least, that's my belief. I can't prove it, but I'll bet a hundred pounds to a hayseed I'm right! Poor Annie went to her death because of that advert!'

Ye gods, Brambell thought bemusedly, Gerry may well be right. If so, he'd certainly haul in the Lazlos for further questioning. Not that Mrs Lazlo had been interviewed thus far. An oversight on Clooney's part?

That Annie had been lured to London deliberately as the sacrificial lamb in a murder plot seemed bizarre on the face of it. 'Why Annie? Why a young girl from York?' he asked Gerry intently.

'Because of the rail link, the ease of the journey. I imagine it's quicker to get to York from London than it is to get to Southend-on-Sea nowadays,' Gerry supplied eagerly. 'No changing, no messing. Why not ask Annie's father? He's a signalman at York Station.'

'Is he still in the building?'

'Yes, the reception area!'

'Good. I'll speak to him at once.' Brambell pressed his desk-buzzer. A young sergeant appeared. 'Sir?'

'There's a Mr Scott in reception. Find him and bring him here at once.'

'Sir!' The sergeant promptly disappeared.

Gerry stood up. 'I'd rather not be here when he comes,' she explained. 'Mind if I hop it?'

Brambell grinned. 'Not at all. I'll be in touch, and thanks, Miss Frayling.'

'For what?'

'Opening a new can of worms?' he suggested quizzically.

Arthur had been upset. This much was obvious, the man was livid, his complexion the colour of lead and mottled purple in the region of his threadveins, which resembled a map of the London Underground, to Gerry's way of thinking, a curious combination of the Metropolitan and Piccadilly lines crisscrossing his cheekbones and the bridge of his nose in careless confusion.

'Oh Arthur, try to calm down,' his wife beseeched him. 'You'll bring on a heart attack if you're not careful. Think of your blood pressure.' Making things worse, not better, 'What did Inspector Brambell say to you exactly?'

'*Say* to me? *Say* to me? Damn near accused me of murdering my own daughter! Asked me a lot of damn-fool questions about my job: railway timetables, if I work night shifts, how often, an' if I'd been on night shift when Annie was killed!'

'And what did *you* say to *him*?' June persisted anxiously.

'Say to *him*? I told him to mind his own bloody business. Asked him who the hell he thought he was – God Almighty? The bloody pip-squeak!'

Gerry groaned inwardly, wishing to heaven she'd kept her mouth shut. Opening a can of worms was one thing, living with the consequences was a different matter entirely.

She said placatingly, 'Well, we're home now. I expect you're hungry, I know I am.'

'Huh,' Arthur snarled, 'wish I'd stayed on at the bed and breakfast. I could at least have nipped into the pub at the end of the street for a couple of pork pies and a sandwich instead of being bloody starved to death.'

'Oh Arthur, how could you say such a thing after all Gerry's done for us?' June's eyes filled with tears.

'Don't worry about it,' Gerry smiled, 'it won't take long to heat up a pan of soup and make sandwiches,' thinking what a good job she'd bought that cooked chicken.

'*Sandwiches?*' Arthur burst forth. 'Is that all? I'm a big bloke, I am, with a healthy appetite. What I need is a fry-up – eggs, bacon, sausages, the full mazuma!'

'Sorry, no can do. I'm flat out of sausages and bacon. Tell you what, though, I'll cook your supper now, shall I? Rump steak, mashed taters, mushrooms, tomatoes, sticky toffee pudd'ns and custard.'

'Huh, that's more like it,' Arthur snorted, 'an' I like my steak well done, think on, not bloody in't middle. How long will it take?'

'That depends on how quickly you can peel the potatoes. The peeler's in the right-hand drawer near the sink, and the sink's over yonder, so the sooner you get cracking, the sooner you'll eat, OK? Do you want to borrow my pinny?'

'Now see here, my girl, peeling spuds is women's work. Let June do it. About time she stirred her stumps for a change, mooning about like a wet week.'

'No, *you* see here, Mr Scott. For one thing I am *not* your girl, for another, if you don't do as I ask, you'll have chicken sandwiches and lump it. You'll see neither hide nor hair of the rump steak, nor will you see egg nor shell of the six-pack and the bottle of whisky I've provided to keep you company on my drawing-room sofa, on which you spent the whole of last night in a drunken stupor, as I recall, on which I fervently hope that you will spend the whole of tonight. Do I make myself clear?'

'You must take me for a bloody fool,' he muttered sullenly, finding the potato peeler, knowing he'd met his match and not liking it one bit.

'Oh, must I?' Gerry said cheerfully. 'What a relief. In which case, no need of pretence.'

When the potatoes had been mashed, the steak suitably kizzened, mushrooms, tomatoes and a couple of fried eggs added to the meal, the sticky toffee puddings microwaved, the custard poured over them, and when Arthur had belched himself into the drawing room with his six-pack and bottle of Scotch, Gerry set about creating a tempting meal of roast ham and salad for June, chicken sandwiches for herself, a pot of tea for both of them.

'I'm really enjoying this,' June said, helping herself to the Heinz salad cream. 'I didn't realize how hungry I was till I started eating.' She smiled wanly, 'I can't remember the last time I had a meal prepared for me, and this is so dainty and tasty, little pieces of hard-boiled egg, a few radishes, and the ham's delicious, not all wet and salty like that pre-packed stuff in cellophane packets.'

'Glad you're enjoying it.' Gerry glanced at the woman concernedly, knowing she was far from happy deep down, just putting on a brave face. She said hesitantly, 'About Annie, the – funeral – is everything all right?'

'Taking her home, you mean? Yes, it's all arranged. We'll be leaving here tomorrow afternoon, not by train from King's Cross, I couldn't have borne that. Inspector Brambell was so kind in offering us the use of a – a mortuary vehicle and a police car and driver for the journey back to York.'

June's face crumpled suddenly. 'It just seems so – awful. Everything, I mean. Like a nightmare. I just can't believe that Annie left home happy and smiling – and *now*!'

'I know, love. I *know*!' Clasping June's hands across the kitchen table, she added truthfully, being Gerry, 'But that's

51

bunkum, isn't it? How could I possibly know what it feels like to lose a child, never having had one myself?'

'But you will have a child, children, one of these days, won't you, when you and your fiancé get married?'

'Yes,' Gerry said decisively, 'lots of children, God willing.' She paused awhile, then said, 'I think you should go up to bed now. I know it's early, but you need to rest, to sleep if at all possible.'

June said, with a spark of humour, 'I might just do that – if you slip me a couple of – "aspirin"! The ones you gave me last night worked wonders!'

'I'm sorry I was a bit hard on your husband,' Gerry said. No way would she refer to him as Arthur.

June's smile faded. 'You don't think Inspector Brambell really believes Arthur had anything to do with Annie's death, do you?' And, 'No, of course not,' Gerry replied unconvincingly.

Six

'**M**r Bretton Sandys?' Inspector Brambell spoke quietly, but the man seated at the desk in a somewhat untidy office appeared startled.

'I didn't hear you knock,' he said confusedly. 'Who are you? What do you want? I'm rather busy at the moment, as you can see. In any case, members of the public are not admitted into my private quarters.'

'I'm sorry, sir. I did knock, and I am not, strictly speaking, a member of the public. I am Detective Chief Inspector Brambell of Scotland Yard. The gentleman with me is Detective Sergeant Briggs, here on official business. Now, Mr Sandys, may we come in?'

'Official business? What kind of business?' Sandys rose to his feet unsteadily, clinging to the edge of his desk for support. 'There's nothing wrong here, I can assure you. My partner and I run a thriving business . . .' His voice trailed away momentarily, then, ashen-faced, 'It isn't my mother, is it? Oh, dear God, please don't tell me she's dead! I couldn't bear it, I really couldn't!'

'No, Mr Sandys, Mrs Lazlo is perfectly well so far as I know. We are here to enquire into the death of a Miss Annie Scott, a former servant in the Lazlo household.'

'*Who*? But I've never even heard of her!'

'Really? I find that hard to believe,' Brambell said coolly, 'since her name has featured strongly in the media of late, in newspapers and on television as a murder victim whose body was discovered in a women's cloakroom at King's Cross Station ten days ago.'

'No! I'm sorry, but no! The name doesn't ring a bell. I seldom watch television, and I am not remotely interested in the gutter press. I have more important things on my mind.

Running a business for one thing. Flowers don't simply grow on their own, Inspector, they need constant attention. Besides which there's so much paperwork to see to. In any case, I fail to see what the death of a servant has to do with me.'

DS Briggs got in on the act. 'You stayed at Bagdale Manor over the Christmas period, did you not? You, your wife and a Mr Alex French?'

'Yes. So what?'

'In which event, you must have come into contact with Miss Scott on more than one occasion,' Briggs reminded him.

'I may have done so of course. If so, I scarcely noticed. I am not in the habit of hobnobbing with servants.'

Disliking the man intensely, weighing up his appearance – lank, over-long fair hair, narrow face, his bony high-bridged nose, weak mouth and indeterminate chin embellished with a straggling goatee beard – Brambell said coldly, 'Possibly your wife's memory is better than yours? If so, I'd like a word with her.'

'She isn't here,' Sandys said quickly. 'She's out shopping in York. The sales are on. She may be some considerable time. She usually makes a day of it; lunching out, etc.' He added grimly, 'Spending money hand over fist. Well you know what women are like?'

Changing the subject adroitly, 'Tell me, Mr Sandys, what is the distance between here and York?' Brambell enquired mildly, assuming his 'country doctor' persona, 'Ten miles? Twenty? At a rough guess, I mean.'

'Fifteen miles precisely,' Sandys supplied loftily, 'the reason why my garden centre has proved so successful. I chose its location very carefully beforehand, I can assure you. Not too far out of town, with plenty of open land on which to establish my glasshouses, and with living accommodation to boot, albeit a house badly in need of repair. *This* house, as a matter of fact, which, as previously stated, is my own private and personal property, inadmissable to the general public, yourself included, Detective Chief Inspector Brambell, and your sergeant. In short, I'm asking you to leave now. I'm certain you can find your own way out. Do I make myself clear?'

'Abundantly so, Mr Sandys,' Brambell acknowledged, admitting defeat at the hands of this long-haired, long-nosed, weak-chinned, self-righteous little twit – not in the habit of 'hobnobbing' with servants, indeed.

As they were about to quit the premises, Sandys' detached house overlooking an acre or so of glasshouses dedicated to the growth of embryo lobelia and alyssum, antirrhinum, salvia, pansies and wallflowers in readiness for the 'bedding out' season of the year, suddenly a thickset, handsome man stepped forward to impede Brambell's and Briggs' departure towards their car, parked in the forecourt of 'Sandys' Garden Centre' emblazoned on a board above the entrance gates of the premises.

Smiling broadly, he said, 'I'm Alex French, Brett's partner in crime, so to speak. Anything I can do to help? Couldn't help catching the drift of the conversation. Well, I remember Annie Scott if he doesn't. What exactly do you want to know about her?'

Brambell and Briggs exchanged glances. French said expansively, 'Let's go to my flat, shall we?' Leading the way upstairs, 'Do sit down, gentlemen, and make yourselves comfortable. Now, what'll it be, tea or coffee, or would you prefer a drop of the hard stuff?'

'Thank you, coffee will be fine.' Brambell glanced round the room as he spoke, a large room with doors leading presumably to the kitchen, bedroom and bathroom, taking stock of the colour TV set near the old-fashioned fireplace, bookshelves in the alcoves, the sideboard on which stood a gadrooned silver tray containing various bottles of liquor, a soda syphon and cut-glass tumblers.

Other furniture included a three-piece suite with faded cretonne covers, a small dining table and chairs near the bay window, a roll-top desk, a glass-topped coffee table in front of the settee on which, returning from the kitchen, Alex placed a tray of cups and saucers, a coffee-pot and a plate of shortbread biscuits.

'I take it you live here alone?' Brambell asked, accepting a cup of strong black coffee, waving aside the sugar basin and biscuits, yet helping himself judiciously to a smidgin of cream from a Sunderland lustre jug.

'Yes, you see, Inspector, I value my independence, as I'm sure Brett and Carla value theirs. In fact, I made separate accommodation a prerequisite of entering into partnership with Sandys.' He smiled urbanely. 'Brett's a good bloke on the whole, the trouble is, he has a one-track mind. All he thinks about, really cares about, is this garden centre of his: making a success of it.'

'And is he making a success of it?' Brambell asked, stirring cream into his coffee.

'You mean financially? Well, yes and no. To be brutally honest, he'd be a damn sight better off without that spendthrift wife of his, a luxury he can scarcely afford. I've told him so often enough, but he won't listen. He's besotted with the woman. Mind you, she *is* attractive, and so she should be, the money she spends on her appearance.' He continued, speaking confidentially as if afraid of being overheard, 'My belief is that she's having a bit on the side.'

'An affair, you mean?' Briggs asked succinctly, entering the conversation abruptly, a man who preferred to call a spade a spade, not a shovel. He added brusquely, 'This is a murder inquiry, not a guessing game. If Mrs Sandys *is*, as you suggest, engaged in an extra-marital relationship, presumably you know with whom?'

'No, I don't. In any case, what has that to do with Annie Scott?'

'Fair enough,' Brambell conceded amiably, with a concili-atory glance in his colleague's direction, 'by all means, let's talk about Annie Scott, shall we? Go ahead, Mr French, we're listening.'

'There isn't much to tell, really,' Alex replied evasively, sore over his brief encounter with the rough side of DS Briggs' tongue. 'She simply struck me as being an odd kind of girl . . .'

'Odd? In what way?' Brambell prompted him gently.

'Well, that's difficult to say. As if she needed to feel important, to be noticed in some way. Not that she was very good-looking, she wasn't, but she had the cheek of Old Nick. Believe it or not, she actually made a pass at me. Several passes as a matter of fact.'

'You mean she – propositioned you?' Brambell asked. 'Invited you to her room?'

'Nothing as blatant as that,' Alex confessed, 'I'd have given her short shrift had she done so. No, she just flirted outrageously. Wherever I went, she'd be there, making sheep's eyes at me. A chap can always tell. It was damned embarrassing, to be honest. More than likely she'd have been given the sack if I'd breathed a word to Elliot Lazlo.'

'Miss Scott *was* given the sack,' Brambell said flatly, 'on the day preceding her murder.'

'You don't say? Well, don't look at me! I didn't blab, if that's what you're thinking.'

'Tell me, Mr French, do you recall Mr Lazlo being called away, on Christmas Eve, by Miss Scott, to speak to a man, a tramp by all accounts, who had turned up on the kitchen doorstep and refused to leave without seeing Mr Lazlo?'

'Yeah, come to think of it. Why, is it important?'

'Certainly, insofar as Annie Scott later discovered the body of a man, in tramp's clothing, in a shallow grave on Hampstead Heath. The man had been murdered.'

'Ye gods! And you think Annie was responsible for his – murder?' Obviously shaken, rising to his feet, French crossed to the sideboard to pour himself a half tumbler of whisky. 'Hope you don't mind,' he apologized. 'But I really need this,' swallowing a mouthful of the hard stuff. 'Quite sure you won't join me? No? Well, suit yourselves! But frankly, Inspector, I'm out of my depth here! Why the hell would Annie Scott, of all people, have resorted to – murder?'

'She didn't,' Brambell assured him calmly, 'someone else did! Presumably the person responsible for Annie's own murder, the reason why we, Briggs and myself, are here, to discover the truth of the matter.'

Alex shrugged his shoulders dismissively. 'Well, I've told you all I know. So who's next on your list of suspects – Carla?' Downing another mouthful of whisky, 'A waste of time, old chap, believe me. You'll get no change out of her. She'll look through you, not at you: pretend she hasn't a clue what you're on about. What's more, she won't be kidding. What Carla has between her ears, it certainly isn't brains.' He chuckled unpleasantly. 'Someone should tack a sign on her forehead – "Vacant room to let".' As the two policemen rose to their feet, 'Oh, off now, are you? No more shots left in your locker?'

'Just one, Mr French. Tell me, truthfully, how much capital have you invested in the Sandys' Garden Centre?'

'Truthfully?' Alex pulled a wry face. 'Not a bean, old sport, for the good and simple reason that I had no capital to invest. But it wasn't money Brett wanted, far from. His mother forks out the necessary on a regular basis to underwrite her son's so called business venture, and why not? She's stinking rich, God knows. No wonder he went all weak and feeble in that pigsty of an office of his when he thought she was a goner. I mean to say, the thought of all that lovely money passing into the wrong hands if the old girl hasn't made a will!

'The fact is, Brett made me an offer I couldn't refuse. He needed a minder, a kind of human guard dog. I needed somewhere to live, a job of work to do. Brett and I had been at school together. He was bullied unmercifully by the prefects, one boy in particular, a muscle-bound swine called Agnew, who had it in for Brett good and proper. Well, to cut a long story short, I gave Agnew a damn good hiding: told him to lay off Brett or he'd get more than a cut lip and a bloody nose next time, and told him to pass on the message to his pals.

'From then on, I assumed the role of a hero in Brett's eyes – bloody embarrassing really. Well, the long and short of it is, I landed myself in a spot of bother with the police a while back – a dodgy business deal that back-fired.' Alex smiled disarmingly. 'Might as well come clean. You'd have found out sooner or later anyway. So here I am, living under false pretences. Just one thing, Inspector, I had nothing whatever to do with the murder of Annie Scott!'

Strangely enough, Brambell felt inclined to believe him.

'Now where to, sir?' Briggs asked, driving away from Bretton Sandys' garden centre.

'To the nearest pub for a beer and a bite to eat,' Brambell replied, 'to take away the taste of that bloody awful coffee.'

Over two pints of Tetley's and plates of roast beef sandwiches, DS Briggs voiced his opinion that something fishy was going on at Sandys' Garden Centre, warranting further investigation. After all, a long-haired twit with an Oedipus complex, a spendthrift wife more than likely engaged in an adulterous affair with the local squire, not to mention a minder with a criminal record.

Swallowing his last mouthful of bitter, 'Quite right, Bert,' Brambell said regretfully, 'the trouble is, we can scarcely proceed further until all the guests at the Lazlos' Christmas house party have been interviewed, including Dorothea Lazlo, the hostess, who can scarcely deny having known Annie Scott, since she may have been instrumental in employing the girl in the first place.'

'*May* have been?' Bert Briggs frowned. 'Why? I thought it was she who wrote to Annie, who sent her a rail-ticket to London for the interview?'

'Supposition for the time being, laddie,' Brambell reminded him, shrugging into his overcoat and applying his hat, a brown felt trilby, to his head, 'the reason why I intend paying a visit to Bagdale Manor tomorrow morning. You'll accompany me, of course?'

'Of course, sir,' Briggs responded happily. 'It wouldn't be a show without Punch!'

A bond of respect and affection existed between Brambell and his colleague. The DCI placed utter reliance in the younger man's dedication to his job, his devotion to his wife and children. Briggs equally admired Brambell's sense of justice and fair play, his quirky sense of humour, the astuteness of his razor-sharp mind belied by his occasionally assumed persona of an absent-minded professor, a parson or a country doctor.

'Where to next, sir?' Briggs asked, seated behind the steering wheel of Brambell's Mercedes. 'London?'

'Not quite yet,' Brambell murmured apologetically, 'to a village on the outskirts of York, a few miles from here. Whitwell, or some such name. You see, Annie Scott's funeral is due to take place there, in the village church at two o'clock, and I'd like to pay my respects, if you don't mind, that is.'

'Mind? Of course not, sir! I'll be honoured to come with you,' Briggs replied, 'though I'm not really dressed for a funeral.'

'Neither am I, come to think of it,' Brambell confessed, 'but we'll sit at the back. I don't suppose anyone will notice. I did think to bring a couple of black ties, however. They're in a plastic bag in the glove compartment.'

'If I'd known beforehand, I'd have sent flowers,' Briggs said ruefully.

Brambell smiled, 'Not to worry, laddie, you already have, daffodils and tulips. I ordered them yesterday, from thee and me, just a spray. I figured that Annie would like spring flowers.'

Briggs, the father of a teenage daughter, blurted savagely, 'The person responsible for Annie's murder will be brought to justice, won't he?'

'Oh yes,' Brambell replied grimly, 'you can depend on it!'

Gerry had also sent flowers, two dozen red roses, from Bruno, the name of Annie's dog.

She had driven from London to Whitwell, setting off in the early hours of the morning, wanting to attend the funeral for June Scott's sake, and as a mark of respect for Annie.

In floods of tears, June had clung to Gerry as to a lifeline when she had called at the house to offer her condolences, begging her to return to the house after the funeral, to stay overnight if possible, offers which Gerry gently but firmly refused, knowing that to spend time beneath the same roof as Arthur Scott was a sheer impossibility, saying she must return to London after the service, since snow had been forecast, which was perfectly true, and she didn't fancy getting stuck in a snowdrift. Equally true.

Seated at the back of the church, berating herself as a blithering coward, Gerry's heart lifted when she caught sight of Brambell and Briggs sliding into the same pew as herself. Thanking God for the long arm of the law, help was at hand, she thought, should she need to fire a rocket from a snowdrift, a distinct possibility since snow was beginning to fall quite thickly now; flakes as big as goose-feathers, not the wet, clingy stuff.

The church was packed with villagers, minor local dignitaries, members of what Bill referred to as 'The Press Gang'. There were TV cameramen in the graveyard ready to record the arrival of the cortège. Gerry could imagine the newscaster's commentary on the six o'clock news, spoken in a level voice devoid of emotion, simply referring to poor Annie as the victim of 'the King's Cross Murder'. End of story. The end of Annie, whose body had duly been buried in the Whitwell Church cemetery, amid a flurry of thickly falling snowflakes.

'I thought I might find you here,' Brambell said gently, leading Gerry away from the graveside for a quiet word. 'Have you any immediate plans?' Casting an eye at the low-hanging clouds and the whirling snowflakes. 'My sergeant and I are heading to London straight away.'

'Me too,' Gerry replied, shivering with cold and fatigue. 'Mrs Scott invited me to stay overnight, but I refused. I just want to go home.'

'But are you fit to drive?'

'Fit or not, that's what I intend doing. I can't stay here, I just *can't*.'

'Of course not, nor should you. On the other hand . . .' A thought occurred, 'Would you consider coming with me? Letting Sergeant Briggs drive the Mini?'

'The way I feel right now, I'd consider anything: walking, thumbing a lift, riding pick-a-back,' Gerry said, her gutsy sense of humour gaining the upper hand, 'so yes, Inspector, and thank you, if you're sure Sergeant Briggs won't mind exchanging a Merc for a Mini.'

Briggs smiled. 'I like Minis,' he assured her, 'especially red ones.'

So all was settled. After a brief farewell to June, assuring her that she would keep in touch, Gerry strapped herself into the passenger seat of Brambell's Mercedes, sighed blissfully, and promptly fell fast asleep.

She was going home!

Seven

B rambell felt as if he were treading on eggshells on his arrival at Bagdale Manor to interview Dorothea Lazlo. Not only was this a world-famous artist, but words had passed between himself and Inspector Clooney when he'd told his Hampstead colleague of his intention to question her personally.

In short, Clooney had taken the huff. 'Are you implying that I am incapable of conducting my own interviews?' he'd demanded sourly.

'Not at all. But time is of the essence in this inquiry, and to the best of my knowledge and belief, Mrs Lazlo has, so far, not been interviewed at all,' Brambell reminded him. 'Correct me if I'm wrong, Inspector!'

Deflated, Clooney had conceded the high ground to his superior officer. Knowing full well that he should have interviewed Dorothea Lazlo himself, and had failed to do so, had caused Clooney sleepless nights, of late. Now, apparently, he was being made to suffer the consequences of his dereliction of duty. A bitter pill for a man of his age and rank to swallow.

Not that Brambell had been either dictatorial or demanding, nor had he mentioned his failure to report details of the Lazlos' Christmas guest list. Glossing over that further dereliction of duty on the part of his subordinate, Brambell had simply requested him to interview a literary agent called Dumas at his offices in North Audley Street, adjacent to the Roosevelt Memorial in Grosvenor Square. Another slap in the eye so far as the touchy Clooney was concerned.

Entering Bagdale Manor, accompanied by DS Briggs, awaiting the arrival of Dorothea Lazlo in the comfortably furnished drawing room into which they'd been ushered by a stout woman with an ultra-refined middle-class accent, Brambell experienced a feeling of trepidation at his forthcoming interview with a world-renowned artist.

Stepping closer to the fireplace, 'Now that's what I call a painting,' he said, gazing up at a picture of lilacs on a windowsill against a background of falling rain, so vivid that one could fairly catch the fragrance of the lilacs and hear the beating of the rain on the windowpanes.

'I hadn't reckoned you as an art lover,' Briggs remarked drily.

'I'm not. I just know what I like, and I like that,' Brambell replied, edging closer to the fireplace.

'With respect, sir, that's a coal fire in the grate, and – whoops!' Nudging Brambell aside and grasping hold of hefty brass firetongs from the Victorian hearth tidy, quickly Briggs tossed back into the fire a sizeable lump of red-hot coal.

'Holy smoke,' Brambell muttered. 'If that had landed on my foot! Thanks, Briggs. Well fielded, laddie!'

'Well done indeed, young man!' Dorothea had entered the room unnoticed. Turning, they beheld on the threshold of the room a tall, slender, grey-haired woman wearing a long black dress and a matching scarlet-lined velvet cloak with a stand-up collar framing a still remarkably beautiful face.

Gliding forward, smiling, a slender be-ringed hand extended in greeting, 'I am Dorothea Lazlo, and you must be Inspector Brambell and DS Briggs? I hope I haven't kept you waiting?'

'Not at all, ma'am,' Brambell murmured respectfully.

'So you admire my *Lilacs in the Rain*, do you?' Dorothea enquired charmingly of DCI Brambell. 'I'm quite attached to it myself as it happens, since it was one of my first efforts, painted a long time ago, in the springtime of my life, long before I embarked on my more serious volume of work.'

She paused momentarily then added wistfully, 'I'd so like to show you my studio, if you can spare the time, that is? If so, please come with me. Catering to the whims of an old woman, if you like, whose glory days as an artist have long since gone, due to failing eyesight and arthritic hands. Inevitable consequences of illness and increasing old age, I fear.'

'But of course,' Brambell acquiesced, intent upon visiting

Dorothea Lazlo's studio, deeply aware of his gut feeling, as a seasoned police officer, that he was being led, by the nose, up or down a garden path, whichever, by a very clever woman, neither short-sighted nor arthritic, judging by those slender be-ringed hands of hers, and her sparkling, wide-awake eyes. So just what the hell was going on here?

Quitting Bagdale Manor by a side door, following in the wake of Mrs Lazlo, he received something of a jolt when he found himself in the walled garden to the rear of the main house, approaching a smaller, one-storey building set in a plantation of thickly crowded trees, leafless at this time of year, a dense shrubbery of spotted laurels and what appeared to be rhododendron and azaleas. A formidable barrier lining a narrow concrete path leading to the door of the studio.

Awaiting the unlocking of the door, gazing about him at the rest of the garden, staring up at the high, tree-lined walls, noticing a maze of cracked concrete paths, sprouting grass, leading to the main house, weed-choked borders and flower-beds, a rusty iron gazebo and a stagnant fish pond, Brambell shivered slightly despite his warm winter overcoat, repelled by the garden's state of neglect, wondering why the devil it had been allowed to fall into such a state? Surely the Lazlos, monied people by all accounts, could afford at least a jobbing gardener to keep their property in a better state of repair?

At the far end of the garden, Brambell noticed a series of iron steps leading to a verandah fronting, presumably, the first-floor rear windows of the manor? A nice look out, he thought, for guests of the Lazlos, rising from their beds to contemplate nothing more than cracked concrete, rusted ironwork and a stagnant fish pond. Ah well, so far as he knew, there was no law against the peculiarities of the human race, not unless such peculiarities included murder, or cruelty to animals.

Then suddenly, animals, he thought, catching sight of a dog-kennel in the vicinity of Dorothea's studio. A kennel with an iron dog-collar attached to a rusted iron chain. And, Annie's dog, he remembered. Poor Annie Scott's dog. The poor brute who had lain beside her, whimpering, on the night she was murdered; strangled to death with the creature's own lead.

Having opened the door of her studio and switched off the

64

burglar alarm system, 'Do please come this way, gentlemen,' Dorothea said invitingly, leading the way up a twisting iron staircase to an upper room, raftered, and bearing the hallmarks of a professional artist – a throne mounted on a dais, long tables cluttered with paintbrushes, palettes, bottles of turpentine, sticks of charcoal, easels and canvases. 'Well, here it is, my spritual home. At least it used to be in my glory days, though I still come here quite often – to recapture those days. Unsuccessfully, I'm afraid, since my recent illness.'

Brambell said conversationally, 'Tell me, Mrs Lazlo, when you hired Alex French as your son's bodyguard, were you aware of his criminal record?'

Dorothea's smile faded. 'Really, Inspector,' she said coolly, 'I thought you came to look at my studio, not to shock me into an admission of some kind.'

'Actually, Mrs Lazlo, I came in my capacity as a police officer engaged in a murder inquiry, to ask questions, hopefully to receive answers. I thought that was clearly understood when you granted me access to your home. If my question startled you, I'm sorry. But you still haven't answered.'

Dorothea shrugged her shoulders dismissively. 'Very well then. Of course I knew. But Alex had served his term of imprisonment. My son needed someone to look after his – interests. He and Alex had been at school together. Brett has never been physically robust. He liked and trusted Alex and so, when he was released from prison, I got in touch with him. What's wrong with that? Or is there a law against a mother acting in her son's best interests?'

'Not that I know of.' Brambell smiled placatingly. 'Thank you for being so candid.' Glancing at his watch, 'Now, with your permission, may we return to the house to continue the interview? Just a few more questions, then my sergeant and I will be on our way.'

'More questions?' Dorothea uttered distastefully. 'Tell me, Inspector, do you enjoy prying into people's private affairs?'

'Unfortunately, ma'am, "Murder will out", as the saying goes,' Brambell reminded her, as they returned to the Bagdale Manor drawing room.

*   *   *

65

'Well, sir, what did you make of all that?' Briggs asked, heading the car towards Scotland Yard.

'More to the point, what did *you* make of it?' Brambell insisted quietly. 'Two brains are better than one, and I'd value your comments.'

'I think that Mrs Lazlo was playing for time when she invited us to her studio, and to create an impression of herself as a – clapped-out geriatric – which she obviously is not. Failing eyesight and arthritic hands, my foot!'

'Ah, so you twigged that too?' Brambell sighed deeply. 'Go on.'

'And when you asked her about that letter she had supposedly written to Annie Scott, enclosing a return ticket, photographs of Bagdale Manor and so on, what a performance! An artist? More of an actress, I'd say! She'd make a marvellous Lady Macbeth!'

'I hadn't figured you as a Shakespeare buff,' Brambell said teasingly.

Briggs grinned. 'Is sir extracting the Michael, by any chance?'

'As if. Pray continue. And get a move on, otherwise it'll be bangers and baked beans for us, my lad!'

'As for all that tarradiddle about Annie being chosen from a long list of applicants, and thinking the world of her, and knowing nothing whatever about the tramp who came to the house last Christmas Eve, who did she think she was kidding? I didn't believe a word of it. Do you mean to tell me that a husband wouldn't tell his wife there'd been a bloke at the back door making a nuisance of himself? I'd tell my wife, right enough, and even if I didn't, she'd find out in two shakes of a lamb's tail.'

'So you think Mrs Lazlo was lying?' Brambell mused.

'I'd stake my life on it,' Briggs replied. 'Oh, sorry sir, I didn't mean to utter the "s" word.'

'Steak, you mean?' Brambell sighed deeply. 'Tell you what, I know of a nice little restaurant not far from here. What would you say to a man-size porterhouse steak, and chips?'

'Yes, *sir*!' came the immediate response.

Later, nearing repletion, chasing a remaining chip round his plate, and the last morsel of steak, Briggs said, 'If only we had a lead on the tramp's identity. It bothers me to think of the poor devil "on ice", so to speak. He must have come from somewhere before ending up on Hampstead Heath. A hostel of some kind, for down and outs? Someone must have given him that balaclava and the army greatcoat. There must have been a reason why he turned up at Bagdale Manor on Christmas Eve. The back entrance strikes me as being significant. He obviously knew his way down the steps to the basement kitchen, which suggests he'd been there before. So why the heavy pall of silence?

'My guess is that someone in that house knew who he was, and the reason for his visit. All right, so perhaps he was just a beggar in need of a handout. If so, why did his killer remove all evidence of his identity? Come to think of it, why crack his skull, then fire a bullet into him when he was already as dead as mutton? It doesn't make sense, not unless his killer wasn't sure if that blow to his head had merely rendered him unconscious, and wanted to make damn certain that he really was dead.' Pushing aside his plate, 'So where do we go from here? I mean to say, we can't keep the poor bloke in cold storage indefinitely. What about the inquest? OK, so the verdict would be murder by a person or persons unknown, but at least we'd be able to give the poor sod a decent funeral.'

'Patience, laddie,' Brambell reminded him. 'When that funeral takes place, I want to see a name engraved on the head-stone. *His* name, along with his date of birth and "the beloved son of . . ." We owe him that much, don't you think?'

A thought occurred: 'What we need right now is someone to do a bit of snooping on our behalf. Someone, professing to be a relative of a missing person, poking and prying into hostels in the vicinity in search of her husband, brother, father or whatever.'

Briggs looked startled. 'A private detective, you mean?'

'Not as such –' Brambell smiled reflectively – 'more of a "Miss Marple" with a way of winkling out the truth, as she did in last year's "Antiques Murders", remember?'

'You mean – Geraldine Frayling – the crime novelist?' Briggs asked, disbelievingly. 'The girl I met yesterday at Annie Scott's funeral, whose Mini I drove back to Hampstead with my knees tucked under my chin?'

'The self and same,' Brambell assured him. 'A highly

intelligent lady with a specific interest in two murders, those of the tramp and Annie Scott, since she was on Hampstead Heath, with Annie, and her dog, at the scene of the tramp's murder, and it was she who came forward to help in our enquiries at the discovery of Annie's body in that cloakroom at King's Cross Station.' He paused momentarily to settle the bill for two porterhouse steaks, chips, soup, bread-rolls and two glasses of lager, then, 'Now do you see why I'd like to get Geraldine Frayling in on the act?'

'Yes, sir,' Briggs replied, not sounding too sure.

'Which reminds me,' Brambell frowned, 'I must discover the whereabouts of Annie Scott's dog.'

Inspector Clooney's interview with Jeremy Dumas, a pompous, elderly man who looked as if he'd been buffed with a chamois leather, had yielded nothing of importance pertaining to the identity of the tramp who came to Bagdale Manor last Christmas Eve.

'A tramp, you say? Good grief, man, do I appear the kind of person to associate with down-and-outs? Look here, Inspector, my wife and I were guests of the Lazlos on that occasion. I have acted in my capacity as Elliot Lazlo's literary agent for the past fifteen years, very successfully I might add. Lazlo and I spent some time together, in his study, discussing ideas for his next book. At no time did any mention of a – tramp arise. Why should it? Elliot had more important things on his mind. Knowing Lazlo as well as I do, if such a fellow had come to the house making a nuisance of himself, he would have dealt with the matter with a minimum of fuss, sent the fellow about his business, then forgotten all about it.'

Curiosity getting the better of him, Dumas asked, frowning slightly, 'But why all these damn-fool questions? Had the fellow a criminal record? Did he attempt to extort money from Lazlo? Threaten him in some way?'

'Not so far as I'm aware,' Clooney said narrowly, studying Dumas's face intently, disliking what he saw, that high-domed forehead of his, lantern-jaw, long bony nose on the bridge of which rested a pair of executive-style glasses, his narrow-lipped mouth and receding chin, his womanish hands drumming nervously the surface of his highly polished mahogany desk. 'Quite the reverse. That tramp ended up in a shallow grave on Hampstead Heath with a fractured skull and a bullet wound in his chest. In short, Mr Dumas, he's been murdered!'

'Good God!' Dumas uttered briefly. 'But who could have done such a thing, and – *why*?'

'That's why I'm here,' Clooney reminded him. 'To find out why.'

'But surely to God, you don't suspect *me*, do you?' Dumas blustered, wiping beads of sweat from his forehead with a white silk handkerchief. 'I tell you, Inspector, I knew nothing at all about that – tramp. You've got to believe me!'

Rising to his feet, Clooney said coolly, 'I'll be in touch with you again, Mr Dumas, if necessary. Just one thing more, if you intend leaving town, you will keep me informed of your whereabouts, won't you?'

To Clooney's infinite satisfaction, Dumas seemed incapable of leaving his office chair, for the time being, let alone London.

Next day, 'Good of you to come at such short notice, Miss Frayling,' Brambell said pleasantly, ushering her into his office. 'I trust you've recovered from the trauma of Annie Scott's funeral and the journey back to London?'

Gerry pulled a face, 'To be honest, Inspector Brambell, I scarcely remember anything about that journey, seeing I was asleep most of the time.' She added anxiously, 'I didn't snore, did I?'

Brambell laughed, 'Not that I noticed, but the windscreen wipers were going like the clappers, besides which I had a new tape to listen to, a Christmas present from my wife. I have a fondness for Tchaikovsky, you see? Particularly his *1812 Overture*, when the cannons start firing.'

'Oh Gawd,' Gerry uttered bleakly, 'as bad as that, was it?' She added sagaciously, 'But I doubt you sent for me to discuss my adenoidal defects, so why did you?'

'To offer you a job,' Brambell confessed, 'which you may not feel inclined to accept. An unpaid job involving a lot of legwork, a modicum of acting ability, and a hide like a rhinoceros. In short, Gerry, may I call you Gerry, by the way?

I want you to discover the identity of the tramp that you and Annie Scott discovered on Hampstead Heath. A tall order, I know, but he couldn't have sprung from nowhere. You see, Gerry, we really need to know who he was and why he turned up on the doorstep of Bagdale Manor, last Christmas Eve, prior to his murder, without which information, we, that is to say, myself and my Scotland Yard colleagues, are virtually hamstrung.'

Gerry *did* see. She said quietly, commonsensically, 'So when shall I start? Would tomorrow morning be soon enough?'

'You mean you really don't mind? Bearing in mind that it could be dangerous?' Brambell reminded her gently.

'Of course I don't mind,' Gerry assured him. 'Shall I wear a beard and a false moustache; carry a white stick and a begging bowl, or should I simply sail in where angels might fear to tread, as my own sweet self?'

'I leave all that to you. Why not consult Virginia Vale?' Brambell suggested, tongue in cheek, referring to Gerry's fictitious super-sleuth.

'Now why didn't I think of that? Knowing Virginia, she'd set about discovering drop-ins for dropouts. Do they still have soup-kitchens, I wonder? Hmm, I'll get in touch with the Sally Army and Social Services, make a list, buy a map.' She paused, then asked, 'Why me, by the way? I imagine you have scads of WPCs who would jump at the chance of a bit of sleuthing?'

'True enough,' Brambell conceded, 'but I figured that you would want to get in on the act, for Annie's sake. Also I admired the way you tackled that smuggling racket in Robin Hood's Bay, showing remarkable courage and resourcefulness in my estimation. If it hadn't been for you, we might never have tied in Christian Sommer and the rest of the gang in the so-called "Antiques Murders".'

'I couldn't have done it without Bill Bentine,' Gerry supplied modestly. 'If it hadn't been for him, I'd probably be blowing about in the wind on Hampstead Heath, right now. Getting into people's eyes and up their noses.'

'Ah, Bill Bentine, the man you're engaged to marry?' Brambell nodded. 'When is he due home, by the way?'

'I'm not certain, but it can't be soon enough for me.' Gerry sighed wistfully, then, springing up from her chair like a jack-in-the-box, 'Well, I'd best get going. I'll start phoning around right away, then I'll have an early night and start sleuthing at the crack of dawn.'

Pausing on the threshold, she said, 'Thanks, Inspector, for offering me this job. I'll do my best not to let you down.'

Eight

If she were Virginia Vale, about to embark on a mission impossible, where would she start looking for a faceless, nameless, murdered tramp in the purlieus of the Greater London area? Gerry asked herself.

Well, certainly not in the West End. Hardly likely he'd have booked in at Claridges, the Grosvenor Hotel, or the Ritz for a couple of nights prior to his back-door visit to Bagdale Manor, presumably in search of a handout from Elliot Lazlo. But why Lazlo? Why Bagdale Manor in particular?

Deep in thought, Gerry reckoned she'd best begin her search in the Hampstead area, wearing old clothes, comfortable walking shoes, a secondhand coat purchased from a charity shop, no make-up, and with a muffler tucked under her chin. But as what? The deceased's abandoned wife? His daughter? His 'bit on the side'? She rather fancied the latter, truth to tell, imagining herself whining tearfully, 'Oh Gawd, sir, I've just gotta find 'im, the fix I'm in. 'Is name? I dunno for sure. But 'e's tall an' good-lookin', wearin' an army greatcoat, boots, an' a balaclava 'elmet wot I knitted for 'im wiv me own two 'ands. If you've seen 'im or know where 'e is, for Gawd's sake tell me! Me bein' four months gorn, an' all!'

Well, perhaps not? Gerry thought. No use over-egging the pudding. Best settle for a role as his daughter, along the lines of, 'It's my ma I'm so worried about. They'd had a blazing row, you see, the night he walked out on us wearing his old army greatcoat and boots, and his balaclava helmet. Very angry and upset he was, at the time. But we miss him so much, and want him back home again as soon as possible.' And yes, Gerry thought, that sounded far more plausible.

But, despite her first day's intensive sleuthing, à la Virginia Vale, Gerry returned to her eyrie, at dusk, none the wiser as to the identity of the tramp than she had been when she'd set out early that morning. Having visited a number of hostels – cheap lodging houses and overnight dormitories for the down-and-out population of alcholics and drug-addicts in the area – apparently no one had so much as clapped eyes on a tramp wearing an army greatcoat and a balaclava helmet.

Solving the Antiques Murders had been a doddle compared with this, she thought, stripping off her sleuthing outfit and running a bathful of hot, scented water. At least she was getting plenty of exercise, she reminded herself, and not much to eat. All she'd had since her muesli and banana breakfast was a bacon butty and a mug of coffee from a caff near Hampstead Station.

Thinking of bacon butties reminded Gerry of Maggie and Barney Bowler's hamburger joint in the Old Kent Road. Recent events had made her plans to stay with them for a while virtually impossible. Now seemed as good a time as any to rectify that omission. Staying with Maggie and Barney, she'd be close to a wider field of investigation, far removed from the more upper-crust areas of London.

Finishing her bath, having paid special attention to pumice-stoning her feet, Gerry, warmly bundled up in a favourite old dressing gown of hers, went down to the kitchen to cast an anxious eye at the contents of the refrigerator. Oh Gawd, she thought, nothing but cold chicken and salad, when what she really needed was comfort food, and lots of it. Pork pie and chips. Bangers and mash. Eggs and bacon. Black Forest gateau. Chocolate ice-cream. Oh, very well then, cold chicken and salad it would have to be, the lettuce and tomatoes embellished with dollops of the Heinz salad cream she'd bought to please June Scott.

Suddenly, the phone rang. Picking up the receiver, 'Bill, is that you?' she asked anxiously.

'Sure it's me,' he assured her. 'Why? Who else?' Then, less lightheartedly, 'Say, Gerry, are you all right? You sound a bit uptight, that's all.'

'That's because I *am*! Up tighter than catgut on a violin! So would you be if you'd spent the day in and out of doss houses in search of a murder victim!'

'Good God! Don't tell me one has gone missing?' Only Gerry, he thought, could mislay a cadaver.

'He hasn't gone *missing*. We don't know who he is, and I'm not having fun trying to find out.'

'*We*, being?' Bill asked perplexedly, thinking this must be a bad connection and he wasn't hearing properly.

'Scotland Yard – and me,' Gerry supplied modestly.

'Good grief! Don't tell me you've joined the Force!'

'Well yes, in a manner of speaking, as an undercover agent. A kind of plain-clothes detective. And I *do* mean plain-clothes. Honestly, Bill, you should see my get-up! I had all on convincing one doss-house owner that *I* wasn't after a bed for the night!'

'Ye gods! And after you promised me faithfully that you'd keep out of trouble! What is it with you? Have you a death wish or something? Here am I in New York, slaving my guts out to get a deal for your current novel. And there are you, my soul-mate, my one and only, risking life and limb poking about in – doss houses!'

'Oh, Bill! Say it again,' Gerry beseeched him, coming over all romantic.

'I said, risking life and limb poking about in doss houses!'

'No. I meant before that. The bit about my being your soul-mate. Your one and only. Did you really mean it?'

'Of course I did! The fact remains, I'd sooner come home with a wedding, not a funeral, in mind!' He added briefly, 'Sorry, love, gotta go now. A nice publisher has me earmarked for a slap-up meal of lobster mayonnaise, New England turkey plus all the trimmings. Pecan pie with chocolate ice-cream, washed down with vintage champagne, and I mustn't keep him waiting. Otherwise he might change his mind about handing me a six-figure cheque for your latest brainchild. So 'bye for now, Gerry love. Be seeing you soon.'

'How soon?' Gerry asked. But the line had gone dead. Reluctantly, she returned to the kitchen to face her slab of cold chicken. Then, on a sudden impulse, returning to the telephone, she dialled the number of Barney's hamburger joint. Maggie answered the call.

'Look, Maggie, Gerry here,' she said urgently. 'Is my room still vacant? It is? Oh, thank God! I'll be there in an hour or so, if that's OK? Maggie, you're a gem! And I'm bloody hungry! So how about *what*? A double beefburger and chips? Oh, yes, *please*! With a double helping of chips, plus a bacon butty!'

As Gerry entered the hamburger joint an hour and a quarter later, having ditched the cold chicken and salad into her outside dustbin, and exchanged her dressing gown in favour of her sleuthing get-up, Maggie said succinctly, 'What the hell's up with you? You look like the Wreck of the Hesperus, and then some!'

'I know. But I'm in disguise for the time being. I'll tell you why, later. What I need, right now, is food! Lots and lots of food!'

'But what about your diet? And what have you done to your hair? And where the heck did you get that coat you're wearing? All right, I can wait. So sit yourself down and get something to eat inside you. Gawd's truth, girl, you look worse than some of them tramps wot come in here for their early morning breakfasts!'

'*Tramps?*' Gerry asked eagerly. 'What kind of tramps? Where from? What do they look like?'

'Like – *tramps*,' Maggie said briskly. 'You know! Pretty much the same as you do right now! Mind you, they're not all dropouts. Far from. Just down on their luck for the time being. And some of 'em ain't tramps at all, just actors. There's been a lot of filming going on recently for one of them television series: *The Bill*, or whatever. Darned if I can remember which one. There's so many of them on telly, these days.'

Actors, Gerry thought deeply, awaiting the arrival of her double hamburger and chips. So what if she'd been wasting her time scouring the doss houses of Hampstead if the tramp she was in search of had been, not a bona-fide tramp at all, but an actor? Only one way to find out. But not right here and now! Not until she had bitten deeply into a bread bun containing Barney's specialité de la maison, a hamburger topped with melted cheddar cheese, alongside a plateful of chips, thick-cut chips, crisp on the outside, floury within, served with a separate dish of sweet pickle relish.

'Feeling better now, are you?' Maggie asked discerningly, removing Gerry's empty plate from the formica-topped table.

'Ready for your bacon butty? Or will you settle for a mug of coffee? Your eyes being bigger than your belly?'

'Yeah, thanks, Maggie,' Gerry conceded. 'A cup of coffee will do me fine. I'll have the bacon butty for breakfast first thing tomorrow morning, if that's OK with you?'

'Anything you do is OK with Barney and me,' Maggie reminded her. 'Just as long as you are not in danger. As you were the last time you stayed here. Remember?'

Gerry shivered slightly, vividly recalling the last time she had sought refuge in the Old Kent Road, at the time of the 'Antiques Murders', last autumn. A series of bizarre murders in which she had originally featured as the redoubtable Inspector Clooney's prime suspect.

She said, 'Believe it or not, Maggie, but this is a bona-fide mission I'm on. I'm a police snout.'

'A – *what*?'

'An undercover agent.'

Maggie sniffed audibly. 'Well, they do say, if you can't beat 'em, join 'em! So what are you snouting after?'

'A man. A dead tramp.'

'Huh! Ask a silly question,' Maggie said huffily. 'Now see here, my girl. What you need is a good night's sleep. Either that or a piecryatist! So the sooner you get to bed, the better. A dead tramp indeed! The very idea!'

Glancing about her fearfully, 'Sssshhh, Maggie,' Gerry hissed. 'Someone could be listening. The last thing I want is to blow my cover.

Conscience-stricken about breaking her diet, next morning Gerry went downstairs to order poached eggs on toast instead of a bacon butty. There were already a few regulars tucking into 'Barney's Breakfast Bonanza' – eggs, bacon, bangers, baked beans, tomatoes and fried bread. Most of the regulars were lorry drivers or overnight shift workers. All were rough looking with 'six o'clock shadows'. Badly in need of a shave.

Gerry felt that she fitted into the picture quite nicely in her down-and-out get-up, with her hair dangling down like a spaniel's ears. Maggie and Barney had reacted magnificently to her appearance in the caff. Ignoring her completely apart from Maggie asking her what she wanted to eat and calling to Barney, 'Two floaters on toast an' a mug of tea.' But did she really have to bring out that can of air freshener?

Dipping toast into her 'floaters' and slurping the tea, glancing about her surreptitiously, her ears flapping to catch snippets of conversation from her fellow diners and glancing furtively at the door whenever it opened to admit a new influx of toughs and scruffs. Hopefully actors dressed as tramps. Just her luck, she thought, that vagrants were thin on the ground this morning. Even pretend ones. More than likely, whichever episode of whichever TV drama they'd been filming had been completed and the 'tramps' were now appearing elsewhere as butlers, chauffeurs, or ghillies in *Monarch of the Glen*.

Finishing her breakfast, Gerry shuffled out of the caff to begin another day's foot-slogging in search of clues leading to the identity of her missing 'pater familias' whose name she didn't even know. Little wonder she'd been given some mighty funny looks the day before, when she'd been asked the name of her 'father' and she had been obliged to admit that she couldn't, for the life of her, remember his name.

'So what's *your* name?' one doss-house keeper had asked her. To which question Gerry had replied, quite truthfully, 'My name is Mudd!'

'Why doesn't that surprise me none?' the doss-house keeper had chuckled evilly. 'Now, hop it!'

Gerry had 'hopped it' obediently.

So now where to? And what next on the agenda? she wondered, traipsing despondently down the Old Kent Road. A phonecall to Inspector Brambell admitting that she'd bitten off more than she could chew? In other words, admitting defeat? No way, she thought mutinously. She'd been given a job of work to do, and come hell or high water, she'd carry it through to the bitter end. What would Bill think of her otherwise? All she needed was a lucky break.

Gerry's lucky break came with startling suddenness.

'For God's sake, girl, get a move on!' The strident voice in her left ear belonged to a wild-eyed young man with a pony tail of hair dangling from a back-to-front baseball cap. 'Shooting's about to commence. The director's in a hell of a temper. So get in there and start acting like a troublemaker.' So saying, grabbing her shoulders, he propelled her smartly down an alley towards a brightly lit film set and shoved her into a throng of actor tramps about to storm what appeared to be a police station.

Surging forward at the director's call for Action, yelling, 'God for Harry, England and Saint George,' at the top of her voice, fame at last, Gerry thought. The Charge of the Light Brigade wasn't in it. She'd probably win a Bafta Award for the best supporting actress.

'*Cut!*' the director barked in a voice like thunder. 'This is supposed to be a protest against police brutality, not the Battle of Agincourt!' Glaring at Gerry from his elevated chair near the camera. 'Just who the hell do you think you are? Dame Judi Dench?'

'No, sir. Sorry, sir,' Gerry murmured contritely. 'I got a bit carried away, that's all.' She added eagerly, 'I could shout "Great Scott" if you'd prefer. Well, I am supposed to be a troublemaker, aren't I?' (A role for which Gerry privately felt herself to be eminently well suited, come to think of it.)

'One more word out of you, young lady, and you'll find out the full meaning of the word trouble,' the director said, between clenched teeth. 'Do I make myself clear?'

'Pardon?' Cupping her left ear with her hand, her mischievous sense of humour coming uppermost. 'I didn't quite catch what you said. A build up of wax in my ossicles, you know? Nothing to worry about, my doctor assures me,' Gerry said, tongue in cheek. 'Though the use of an ear trumpet may be on the cards, later on in life.'

'Look, lady,' the director shouted at her, 'have you any frigging idea how much this delay is costing us? Now, for Pete's sake, get back in line, and keep your lips buttoned this time. OK?'

The director's name was Adrian Sweeting, Gerry later discovered by the simple expedient of asking the guy with the pony tail and the back-to-front baseball cap, whose name was Rafe Barmby. He was flicking through a list of names when she approached him after the filming. 'Why? Do you fancy him?' Rafe muttered, frowning. 'If so, forget it, girlie. He's spoken for. What's your name, by the way?'

'Mudd,' Gerry supplied helpfully.

'Mudd? There ain't no Mudd on my list. Where did you come from?'

'Barney's Hamburger Joint in the Old Kent Road.'

'Who's your agent?'

'Bill Bentine.'

'Bentine? Never heard of him.' Rafe's frown deepened. 'Hey, what is all this?'

'You tell me.' Gerry smiled charmingly. 'I was walking along, minding my own business, when you grabbed hold of me, shoved me down an alley, and told me to start acting like a troublemaker. Which I did. So what's the problem?'

'The problem is, you ain't on my list. Which means you're not entitled to a fifty quid fee for your services.' Regarding her suspiciously. 'Oh, I get it! Thought you'd pull a fast one, did you? Well, I've met your kind before. Wandering on to a film set, hoping no one would notice you. Hoping for a cash handout you weren't entitled to. I've a damn good mind to send for the police.'

Smarting from the 'girlie' appellation, 'Now you listen to me – *laddie*,' Gerry replied coolly, 'I *am* the police!' Not strictly true, but effective. 'As for "wandering" on to a film set, I didn't wander on to it, I was pushed on to it. And *you* did the pushing. Remember?'

Rafe moistened his lips with his tongue. 'All right. Fair enough,' he conceded. 'So what is it you want?'

'Information about a missing person. Possibly an actor. What I'm after is names and addresses. The man I'm after disappeared last Christmas, dressed as a tramp. Wearing an old army greatcoat, boots and a balaclava helmet. He was tall. About six feet. Dark-haired and, I imagine, reasonably good-looking. Difficult to tell, since there wasn't much left of his face when his body was discovered on Hampstead Heath. Moreover, Mr Barmby, he hadn't died of frostbite. He'd been murdered!'

'Ye gods!' Barmby uttered hoarsely. 'And you think *I* did it? Is that it?'

'Not necessarily,' Gerry assured him calmly. 'All I'm asking of you, for the time being, is your co-operation in establishing the murdered man's identity. Records, and so forth, of any actor who went missing from your list at the time in question.'

She paused dramatically. 'I take it that you are willing to co-operate?'

'What? Huh? Oh yeah! Sure! More than willing,' Barmby assured her. 'So what next?'

'A visit to Scotland Yard at, say, ten o'clock tomorrow morning?' Gerry suggested. 'Along with your records, of course. Ask for Detective Chief Inspector Brambell.'

Gerry paused suddenly. Barmby's face had paled to the colour of wood ash. 'Is anything the matter?' she asked him intently.

'Well, yes. That is, I'm not quite sure, but I think I know the name of the man you're after! He'd been on the shoot all along. Not as a supernumerary but a feature actor. Which is why Adrian Sweeting nearly did his nut when the guy went missing without a by your leave or a word of explanation of his absence. A few days short of Christmas, that was.'

'And you know, or think you know the name of that man?' Gerry insisted. 'If so, you *must* tell me!'

'Right then. I will!'

Hearing that name, Gerry drew in a deep breath of relief, knowing that the identity of the murdered man was no longer a mystery. She had recognized his surname the moment she'd heard it.

Nine

G erry's immediate reaction had been to ring Inspector Brambell imparting news of her success; discovery of the dead man's identity would be a feather in her cap. On second thoughts, the more information she could give him, the better.

First and foremost, proof positive of the man's identity. His last known address, for instance. A word with his landlady. Perusal of Barmby's list. Taking nothing for granted à la Virginia Vale, her fictitious super-sleuth.

'Right,' she told Rafe Barmby severely. 'I shall need sight of your records as soon as possible! This is a murder inquiry, think on! I'll expect you to make them available to me by six o'clock this evening at the latest. Understood?'

'Yeah. I guess so,' Rafe conceded miserably. 'At Scotland Yard, you mean?'

'No. At Barney's Hamburger Joint in the Old Kent Road. My undercover address for the time being! I'll be at a table near the counter. Just try not to draw attention to yourself, that's all! Wear your baseball cap the right way round for a change.'

'Now what's going on?' Maggie demanded when Gerry slunk into the caff like a Disney cat, at a quarter to six, still wearing her down and out clothing. 'Where the hell have you been all day? Barney an' me's been worried sick about you! All that stuff you told me, last night, about being a police snout in search of a dead tramp, didn't make sense to me.' Referring to a conversation with Gerry, in her bedroom, the night before. 'I mean to say, why should you be working for the police? Above all that wooden-headed Detective Inspector Clooney?'

'But I'm not working for Clooney. I'm working for Inspector Brambell,' Gerry explained. 'A man as different from Clooney as chalk is from cheese. A really nice man. So please, Maggie, don't be cross with me. You see, I took it as a compliment when he sought my help in discovering the identity of that dead tramp on Hampstead Heath. Please, Maggie! I'm expecting someone! I'll tell you about it later.'

Barmby appeared at ten past six, looking like a fairground tout, a bookie's runner or a dodgy dodgem-car attendant, having exchanged his baseball cap for a checked flat cap several sizes too big for him. To make matters worse, his pony tail, freed from its elastic band, dangled about his shoulders like damp seaweed. He was carrying a white plastic carrier bag, wearing a putty-coloured anorak, shredded blue jeans, white trainers, and dark glasses.

Gawd strewth, Gerry thought. He might just as well have worn a stocking mask and had done with it. He could not have drawn more attention to himself had he also appeared with a burglar's tool kit slung over his shoulder. 'Over here,' she hissed, to Maggie's obvious amusement, as Barmby, as blind as a bat in his 'shades', tripped over the doormat and staggered, knees bent, towards Gerry's corner table near the counter.

'I thought I told you not to draw attention to yourself,' Gerry muttered crossly. 'All I asked you to do was wear your baseball cap the right way round. Not to wear sunglasses in the middle of January! Now everyone's looking at us!'

'Sorry, miss,' Barmby apologized, hefting the carrier bag on to the table. 'But it weren't all that easy getting hold of the information you wanted. Bloody difficult, as a matter of fact, with the director breathing down my neck, wanting to know what I was after in the office filing cabinet. Well, you've met him. So you know what he's like? Not the easiest guy in the world to get along with.'

'All right, Mr Barmby. You've made your point,' Gerry replied starchily, in what she hoped was a Scotland Yard tone of voice. Then, more sympathetically, feeling sorry for the man, 'Which reminds me. Since you are here, how about a hamburger and chips and a mug of coffee? Unless your wife has a cooked meal awaiting your arrival home, that is?'

'*Wife*? What ever gave you that idea? I ain't married. I live alone! See to myself, ta very much!' He sighed deeply, 'Not that I'd say no to something to eat right now! Things being so chaotic at the shoot today, I didn't have time for lunch.'

'Come to think of it, neither did I,' Gerry said wistfully. 'So how about hamburgers and chips for two? My treat.'

Frowning, Barmby said perceptively, 'If you're a Scotland Yard detective, I'm Elvis Presley! So, like I said before, what *is* all this?'

'Believe it or not, Rafe,' Gerry informed him, 'I a*m* working for Scotland Yard in the capacity of an undercover agent. You see, I had the misfortune to be on Hampstead Heath when the body of the murdered man was discovered. Not a pretty sight, I assure you. Now, thanks to you, I know that man's identity. Now, it's up to me to find out more about him. His past life, and so on. Where he lived, prior to his death. Names of his friends, colleagues, and so forth. Above all, who wanted him dead. Who stood to gain financially, or otherwise, from his death.'

'Yeah. Well, you'll find everything you need there in the carrier bag,' Rafe assured her. 'I never cottoned on to him myself. A queer kind of cove, to my way of thinking. A law unto himself. You know the kind? Stuck up wasn't in it. God's gift to women. Or thought he was. Despite his having a prison record, way back.'

'A prison record? For what, exactly?' Gerry insisted.

'Dunno for sure. But it's all there in his file. To do with money. What else?' He paused. 'Look, lady, I'm beginning to wish I hadn't come. I could lose my job over borrowing those files, and I can't afford to do that.'

'Don't worry. I'll have them photocopied and returned to you as soon as possible. Any trouble, and you'll be in the clear. Inspector Brambell will make sure of that. Now, about that hamburger and chips. Don't know about you, but I could eat a horse!'

Rafe said doubtfully, 'How can I be sure this isn't a wind-up? That you are who you say you are? That you *are* working for the police? For all I know you might destroy those files the minute my back's turned. You say you were on the Heath when the body was discovered? Sounds a bit fishy to me. You could have bumped him off yourself! You could want rid of those files to destroy evidence against you!'

'Tell me, Rafe,' Gerry said mildly. 'Have you thought of taking up crime writing as a profession? If not, you should. The first requisite of which is a suspicious mind. And I should know. Have you ever heard of the crime novelist Geraldine Frayling, by the way?'

'Yeah. Sure. Who hasn't? What of it?'

'Because she happens to be a close friend of mine. As a matter of fact, we live under the same roof. Now, let's eat, shall we? Afterwards, I'll drive you to Hampstead to meet her. Not that her real name is Frayling. It's Mudd. Her friends call her Gerry. That is to say, my friends call me Gerry. I prefer it that way. And if you're worried about your files, I have a photocopier in my work room. I'll zip 'em off in two shakes of a lamb's tail, and you can have them back pronto. OK?'

Rafe's mouth sagged open momentarily. Seconds later it was filled with Barney's hamburger and chips. 'There, get that down you,' Maggie, who had been listening intently to the conversation, advised him sotto-voce. 'And thank your lucky stars I didn't throw you out, neck and crop. Comin' in here lookin' like a bloody Belisha beacon; accusin' our Gerry of murder, or as good as. The very idea!'

Later, entering the Eyrie in Gerry's wake; glancing about him in awe at the staircase with its turkey-red staircarpet and shining brass rods, polished banister rail, and the stained-glass window on the half landing:

'Some place you've got here,' Rafe remarked admiringly, recalling his own less spactacular accommodation in Clerkenwell. A stone's throw away from the Smithfield Central Market with its overhanging odour of freshly killed meat. Not even a proper self-contained flat. Just a bed-sitting room and kitchen, with use of a shared bathroom and toilet along the landing. All he could afford on his present salary.

'Come up to my work room,' Gerry said. 'I'll copy the files and give you back the originals. Afterwards, I'll drive you home, then go back to Barney's. He and Maggie are old friends of mine. Salt of the earth.'

'You live here alone?' Rafe asked, on their way upstairs.

'Most of the time. My fiancé, Bill Bentine, stays with me at weekends when he's in London. He's in New York at the moment, wheeling and dealing on my behalf. He'll be home soon.' Gerry's face lit up at the thought of seeing Bill again. 'Well, here we are. This is my work room. My sanctum.'

Crossing the threshold, Rafe noticed Gerry's single divan bed in a corner of the room, her desk near the window, her old-fashioned typewriter, her newly acquired photocopier on a side table; bookshelves, a settee, and a plump cretonne-covered armchair near a low, glass-topped coffee table with a red-shaded lamp and a copper bowl planted with trailing ivies interspersed with African violets.

'That curtained door near the bed leads to the fire escape,' Gerry told him, busying herself with the carrier bag, its contents, and the photocopier. 'This contraption was Bill's idea. He tried talking me into buying a computer. But I couldn't get the hang of it. I prefer my old Olivetti.' She laughed. 'I'm a fuddy duddy at heart, I guess. Hence this house and my love of antiques. I couldn't bear living in a modern bungalow.'

'Were your folks well off?' Rafe asked wistfully.

'Far from.' Gerry laughed. 'I was brought up in a council house in Clapham. I bought this house from the proceeds of my first book, *Virginia Vale Investigates*, and its spin-offs. Film and TV rights in particular. I decided to invest my earnings in a home of my own. A decision I've never – well, hardly ever – regretted.'

Feeding paper into the photocopier and heaving a sigh of relief when the task had been completed, 'There. That's that,' she announced. 'All done and dusted! Now, let's get going, shall we? Where do you live, by the way?'

In Clerkenwell. Number 14 Skinner Road,' Rafe uttered briefly.

'Well, what's wrong with that?' Gerry said cheerfully, getting into the driving seat of her Mini. 'After all, every man's home is his castle.'

Some castle, Rafe thought gloomily, recalling his squalid pad with its spring-busted armchairs and settee, his sofa bed in the sitting room, his minuscule kitchen with its Baby Belling cooker, the size of a postage stamp, and that long trek to the bathroom along the landing whenever he answered a call of nature. Usually to find that someone else had beaten him to it. He said, 'Do you think I stand a chance of becoming a writer?'

Gerry said, 'You'll never know that for sure, will you? Unless you give it a try.'

'So who was that? And where have you been all day?' Maggie wanted to know, perching herself on Gerry's bed. 'And what's all them papers on the dressing table? Well, I'm waiting.'

'Right. So pin your ears back and listen. The man I met earlier on is my "grass". His name is Rafe Barmby. One minute I was walking down the Old Kent Road, minding my own business. Next thing I knew I was on a film set. Acting as a troublemaker, if you must know. Protesting against police brutality towards vagrants. *I* was one of the vagrants.'

'I'm not surprised, in *that* get-up,' Maggie remarked scathingly. 'If Bill could see you now, he'd cancel the wedding and run a mile!'

'I shan't be needing it any longer,' Gerry said dismissively. 'I've brought a change of clothing from the Eyrie. I went there, this evening, with Rafe, to photocopy the information he'd given me.' She sighed deeply with satisfaction. 'I've done it, Maggie! I've discovered the dead man's identity! Isn't that marvellous? Mind you, I couldn't have done it without Rafe's co-operation.'

'Well, that's a relief, I must say. Knowing you've finished with them filthy old rags of yours. The only fit and proper place for them is in a dustbin. So just you strip off. Take a shower, wash your hair, an' kick 'em on to the landing. Meanwhile, I'll nip down to the kitchen for a pair of rubber gloves and a bin-liner.'

'Fair enough,' Gerry conceded. 'But don't you want to know the name of the dead man?'

'Would I know it if I heard it?' Maggie asked. More interested in getting rid of what she thought of as Gerry's 'flea market' apparel, afraid that if she didn't shift it with her own two hands, it might just make its own way downstairs.

'Probably not,' Gerry said, beginning the stripping off process, feeling vaguely disappointed. Maggie had been a tower of strength during the 'Antiques Murders', she recalled. Now she seemed uninterested in this present murder inquiry. Though she had been supportive and sympathetic over the murder of poor Annie Scott.

Standing beneath the shower in the en-suite bathroom, blissfully aware of hot water laving her skin and hair, applying a liberal amount of shampoo to her head and lavender-scented soap to her body, Gerry worked out that Maggie's less supportive attitude had to do with worry that she might be heading for more trouble. Possibly even further attempts on her life if she became too deeply involved in tracking down yet another serial killer. Moreover, she could be right. But no way was Gerry prepared to give in until the murderer of Annie Scott had been brought to book.

Annie had trusted her, had turned to her for help. So how could she, in all conscience, betray that trust?

Duly washed and shampooed, and wearing clean and decent clothing, Gerry went downstairs to the caff to find that Maggie had set the back-room table for a proper home-cooked dinner. A 'Closed' sign hung on the caff door.

Catching sight of Gerry in a neat jumper and skirt, 'Well, now you look like a human bein',' Maggie said approvingly. 'Just you sit down. Dinner's nearly ready. Now, where's Barney got to? He knows we're having roast lamb an' I can't carve for toffee! Oh, here he is! High time too! Huh! Smelling like a barber's cat! Must be that aftershave I gave him for Christmas!'

Gerry laughed. Things were back to normal. Maggie was back to her usual ebullient self. Bustling back and forth from kitchen to dining room: bringing to the table tureens of vegetables, gravy and mint sauce. Finally the roast leg of lamb, cooked to perfection, for her husband to carve, which he did so with the aplomb of a maître d' at Wheeler's Strand Restaurant.

Meanwhile, Maggie had opened a bottle of white wine to complement the meal. 'What is this?' Gerry asked merrily. 'A celebration?'

'Something like that,' Maggie said mysteriously. 'More of a surprise party really!'

'A surprise party?' Gerry wrinkled her forehead. 'So what's the surprise?'

A familiar figure entered the room at that moment. '*I* am, Gerry love,' Bill Bentine said tenderly. 'Well, don't just sit there! Say something! Anything! If it's only What the hell are you doing here?'

'So what the hell *are* you doing here?' Gerry's eyes filled with tears. Next moment, she was in his arms. 'Oh, Bill,' she murmured. 'Why didn't you tell me you were coming home? I thought you were in America, stuffing your face with lobster mayonnaise.'

'Well I'm not. I'm here. About to stuff my face with roast lamb and mint sauce. Thanks to Maggie and Barney.'

Casting a grateful look in Maggie's direction. Now Gerry knew why she had been so insistent on getting rid of her old clothes. Why Barney's aftershave. Why the best china dinner service and the 'Closed' sign on the caff door.

Blowing Maggie a kiss across the room, 'Thanks, darling,' Gerry mouthed silently. Aglow, Maggie said briskly, 'Well, let's eat, shall we? Before it all gets cold. I'll just set another place for Bill. Thanks, by the way, for the table hotplates you gave me for Christmas. Otherwise, everything'd have been lukey warm by now. An' I ain't all that fond of lukey warm grub. Now you, Barney, stop fakin' about with that joint. An' don't cut it too thin, think on!'

Not that Bill and Gerry would notice what they ate, Maggie reckoned fondly, in their present state of euphoria. Gazing into each other's eyes like Romeo and 'Julia'.

At Maggie's suggestion, Bill and Gerry went home to the Eyrie after dinner. 'Look, love,' she said, 'you have a lot of talking over to do. A bit of canoodling too, I shouldn't wonder.'

Gerry wasn't too sure about that. Unless she missed her guess, Bill appeared to be suffering from jet lag. She felt pretty tired herself, come to think of it.

Helping Bill indoors with his luggage, 'Why not go into the drawing room? Sit down and relax whilst I make some coffee,' Gerry advised him. 'Switch on the fire. Pour yourself a drink.'

'Thanks, darling,' he said gratefully. 'Oh, Gerry, I'm so glad to be home. Let me look at you.'

'All right. But not too closely! Truth to tell, I feel like a tramp.'

Holding her at arm's length: 'You certainly don't look like one. And you smell divine. What is it? Madame Rochas?'

'No, just lavender soap and John Frieda shampoo. Over four quid a tube, would you believe?'

'You *look* lovely too. Hey –' turning her sideways – 'I believe you've lost weight. Have you been dieting?'

'Well, on and off. Now and then,' Gerry supplied modestly. 'Can you really tell the difference?'

'I'll say I can. So what have you been eating?'

'Mainly hamburgers and chips. But I've been running about a lot lately. Jogging, and such like.'

When Gerry, all aglow, returned to the drawing room with the coffee, Bill was fast asleep in his favourite armchair near the fire. Just her luck, she thought. Even so, she hadn't the heart to disturb him – her darling, handsome, beloved Bill.

Silently drawing the curtains and placing a rug over his knees, turning on the threshold to switch off the lights, quietly Gerry went upstairs to her room. Filled with an overwhelming feeling of happiness, how wonderful, she thought, to wake up tomorrow morning knowing that he would be there, most likely in the kitchen cooking her breakfast, to greet her, to hold her, to kiss her good morning. To whisper, 'I love you.'

Having made up his sofa bed for the night and secured his pony tail with a rubber band, he'd quite enjoyed his encounter with the authoress woman, Rafe Barmby thought, wondering if she'd really meant what she'd said about giving writing a go. Well, why not? He could churn out quite a good crime novel given his experience of the TV game and some of the oddballs he'd come across as a result.

Not just oddballs neither, but downright villains. Take that dead bloke Gerry Frayling was so interested in, for instance. Rafe had had him sussed as a low life from the word go. No wonder he'd been done in, the arrogant sod. And him with a prison record and all. Funny how some blokes got away with murder, fraudulent conversion, perversion of the course of justice, or whatever. Usually pratting about in open prisons, being given special treatment: weekends off to visit their families and suchlike. Dependent on their upper-crust accents and friends in high places. Bloody unfair, in Rafe's opinion, walking along the passage to the lavatory to relieve his feelings, before settling down for the night.

He had no premonition of danger. His killer walked on silent feet. No need of a knife or a blunt instrument. Winding

Rafe's pony tail about his neck, pulling it tighter and tighter. Quickly, silently and efficiently, the murderer simply strangled his victim to death with his own hair. Smiling as Barmby's lifeless body slumped to the ground; eyes wide open and staring. A surprised expression on his face.

Ten

'So what's on the agenda today?' Bill asked, over breakfast. 'A visit to Scotland Yard to hand in your notice as a secret agent?'

'Not quite yet,' Gerry said meekly. 'Sorry, Bill. I know you disapprove, but I have important leads to follow up, and I can't leave my work unfinished.'

'That's all well and good, darling, but try to see things from my point of view. You're a writer, for heaven's sake, not a detective. So why not stick to writing and leave the sleuthing to the professionals? Just hand over those files to DCI Brambell and let him sort things out?'

'I can't, Bill.' Gerry shook her head. 'Because of Annie Scott. She trusted me, you see? The thought of letting her down is – unbearable.'

Bill said huskily, 'So is the thought of losing you. I damn near did so last year, remember? I wouldn't want to go through that again.'

'Thanks, love.' Reaching for his hand across the table, 'You say the nicest things. Even so, I really do need to bring this job to a satisfactory conclusion, preferably with your blessing.'

'I see.' Bill sighed deeply. Kissing Gerry's hand, he said, 'Very well, then. You have my blessing.' Against his better judgement, 'Go ahead. Just promise me one thing. Steer well clear of danger.'

'I promise! But all I want to do is find out more about the dead man's background. Take a look at his last known address. What harm in that?' Changing the subject adroitly, 'So what will you be doing today?'

Bill pulled a face. 'Visiting my office, what else? Finding out what's been happening during my absence. Whether or not Clarinda Clarkson has honoured her three-book contract, which I doubt. Knowing Clarinda, more than likely she'll be on the verge of a nervous breakdown – not to mention her publishers.'

He grinned wryly. 'Never mind, eh? These things are sent to try us. What shall I bring home for supper, by the way?'

Starting the washing-up, 'Hmm,' Gerry pondered, 'how about an anchovy and tomato pizza from that Italian takeaway in the High Street?'

'Anchovy and tomatoes?' Bill protested. 'If there's anything I hate, it's anchovies. What's wrong with bangers and mash? Fish and chips?'

'Nothing at all,' Gerry said blissfully. 'Bangers and mash sounds fine to me. Plus anything else you fancy. A few smoked bacon rashers, a bit of black pudd'n, a loaf of bread, oven chips, Black Forest gateau, a nice little duck for tomorrow night's dinner. It's up to you entirely, Bill darling.'

Upstairs in her sanctum, Gerry perused the files Rafe Barmby had given her. Discovering Aubrey Sandys' last known address should not prove too difficult.

Aubrey Sandys, Gerry mused, Dorothea Lazlo's ex-husband, an actor, a con man, who had ended up dead in that shallow grave on Hampstead Heath. Not exactly a pillar of the community, she thought, recalling Barmby's assessment of Sandys as a queer kind of cove, a law unto himself: stuck up, believing himself to be God's gift to women.

Scarcely surprising, Gerry figured, that a man of his ilk had flouted the law to the extent of a prison sentence for theft, by way of a series of unpaid debts to various prestigious hotels in the West End of London: the Savoy, Claridges, the Ritz, and so on, amounting to several thousands of pounds, until he was finally caught and sentenced to a three-year term of imprisonment to suffer the consequences of a flamboyant lifestyle beyond his means to afford from his own resources as a, presumably, second-rate member of the acting profession.

Little wonder, therefore, Gerry surmised, that he'd ended up dead, with a fractured skull and a bullet in his greatcoat – or someone else's gear. Odd that he had chosen to visit Bagdale Manor in his tramp get-up. A means of diguise, she wondered?

Obviously, he had still been in possession of his Equity card, free to assume his acting career when he came out of clink. Unlike rogue doctors, solicitors and their ilk, he not been struck off whatever register pertained to members of Equity. Perhaps there wasn't one? Even high-ranking Members of Parliament appeared to come out of choky, nowadays, smelling of violets.

But first things first. Having found Sandys' last known address, getting into her Mini, she headed towards Blackfriars, in search of Queen Victoria Road.

Unsurprisingly, the house she was after was a Victorian villa, bay- and sash-windowed, set back from the road behind an untidy privet hedge, with an iron gate and a tiled path leading to a brass-letterboxed front door.

Heavy curtains were drawn across the lower bay window. The sash windows had half-drawn Venetian blinds with dangling ivory acorns. The small front garden was weed-choked. Tufts of grass sprouted between the tiles, the letterbox and the brass bell-pull were dingy with neglect. Paint was peeling from the front door. There was no sign of life. Even so, Gerry rang the bell, and waited.

After what she considered to be a decent interval, glancing quickly about her to make sure nobody was watching, Gerry went round the angle of the house to the back door. There was a long, overgrown rear garden with a rickety wooden fence, kitchen windows stuck up halfway with a kind of gummed and patterned paper of the kind fashionable in the 1920s. Not that Gerry remembered the 1920s. She had, however, seen a re-run of Noël Coward's *This Happy Breed* recently on television. An era in which sticky fly-catchers had dangled from kitchen ceilings alongside clothes' airing racks.

Making her way past the kitchen windows, she came across the back door with frosted upper glass panels. Further along, there was a second bay window, with drawn-back curtains.

Standing on tiptoe, Gerry craned her neck to peer inside. This had obviously been a dining room, judging by the table and chairs, a heavy oak sideboard and a Welsh dresser arrayed with various items of dusty china.

Had this really been Aubrey Sandys' pied-à-terre? Gerry wondered. Presumably a man of the world, into entertaining?

Wouldn't he have been more likely to have lived in a modern flat? Why this run down Victorian monstrosity?

Fairly itching to get inside for a look round, she tried pushing up a window. To no avail. It wouldn't budge. Returning to the back door: rattling the handle, she met with the same result. Short of smashing the upper panel of the back door and laying herself open to a charge of breaking and entering, now what? Gerry wondered. And then. Was it remotely possible, she asked herself, having stumbled over a row of plantpots near the kitchen door, that the key of the back door could be hidden under one of them? If so, this was one of the oldest tricks in the world, and one of the silliest. Nearly as daft as leaving a doorkey suspended on a string to be hauled up through a letterbox. But there right enough was the back door key, dangling from the upright letterbox between the frosted glass panels, Gerry discovered when she went 'fishing'.

Heart beating madly, stepping inside the kitchen, glancing about her, she noticed a cobwebby alcove containing a gas cooker with an eye-level grill, of post-war vintage. A là Bette Davis in *All About Eve*. 'What a *dump!*' Gerry murmured, sotto voce, beginning to wonder if she had broken into the right house, which had obviously stood empty for some considerable time.

This may well be Aubrey Sandys' last known address. Scarcely likely, however, that he had lived here on a permanent basis. If ever. In which case, why hadn't he got rid of it ages ago? The bit firmly between her teeth, Gerry intended to find out why.

The dilapidated kitchen door led to a passageway with a flight of stairs leading to the upper rooms. Other doors led from a narrow hall into a sizeable, bay-windowed drawing room, a much smaller living room, and the bay-windowed dining room she had already glimpsed from a tip-toe position in the back garden.

Each and every room, she discovered, was fully furnished with poor-quality tables, chairs, sideboards, sagging settees and armchairs, and littered with gimcrack ornaments of the kind easily obtainable from junk shops the length and breadth of the East End of London. From market stalls or fair-grounds.

Somehow, to Gerry's way of thinking, this simply didn't make sense. Would a man, once married to a world-renowned artist of the calibre of Dorothea Lazlo, really have chosen to display, on his walls, a cheap-jack print of a green-faced woman, for instance?

Another thought occurred. Could this house possibly have been the marital home of Aubrey Sandys and Dorothea in the early days of their marriage? Had he loved it so much that, following their divorce, he had felt unable to part with it? Loving Dorothea so much, had he felt it necessary to turn up on the doorstep of the basement kitchen of Bagdale Manor, last Christmas Eve, dressed as a tramp, in the hope of seeing her again? Instead of which, he had exchanged words with, not Dorothea, but her present husband, the wealthy, charismatic biographer, Elliot Lazlo?

Sensing danger, had Elliot Lazlo invited Sandys into his study, cracked his skull with a blunt instrument, dragged his inert body to his car, dumped him in a hastily scooped-out grave on Hampstead Heath? Then, to make certain that he was really a goner, have fired a bullet into him, at close range, for good measure?

A strong possibility, Gerry pondered, moving from room to room of the silent, derelict house. But now did the murder of Annie Scott fit into the picture? Scarcely likely that Lazlo, having sent Annie, by taxi, to King's Cross Station, with Bruno beside her, would have followed her surreptitiously, to strangle her to death with the dog's lead. Why bother, when he might far more easily have put paid to her at Bagdale Manor and dumped her lifeless body on Hampstead Heath? Or, even more possibly, within the confines of that mysterious walled garden to the rear of Bagdale Manor?

One of these nights, Gerry decided, making her way upstairs to the first landing of Aubrey Sandys' broken-down villa, she would gain entry to that walled garden, by fair means or foul. Most probably the latter. Most certainly without Bill's knowledge or consent.

There were three rooms on the upper landing. Two bedrooms and a bathroom. The latter boasted a claw-footed enamel tub with brass taps, a cracked wash basin, and a badly stained lavatory with a wooden seat and, for want of a better description, a 'bell-pull' handle dangling from an old fashioned thunder box. Sandys might at least have chucked bleach down the loo occasionally, Gerry thought, pulling a face.

What she assumed to be the master bedroom contained a double bed with a sagging mattress and a brass-knobbed bedstead, a double wardrobe devoid of clothing, a dressing table with a triple mirror and a tall chest of drawers. The second bedroom had been used as a work room of some kind judging by a number of benches and work surfaces littered with various tools, hammers, a fret-saw, and screwdrivers. There were also coils of wire, tins of paint, brushes, bottles of turpentine. As if someone had anticipated making alterations or improvements and changed his mind for whatever reason. Possibly detainment at Her Majesty's Pleasure?

What a queer set-up, Gerry thought, pondering the time factor. Far more research was necessary, she considered. If this strange house had been the marital home of Aubrey and Dorothea Sandys, how long ago would that have been? How had they met? Where had their marriage taken place, and when? How long had that marriage survived before their divorce and Dorothea's marriage to Elliot Lazlo?

When had Dorothea's work, her paintings, become famous? How long had Aubrey Sandys been a member of Equity? Had he ever made his mark as an actor? If only she *knew*. She didn't, therefore she must find out.

Feeling decidedly chilly and more than slightly depressed in this ice cube of a mausoleum, Gerry went upstairs to the attics on the top floor of the house. Both were dim and dusty with skylight windows admitting pale rays of daylight on to bare floorboards.

About to call it a day, to quit the house before she contracted pneumonia, suddenly she felt a chewing sense of excitement in the pit of her stomach. It was the kind of gut churning she experienced when her alter ego, Virginia Vale, was about to seize a serial killer by the short and curlies. She saw, on the floorboards of the front attic, dried splashes of paint, like confetti.

So Dorothea Lazlo *had* lived here? It must have been here, beneath a push-up skylight, that she had begun her painting career. Why else the dried-up splashes of colour caked on the floor? Why else a dozen or so canvases propped up in a corner of the attic, their backs to the room? Why a long trestle table stacked with sketch pads, dusty bottles of turpentine, a pottery jar containing sticks of charcoal, crayons and pencils?

Forgetful of her coldness, the chilliness of her feet and fingers, what if, Gerry thought eagerly, she had chanced upon a cache of Dorothea Lazlo paintings worth a fortune? To her intense disappointment, turning the canvases, she discovered that all were blank. But what about the sketch pads? Possibly even Dorothea 'doodles' would be worth a great deal of money nowadays? Michelangelo hadn't done too badly from *his* 'doodles', Gerry recalled. Leastways, he wouldn't have done so had they come to light during his lifetime. Mere guesswork on her part. Frankly, Gerry knew as much about art as she knew about computers.

The sketch pads also proved disappointing. Most of the pages were as blank as the canvases, apart from hastily scribbled shopping lists with reminders of common-or-garden household requirements such as butter, sugar, eggs, toilet rolls, lamb chops, potatoes, and so on. And yet, one entry held Gerry in thrall. A kind of memo, a reminder of a special event in Dorothea's life, which read: 'Foyles. 11.30 a.m. Meeting with E.L.'

Foyles Bookshop, of course, Gerry realized, prestigious for its signing sessions, literary luncheons and launchings. More than likely an author of Elliot Lazlo's calibre would have been well and truly launched with champagne and caviar. Had Dorothea been a guest at one of those wingdings? A strong possibility. By no stretch of the imagination could Gerry envisage a clandestine meeting between Lazlo and Dorothea behind the book shelves.

Food for thought. Which reminded Gerry that she stood in dire need of sustenance. Hot coffee and a cheeseburger would be nice. There was bound to be a snackbar in the vicinity. Hurrying downstairs, she let herself out by the back door and pushed the key back through the letterbox to dangle on its piece of string.

In his office at Scotland Yard, DCI Brambell wondered what

had become of Geraldine Frayling. He had tried her mobile, but it was either switched off or the batteries had run out.

Beginning to doubt his sagacity in asking her to undertake what could prove to be a dangerous mission, he confided his fears to DS Briggs, who had entered the office to inform his superior officer of a new murder. That of a man called Rafe Barmby, who had, bizarrely, been strangled by means of his own pony tail.

Holding back the information until Brambell had finished speaking on the subject of Miss Frayling, realizing that the 'old boy' stood in need of reassurance, Briggs said sympathetically, 'Not to worry unduly, sir. I'm certain that she is a lady well able to take care of herself.' Thinking it best not to add that he'd had his doubts all along about the wisdom of hiring a crime novelist as an undercover agent.

'This report has just come in, sir,' Briggs continued. 'The body of a young man, one Rafe Barmby, was discovered in the early hours of this morning by a fellow lodger wishing to use the bathroom. A peculiar aspect of the murder, Barmby had been strangled with his own hair.'

'Good God!' Brambell said, betraying a sneaking admiration for any man capable of growing that amount of hair. 'It must have been a hell of a length!'

'Apparently he was very proud of it,' Briggs commented drily. 'The old boy who found him said he'd told him often enough to get it cut. Had warned him it was "sapping his strength".'

'Bet Delilah told Samson pretty much the same thing before she gave him a short back and sides!' Brambell sighed deeply. 'Sorry, Briggs. You were saying?'

'The murder took place in Clerkenwell. A lodging house, by all accounts. Cheap, but not particularly cheerful. Barmby and the old man who discovered his body, a Mr Simon Entwhistle, occupied rooms on the same landing. Ground-floor rooms are occupied by the landlord, a Mr Fred Blunt, and his wife Delia. Two couples, a Mr Hubert Sangster and his partner Marlene, plus a ménage à trois, a brother and sister and the brother's boyfriend, namely Arabella and Hugo Simpkins and Hugo's partner, Colm Carmody, are on the top landing.' Briggs added briefly, 'It's a queer case, sir, and no mistake.'

At that precise moment in time, DCI Brambell felt inclined to believe him. Meanwhile, where was Geraldine Frayling?

Gerry had spent that chilly winter afternoon sussing out information about Sandys and his former wife, Dorothea, from records stored in the archives of the Public Records building, formerly Somerset House.

Their marriage had taken place on the 1st of August 1972. The bride had been an art teacher by profession: date of birth 21st of April 1947. The bridegroom, an actor, had been born on 29th September 1948. Never good at mental arithmetic, Gerry worked out, on her fingers, that Dorothea was now fifty-five – a comparatively young woman, despite Annie Scott's reference to her mistress's 'airy fairy' moods and her predilection for breakfast in bed. Yet Annie had fairly jumped down her throat when she, Gerry, had innocently assumed that Mrs Lazlo was bedfast.

'The mistress ain't bedfast,' Annie had snapped back at her. 'She just likes her breakfast in bed, if it's any of your business.' An odd reaction, come to think of it, as if Annie had taken umbrage at Gerry's reference to the Last Rites, administered to a dying woman by a Roman Catholic archbishop, no less.

Deeply puzzled and perplexed, Gerry knew that she had not dreamed up that Press report of a seriously ill woman, a famous artist, close to death, receiving Extreme Unction from a high-ranking member of the Catholic hierarchy on, presumably, her deathbed?

So how come that a woman, at death's door one minute, had been miraculously been restored to life, the next? To the extent of appearing, as large as life, at Bagdale Manor, to organize a full-scale Christmas house party. It didn't make sense, to Gerry's way of thinking. So what price the airy fairiness Annie had referred to? Would an airy fairy semi invalid have been capable of organizing a doll's tea party, let alone a house party? No. Something was up! Just what, she hadn't a clue. But *something*!

Arriving home later that afternoon, she discovered Bill in the kitchen, a pan of water bubbling on the stove, a mound of peeled potatoes on the draining board, two sizeable portions of rump steak plus several jumbo sausages on a work surface.

Brandishing a rolling pin, 'I've just given the steak a good bashing,' he explained, popping the potatoes into the pan, and pricking the bangers. 'The grill's hotter than the devil's pitchfork, so supper will be ready in half an hour.'

'Oh Bill,' Gerry sighed, 'know what I like about you? You're so romantic.'

Grinning wickedly, hauling her into his arms, he kissed her soundly on the lips to the background accompaniment of bubbling water and spitting noises from the grillpan. Then, letting go of her, he said, 'Whoops! The trouble with you, Gerry love, is you have a way of taking a man's mind off his work. Tell me, where did you learn to kiss like that?'

'I used to blow a bugle for the boy scouts,' she replied airily, heading for the stairs to wash her face and hands, comb her hair and change into a long black skirt and sweater. When she was halfway up the stairs, the phone rang. 'I'll get it,' she called out, hurrying down to the hall. 'It's probably Maggie, checking up on me.'

Re-entering the kitchen several minutes later to discover Bill draining the potatoes, she said bleakly, 'Oh, Bill!' Then, to his dismay, he saw that tears were rolling down her cheeks.

Holding her close in his arms, forgetting about the potatoes completely, 'What is it, Gerry love?' he murmured concernedly. 'Bad news?' Not about Maggie, he prayed inwardly, or Barney, the two people Gerry loved most on earth, apart from himself.

'No. It's about a man I met recently. Remember, I told you about him at breakfast, this morning? Rafe Barmby?'

'Yes, darling, I remember. So what about him?' Bill asked.

Staring up at Bill with tear-filled eyes: 'He's dead, Bill! He's been murdered! And *I'm* to blame! It's all my fault!'

Eleven

It took a deal of persuasion on Bill's part to convince Gerry that she was not to blame for Rafe's murder. Maggie had read about it in the evening paper and she had rung Gerry to spare her the shock of finding out for herself. Bill hadn't quite worked out the logic of that idea. Maggie had meant well, of that he was certain. His 'one and only' was bound to be upset anyway, he figured, that her informant had met with so violent an end. Strangled with his own hair, for heaven's sake. The worst feature of the case so far as Gerry was concerned. It was so – sick. So bizarre.

'Look, love,' Bill said patiently, sympathetically, handing her a clean hanky. 'First thing tomorrow morning, you really must place this matter in DCI Brambell's hands. Agreed?'

'Yeah, I guess so,' Gerry complied reluctantly, dreading the thought of a confessional in Brambell's office. Admitting to her shortcomings as an undercover agent. Swallowing her pride that, having discovered the identity of the occupant of that grave on Hampstead Heath, she had not fed him that information right away. Had she done so, Rafe Barmby might well still be alive and kicking, she reckoned, blaming herself for his murder. Such a nasty, cruel, unnecessary murder, she thought, perpetrated on a somewhat gauche, impressionable young man who had done his best to help her.

So who was responsible for his murder? That arty-farty film director, Adrian Sweeting? Darned if she knew. Besides which, she, Gerry, was too tired, too upset, too hungry to think clearly any more. She said faintly, 'OK, Bill. You win! I'll go to Scotland Yard the first thing tomorrow morning! Right now, all I want is—'

'Don't tell me! Let me guess!' Bill said understandingly.

Knowing his 'one and only' so well. 'Something to eat, unless I'm much mistaken?'

'Well, yes,' Gerry confessed awkwardly. 'What I mean to say is, it would seem a pity to let good food go to waste, wouldn't it?'

'That it would,' Bill concurred amiably. 'So how do you fancy lukewarm mashed potatoes, overcooked steak and sausages?'

'Fine. Just fine,' Gerry said mistily. 'If there's anything I love in this world, more than you, it's lukewarm mashed potatoes!'

It was then, Bill realized, with a deep, sweet feeling of relief, that his girl's sense of humour was back. She smiled. 'I was about to say, before I was so rudely interrupted, that all I want is a good hot bath and an early night. Now I'm not too sure about the early night. It's just that I have a lot on my mind. It's been quite a day one way and another.'

'And you'd rather not tell me about it?' Bill queried, seeing to the food. 'Why? What have you been up to?'

'Apart from trespassing on private property, you mean?' Gerry looked sheepish. 'And before you blow a gasket, I didn't ram-raid the joint. I found a key to the back door on a piece of string.'

'Oh well, that makes it all right and proper then, doesn't it? All legal and above board? And you wonder why I worry about you? Honestly, Gerry! It might have been – booby-trapped!'

'I'd have been in the right place then, wouldn't I?' she said mildly. 'Having problems with the potatoes, are you?'

'Have you ever tried mashing lukewarm potatoes?'

'Can't say I have. So why not cut 'em up and fry them?'

'Hey, that's not a bad idea!' He paused. 'Can *you* cook, by the way?'

'When the need arises,' Gerry said loftily. 'Now where was I?'

'Breaking and entering, as I recall,' Bill reminded her, cutting up the spuds.

'Oh, I didn't break. I just entered.' Gerry plumped herself down at the kitchen table. 'Honestly, Bill, I felt as if I'd strayed on to a 1920s film set! It really was revolting! Squalid, to put it mildly. Mind you, the house was Victorian. Talk about

Gaslight. You know, that old film with Ingrid Bergman and Charles Boyer? The one where the husband tries to drive his wife potty?' A thought occurred. 'I wonder if Aubrey Sandys was trying to drive Dorothea potty? Perhaps that's why she took up with Elliot Lazlo? What do you think?'

'Frankly, Gerry love, I haven't a clue what you're on about,' Bill confessed bemusedly. 'Why not begin at the beginning and go on from there?'

'Right then. I will.' And so Gerry told him the whole story from beginning to end, including the information she had dug out of the Somerset House archives, pausing momentarily now and then to offer Bill advice on matters pertaining to the cooking of chips and the advisability of giving the steak and sausages a quick whirl in the microwave. So why, Bill asked her, hadn't he simply bunged the potatoes in the microwave as well? To which Gerry replied that she hadn't thought about it at the time. But then, she was a crime writer, not Delia Smith.

'So what are you really saying, Gerry?' Bill asked when the food was finally on the table. 'That you believe Dorothea Lazlo to be an impostor? That's a bit far-fetched, isn't it?'

'Yeah, I guess so,' Gerry admitted, biting into a jumbo sausage. 'I do tend to get carried away, at times, don't I? It just struck me as odd that a seriously ill woman, at death's door one minute, having received the Last Rites, should have made so miraculous a recovery in so short a time. I remember reading about it in the *Sunday Times*, thinking how sad that such a wonderful artist had been struck down in the prime of her life. Then what happened? Nothing, that's what! No obituary notices in the newspapers. No articles summing up the poor woman's contribution to the world of art. No memorial service in Westminster Abbey or wherever. No mention of her death on television. No mention of her miraculous recovery neither, which struck me as being decidedly odd. Apparently she just hopped out of bed one morning, said she felt fine, and went home to Bagdale Manor to carry on with her life as per usual, which strikes me as being more than slightly fishy! Sorry, Bill, but that's the way I feel.'

Laying down her cutlery, 'Guess I'm not as hungry as I thought I was. Nor as thick-skinned neither. Three people have been murdered so far. Aubrey Sandys, Annie Scott and

Rafe Barmy, and I can't help feeling that I'm connected in some way.'

'Look, Gerry darling. Why not have that early night after all?' Bill suggested quietly. 'I'll do the clearing away down here, then hit the sack myself. And if you're worried about tomorrow morning, I'll go with you to Scotland Yard, if you like.'

'Thanks, Bill. I'd like that very much,' Gerry said gratefully. She added shyly, 'And I'd rather not sleep alone tonight, if you don't mind.'

'*Mind?* Of course not! But only if you are certain that's what you really want.' Knowing Gerry's reservations about physical intimacy before marriage, he felt strangely reluctant to take advantage of her present need of him as a source of comfort, not joy.

In the event, when he had done the clearing away and the washing-up, had bathed and shaved and gone upstairs to her room, he found her fast asleep. Deeply and profoundly asleep. And so, bending down to kiss her forehead and switching off her bedside lamp, he went silently downstairs to his own room.

Loving her so much, he wanted Gerry as a happy bride, on their honeymoon. No hang-ups, no reservations. Nothing to spoil their first blissful physical union, when it happened. Hopefully aboard the Orient Express on their way to Venice.

Minutes later, unable to settle, he went back upstairs carrying a pillow and duvet, and lay down on the settee in the far corner of the room. Having expressed a desire not to sleep alone that night, the least he could do was to be there for her if she awoke in the early hours, in need of company, a shoulder to cry on. But Gerry did not wake up during the night. She was still fast asleep when, at half past six next morning, Bill went down to the kitchen to make a pot of coffee.

Drawn by the aroma, Gerry came down a little while later wearing her favourite old dressing gown. She said, 'Sorry, Bill. I didn't mean to fall asleep. But thanks for being there.'

Bill said, 'Look, Gerry love. Do we really need to wait till September to – pledge our plight? What's to prevent us getting spliced right away?' He added, tongue in cheek, popping bread into the toaster, 'You see, I have a surprise honeymoon in store for us. A really darling small hotel in Budleigh Salterton. In East Devon. The birthplace of Sir Walter Raleigh, no less!' Pouring the coffee and buttering the toast, 'So what do you say?'

Knowing Bill so well. Loving the teasing quality of their relationship so much, Gerry replied primly, 'And there was I looking forward to a surprise honeymoon in Wigan!' Relishing the by-play between them, 'So where do your really intend taking me to on our honeymoon?'

Bill chuckled. 'The sooner you marry me, the sooner you'll find out,' he reminded her. 'Until then, my lips are sealed. So how about tying the knot tomorrow, or the day after?'

'Huh? You've got to be kidding! Look, Bill, when we get married, I want a proper church wedding. A top hat and tails affair, with me in a white dress and a veil, carrying a bouquet of red roses. Walking down the aisle to the strains of – "The Arrival of the Queen of Sheba". So there!'

'Sure you don't mean "The Entry of the Gladiators"?' Bill asked teasingly. Then, more seriously, 'Sorry, darling. If I really must wait till September to whisk you off to Wigan, so be it.' Glancing at his watch: 'Right now, we'd best be getting ready for Scotland Yard. Our meeting with DCI Brambell.'

Brambell and Bill took to one another on sight, to Gerry's relief. He, Bill, and Detective Inspector Clooney, their old protagonist in the 'Antiques Murders', had never exactly hit it off together. But Brambell and Clooney were as different as chalk from cheese, Gerry thought gratefully, entering Brambell's office with Bill in her wake. Brambell and Bill possessed a similar sense of humour totally lacking in DI Clooney.

Rising from the swivel chair behind his desk, hands extended in greeting, 'My dear girl,' Brambell said warmly, with evident relief. 'I've been worried sick about you!' Then, smiling at Bill, 'You, I imagine, must be Bill Bentine?' Clasping Bill's hand in a vice-like grip, 'Delighted to make your acquaintance, I'm sure. Now, do please sit down, the pair of you, and let's get down to business, shall we?'

Gerry said nervously, glancing towards Bill for support, 'I have a confession to make, Inspector Brambell. The truth is,

I discovered the identity of the murdered tramp on Hampstead Heath some days ago. His name was Aubrey Sandys. An actor by profession. He was also the former husband of Dorothea Lazlo.'

Her bottom lip quivering slightly, Gerry continued shamefacedly, 'I'm sorry, Inspector, I should have told you this at the time. I'd come by information which led me to believe that the tramp might have been an actor. Following that lead, I met a man on a TV film set who later gave me various folders borrowed from the office files, which I photocopied before giving him back the originals. The name of that man was Rafe Barmby.'

Brambell whistled softly between his teeth. 'Barmby, eh?'

Bill said, 'We've brought the folders with us. I have them here, Inspector. The thought occurred that the originals might have gone missing. Assuming that Barmby was killed by someone who knew he had them in his possession.'

Brambell said quizzically, 'Tell me, Mr Bentine, have you ever considered becoming an undercover agent?'

Bill chuckled. 'Can't say I have, sir. I leave the imaginative stuff to Gerry. I just do the wheeling and dealing.'

'A highly successful combination from where I'm sitting,' Brambell remarked. 'We all need back-up. I'm fortunate to have an understanding wife and a tolerant sergeant. Which reminds me.' Pressing his desk-buzzer, he called DS Briggs into the office.

'You and Miss Frayling have already met,' he said. 'This is Mr Bentine, Geraldine's fiancé. Now, any developments in the Barmby murder case?'

'Nothing much, sir.' Briggs consulted his notepad. 'Apart from the old gent who found the body, no one else in the house knew about the murder until he, Mr Entwhistle, raised the alarm. In a right state he was too, by all accounts.'

'Scarcely surprising. A nasty business. Go on, laddie.'

'It's a pretty basic set-up. The accommodation poorly furnished. I gather the residents are on social security. The landlord, Frederick Blunt, and his wife, Delia, live on the ground floor. Mr Entwhistle and Barmby shared a bathroom on the first landing. Entwhistle lives at the front of the house. Barmby's room was at the back, overlooking the garden and the fire escape. There's a Mr Hubert Sangster and his girlfriend, Mrs Marlene Fewter, on the top floor, plus a rather unusual trio, a brother and sister, Hugo and Arabella Simpkins, and Hugo's boyfriend, Colm Carmody.'

Brambell sighed deeply. 'Right. We'll trot along later for a look-see. Anything missing from Barmby's room, by the way?'

'Nothing at all, according to the landlord,' Briggs said. 'The room hadn't been trashed. Just one thing, sir. The fire-escape door was open. The killer must have gained access to the house that way. More specifically to Barmby's bed-sit. The fire-escape door leads into his room. It's covered with a curtain. The killer must have waited on the fire-escape landing till Barmby went along to the bathroom, then slipped into the room and followed him.'

'Quite so. Thanks, Sergeant. See you out front in half an hour? We'll take my car. Meanwhile, I'll have another word or two with Miss Frayling who has, by the way, discovered the identity of the tramp,' Brambell added, with a glance in Gerry's direction, betraying his inner satisfaction. 'Wait for it! He was none other than Aubrey Sandys. Dorothea Lazlo's former husband. Presumably also the father of her son Bretton!'

'Well, sir, that is good news,' Briggs responded warmly. 'Which means another trip to the Sandys Garden Centre, I imagine? Congratulations, Miss Frayling.'

'Thanks, Sergeant,' Gerry uttered bleakly. 'I had a lucky break, that's all! I couldn't have done it without the help of – Rafe Barmby.' Her eyes filled with tears.

'Steady, love,' Bill murmured tenderly, clasping her hand. 'Just tell Inspector Brambell the rest of the story, then we'll be on our way.'

'About my trespassing on private property, you mean? And my visit to Somerset House?' Gerry demurred.

'*Everything*,' Bill insisted gently. 'Not to worry, darling. If you end up in jug, I'll visit you every day. Bring you little mutton pies. Bake you a cake with a file. Advise you on the best method of picking oakum without ruining your fingernails.'

Brambell laughed. 'And you said you left the imaginative

stuff to Gerry? Mr Bentine!' Then, more seriously, 'Bill's quite right, you know? I need every scrap of information you can give me, to stand a chance of bringing a dangerous serial killer to justice. Please, Gerry, don't deny me that chance!' And so Gerry spent the next half hour filling in details of her visit to Sandys' last known address. 'He has a prison record,' she went on. 'Sorry, *had* a prison record. I'm not sure when.'

'Not to worry. We can check that out.' Brambell glanced at his watch. 'Well, duty calls. Briggs will be waiting.' Shrugging on his overcoat, 'I'll walk with you to Reception.' There, he said, shaking hands, 'I can't thank you enough for coming in to see me. You've done a first-class job of work, Gerry, for which I am more than grateful. It was a pretty rotten assignment, but I had a hunch you were the girl to come up with the goods.'

'You mean – that's it? But I've barely got started,' Gerry said, in dismay. 'There's lots more to find out. About Dorothea Lazlo, for instance, and where Aubrey Sandys was really holed up before he ended up on Hampstead Heath. About his acting career and so forth. Be fair, Inspector, you can't take me off the case now, before I've really got cracking. *You* tell him, Bill!'

'Hey, don't drag me into this,' Bill laughed. 'I have an office to run, a living to earn, in case you've forgotten. In any event, so have you. The good news is, you're inching your way to the top of the American bestseller list, and they're fairly drooling for your next Virginia Vale novel. So much so that I had to come up with a spur of the moment title for it.'

'So what did you call it? *Murder of a Literary Agent*?'

'I'll leave you two love-birds to fight it out between you,' Brambell chuckled, heading towards his car and the stalwart figure of DS Briggs seated at the steering wheel; jamming his brown felt hat on his head as he did so.

When the car had driven away, Gerry said, 'Look, Bill, I'm not ready to start another book yet. I'm not a sausage factory, you know? I need time to think up a new plot for a novel. Oh, I know you're glad, not sorry, that I've been given the bum's rush. But I really felt I was doing a good job of work as an undercover agent. Well, what do you want, Bill? A sausage-factory author or a fulfilled human being with a – mission?'

'You mean I have a choice?' Bill sighed deeply. 'All right,

Gerry, you win. Go ahead with your mission, if that's what you want. All *I* want is *you*! If that's not enough, so be it!'

Never having seen him angry or upset before, she said worriedly, 'Of course it's enough! I love you, Bill. You *know* that!'

'Do I?' he said grimly. 'You could have fooled me!' Walking with her to his car, parked in the forecourt, he added, 'I'll drive you home first, then get back to my office. *My* work is as important to me as your – mission – is to you!'

On their way to the Eyrie, Gerry said, 'I'm sorry, Bill. I know how much your work means to you; how hard you've worked to get me where I am today. My success as a writer is down to your faith in me from the very beginning, and I'll never forget that. Nor shall I ever forget the way you took care of me during the "Antiques Murders". Remember? I called you my watchdog, my guardian angel, my knight in shining armour? I owe you my life, Bill. I might have died that night, in Whitby Hospital, when Lisl Berenger attempted to smother me, if you hadn't been there to stop her.

'Even so, despite all my so-called fame and fortune, I can't help wishing I could do more with my life than gloat over my bank balance and churn out more bestselling novels. I Can't explain how much it meant to me when Inspector Brambell gave me a real job of work to do in finding out the identity of that tramp on Hampstead Heath, or the way I felt when I *did* find out. You were away at the time, so I couldn't talk to you about it. This was something I had to do on my own. No guardian angel to watch over me this time, more's the pity.

'Believe me, darling, I missed you like hell. As for loving you. You'll never know how much. I loved you almost from the moment I clapped eyes on you. I still do, and I always will. I'd be lost without you. So why don't you go ahead and fix up that "darling" hotel in Budleigh Salterton, Wigan or Timbuktu, for all I care!'

'You really mean that? But what about the top hat and tails? The white wedding dress and the bouquet?'

'Oh, sod all that!' Gerry said. 'I'll wear my old dirndl skirt and sloppy sweater, and you can wear a flat cap and braces.'

'Hmm, well, I'll need to think about that.' Bill smiled, his momentary anger gone and forgotten. Impossible to stay angry with Gerry for very long, he'd discovered. But there were matters he wanted settled between them, necessary to the continuance of their former closeness and understanding.

He said, 'Did you really mean what you said about – "churning out" more novels? I thought you loved writing. I'd hate to think you were being pressurized – by me, of all people. I told you earlier that you had my blessing, and I meant it. But Barmby was alive then, presumably. That's beside the point. His murder, linked to your close connections with the poor devil, made me think twice about that "blessing" of mine.'

Drawing up the car at the front gate of the Eyrie, he continued, 'Try looking at things from my point of view. For whatever reasons, suddenly here you are again mixed up in three murders. Rafe Barmby's too close for comfort, to my way of thinking. Hasn't it occurred to you that you might as well be the next name on the killer's hit list?'

'No, Bill! Honestly, the thought never entered my mind!' Gerry admitted. 'Why should it?'

'My dear girl, because Barmby revealed to you the contents of that bag of folders he gave you. Now do you see why I regret giving my blessing to a venture which could well end in disaster?'

Twelve

No. 14 Skinner Road, Clerkenwell, was undoubtedly seedy and run-down, Inspector Brambell thought, walking up the front path, followed by DS Briggs. 'Not exactly a desirable residence,' he remarked to Briggs, ringing the landlord's bell and awaiting a reply.

'Wait till you see inside,' Briggs replied, sotto voce. 'Hair-cord stair carpet, damp patches on ceilings, peeling wallpaper, cheap furniture, naked light bulbs—' He stopped speaking abruptly as the door opened and the landlord appeared on the top step.

'Ah, Mr Blunt? I am Detective Chief Inspector Brambell of Scotland Yard. You've already met my sergeant, I believe? May we come inside? Just a few questions, you understand, in the present deplorable circumstances?'

Blunt, a short, stout man, balding, and wearing a crumpled roll-neck sweater, scowled ferociously. 'More questions? I've been all through this already. It's unsettling for my tenants having police swarming about the house, asking questions. Poor old Entwhistle's in a shocking state. Damned if I know what more anyone can tell you. Me an' my missus can't add anything to what we've already said. We heard nothing, saw nothing.'

'Even so, Mr Blunt –' Brambell assumed his family doctor persona – 'I'd like to take a look at Mr Barmby's accom-modation, if you don't mind. I have reason to believe that something could be missing. Something of vital importance.'

'Oh, very well then,' Blunt conceded ungraciously, 'you'd best come in. Only make it quick! I run a respectable house here, and I don't want my lodgers upset more than they have been already. I have a living to earn!'

'Quite so, Mr Blunt,' Brambell said mildly. 'Now, if you

111

wouldn't mind showing me Mr Barmby's room?' Following the landlord to the upper landing, he added, 'I take it that the deceased was not in receipt of social security? Unlike the rest of your tenants.'

'Well no, he wasn't,' Blunt admitted. 'So what bearing has that on his murder? The poor sod worked for a television company as a kind of Jack of all Trades. A queer kind of bloke. A bit arty-farty with that long hair of his, but not a mite of trouble. A bit of a loner.'

'Did he have visitors?' Brambell applied his 'tell me where it hurts' technique.

'None that I know of. My wife and I keep a close eye on what goes on here. Like I said, I run a respectable house. No hanky-panky. No funny business.'

'Quite so.' Brambell nodded sagely. 'Does that include the residents on the top landing? Mr Sangster and his lady friend, Mrs Fewster, and the ménage à trois next door to them? Namely Miss Simpkins, her brother and a Mr Colm Carmody?' He smiled benignly. 'Must be a tight squeeze, three folk in a one-bedroom flat. Hmm, who sleeps with whom? I wonder. Not to worry, Mr Blunt. I shall find out, in due course.'

Entering the late Rafe Barmby's bed-sitting room, glancing about him, Brambell registered the pathetic reminders of the poor devil's last moments on earth: his pulled-out sofa bed, made up for the night with pillows, sheets and a duvet, his day-time clothing, exchanged for his night attire – pyjamas and a cotton bathrobe – neatly folded over the back of a spring-busted armchair, a pair of trainers, placed side by side, at the foot of the chair, denoting a tidy-minded individual who had made the best of his frankly squalid accommodation.

As Brambell had suspected, there was no sign of the bag of photocopied folders Gerry had given him on the evening prior to his death, leading inevitably to the plain and simple fact that his killer had been prepared to commit murder in order to lay his hands on whatever vital information was contained in those folders. Not knowing, presumably, that they were photocopies? But that killer would know now, right enough, Brambell surmised correctly. In which case, God forbid, Gerry's own life might well be in danger if the murderer, putting two and two together, had her earmarked as his next victim.

Turning to Briggs, he said hoarsely, 'Tomorrow morning, first thing, it's back to Yorkshire for us, laddie, *and* Geraldine Frayling.'

'Huh?' Briggs frowned perplexedly. 'Sorry, sir, I don't quite get it! Why Geraldine Frayling?'

'Use your loaf, laddie, because her life is in danger. That's why!'

Briggs blew out his lips. 'So when will you break the glad tidings? Besides which, begging your pardon, sir, if her life *is* in danger, what difference would a flying visit to Yorkshire make one way or the other? As I see it, we'd be better off here, trying to track down the evil bastard!'

Brambell sighed resignedly, 'You're right, of course. You have a good head on your shoulders, Bert. So where do you suggest we start looking?'

Briggs said, inspirationally, 'Why not ask Geraldine Frayling?'

'Oh, Inspector, Sergeant Briggs! What a pleasant surprise. Please do come in. Come through to the kitchen. I'll put the kettle on.' Gerry fairly beamed at the sight of her unexpected visitors. 'Have you had lunch, by the way? I could rustle up a few sandwiches. Something more substantial if you'd prefer.'

'Thanks, Gerry. Coffee will be fine.' Brambell and Briggs exchanged glances. Brambell said reluctantly, 'This isn't a social call exactly. To be frank, my dear, certain theories of yours could have a bearing on our enquiries.'

'You mean you want me to go on sleuthing?' Gerry's eyes hit up. 'Oh thanks, Inspector. I have several leads which I'm anxious to follow, to do with Bagdale Manor, Aubrey Sandys' acting career, Last Rites, and so on.'

Briggs broke in unexpectedly, 'With your permission, sir, I think Miss Frayling should be alerted to the possibility of danger in respect of the murder of Rafe Barmby.'

'Oh *that*!' Gerry shrugged her shoulders dismissively, making the coffee. 'I've already had a penny lecture from my fiancé. But, forewarned is forearmed, as the saying goes. I'm built like a sumo wrestler, and I could wear a long black wig and a traffic warden's uniform.' She burst out laughing. 'Well, what do you think?'

'That you mustn't take unnecessary risks,' Brambell said. 'The leads you've given us so far have been first class. Has anything else struck you as being significant?'

'Well, yes. You told me that Bretton Sandys' partner had been in prison. So had Aubrey Sandys. I'd like to find out where and when. Coincidental if they happened to be in the same clink at the same time, hatching plots. The name Sandys would have rung a bell with Alex French, his old school chum's father, presumably also the former husband of a world-famous artist. Plenty of money knocking about. I'll bet a hundred pounds to a hayseed that if they were holed up together, Sandys suggested Alex writing to Bretton, keeping shtum about himself, knowing full well that Bretton would tell his mother he'd heard from his alma-mater palsy-walsy who had tackled the school bully on his behalf.'

'Yes, that makes sense,' Brambell agreed. 'What do you think, Briggs?'

Briggs nodded. 'It would certainly seem so, assuming that French and Sandys did meet in the same prison. A bit of a long shot, but worth investigation. I'll get on to it right away.' He paused briefly. 'Unless you intend a return visit to Clerkenwell to interview the top-floor tenants?'

'No, that can wait,' Brambell said decisively. 'I doubt there's much to be gained from that line of enquiry. Now, Gerry, you mentioned "Last Rites". May I ask why?'

Gerry pulled a wry face. 'Oh lor,' she said, beginning to wish that she hadn't mentioned the subject, 'it was just a barmy idea of mine. I often do get barmy ideas into my head now and then. Ask Bill if you don't believe me. He said, and he was probably right, that my notion of Dorothea Lazlo being an impostor was "far-fetched". Just because the woman had been at death's door, receiving the Last Rites one minute, then up and doing the next. Well, shortly afterwards, anyway!'

Brambell and Briggs exchanged glances, remembering their recent encounter with Dorothea Lazlo. Briggs' words, following that particular interview: 'What a performance! An artist? More of an actress, I'd say. She'd make a marvellous Lady Macbeth!'

Gerry went on apologetically: 'I may be wide of the mark, but I'd really like to visit St Benedict's Hospital to find out what really ailed Dorothea Lazlo. It must have been something quite dreadful to have necessitated the Last Rites administered by an archbishop, no less. A terminal illness of some kind, from which she was not expected to recover. Then, suddenly, there she was, restored to full health, as large as life, on her way back to Bagdale Manor. Not to continue her painting. Oh no! And why not? For the simple reason that the woman who emerged from St "Bennie's" Hospital after her brush with death wouldn't have known one end of a paintbrush from t'other! In other words, she *looked* like Dorothea, *behaved* like Dorothea, but she was *not* Dorothea! Well, not to *my* way of thinking, anyway!'

Ye gods, Brambell thought bemusedly, Gerry may well be right. And if she was, what next? He said slowly, deep in thought, 'If your supposition is correct, if the real Dorothea Lazlo died in St Benedict's Hospital, and an impostor took her place. *Why?* For what purpose?'

Gerry said wistfully, 'That I don't know, Inspector. But I'd sure as hell like to find out!'

'Then why not talk it over with Bill?' Brambell suggested. 'See what he thinks. If he has no objections, then go ahead. The last thing I want is to put the cat among the pigeons.'

Gerry sighed. 'Bill's sure to object,' she said. 'He hasn't got over the 'Antiques Murders' yet. We had a bit of a dust-up, if you must know. When the dust had settled, we came to an understanding. I promised to start a new book if he'd let me get on with my sleuthing, to which he agreed as long as I let him know where I'd be beforehand, and took my mobile along with me. I asked if he'd like me to wear a collar and lead and have myself micro-chipped. Which reminds me, Inspector, where is Annie Scott's dog?'

'In custody.' Brambell chuckled. 'Quite safe, I assure you. His case comes up next week!'

'Huh! Ask a silly question!' Loving the inspector's quirky sense of humour. 'You know, Inspector, you and Bill should team up as a double act. You'd go down a treat at a policeman's ball! Better still, you could go round hospital wards, come Christmas, entertaining the kiddies. They'd love that!'

'Ah well, many a true word spoken in jest,' Brambell laughed, as he and Briggs got up to leave. 'Thanks for the coffee. Now, duty calls. I can tell that my sidekick here is dying to get on with his research into the prison records of French and Sandys. He'll keep you informed, won't you, laddie? Meanwhile, I suppose I'd best return to Skinner Road.'

When they had gone, Gerry's mind went into overdrive. Of course, she thought. What a brilliant idea. No way could she enter St Benedict's Hospital to start asking awkward questions about Dorothea Lazlo without a darned good reason. But there was more than one way to skin a rabbit. A clever disguise for one thing, a dopey expression for another, she reckoned. No problem so far as the latter was concerned. Her dopey expression had to be seen to be believed.

As for the disguise, she would wear her horn-rimmed glasses, a woolly hat pulled well down on her forehead, a duffle coat, a woollen muffler, a long black skirt, fawn fur-lined boots, and carry with her a shoulder bag stuffed with sketch pads, crayons and the kind of gear that art students usually carried around with them during their lunch break from the Slade School of Art, or so she imagined. Adding to her tote bag a packet of corned-beef sandwiches and a flask of coffee, before setting forth to St Bennie's.

Approaching the reception desk, she said haltingly to a smart young woman receptionist behind the counter, 'I'm ever so sorry to trouble you, but, well, you see, as an art student, I'm studying the paintings of Dorothea Lazlo, at the moment, with a view to writing a précis of her life for my written examination early next month. And, well, since I know she was a patient here, from various newspaper reports, a while back, I wondered if you could fill me in with details of her illness, from which, I gather, she made a miraculous recovery.'

Gerry smiled mistily. 'Please, this is really important to me. I'd be so glad of your help.' She added encouragingly, 'I daresay the details are available in your computer?'

'Sorry, that's out of the question,' the woman said. 'Patients' records are strictly private. I doubt even a consultant would divulge details of any patient's illness to other than bona-fide members of their family.'

116

'Yes, of course,' Gerry conceded mildly. 'I'm sorry. It's just that I want to write a really good essay about a woman whose work I greatly admire. I've done lots of research already: studied her paintings, found out that she was an art teacher to begin with, long before she became a world-famous artist. You've heard of her, I daresay? Dorothea Lazlo, whose pictures are worth a fortune nowadays?'

'Well no, not really,' the guardian of the computer confessed, 'I'm not all that interested in art.'

Allowing her underlip to quiver slightly, Gerry murmured, 'The trouble is, if I flunk my written exam, if I fail to gain a scholarship, my ma will be so disappointed. She's worked her fingers to the bone, since Dad died, to pay my fees at the Slade School of Art, bless her.'

Biting her bottom lip, Gerry continued mistily, 'I had intended to end my essay on the life and works of Dorothea Lazlo with an uplifting account of her amazing recovery from a life-threatening illness, here, in St Benedict's, having received the Last Rites from a Roman Catholic archbishop.' Turning away from the desk, a picture of misery, Gerry said pluckily, 'Sorry to have troubled you, I'm sure.'

Relenting her decision not to help an overweight art student in distress, the receptionist called after her, 'Hang on just a sec!'

Gerry hung on, hopefully, as the woman jabbed the keys of her computer. Then, 'Sorry, miss,' the receptionist informed her, 'you must have come to the wrong hospital. No one called Dorothea Lazlo has ever been a patient here.'

Conveying her thanks to the receptionist, humping her hefty shoulder bag through the swing doors of St Benedict's to the pavement outside, now what? she wondered. If Dorothea Lazlo had never been admitted to St Benedict's Hospital in the first place, where the hell was she now? At Bagdale Manor? Miraculously restored to health and strength once more? An impossibility to Gerry's way of thinking, strengthening her belief that the present incumbent of Bagdale Manor was an impostor. Why, she hadn't the faintest idea.

Money? Greed? Blackmail? A cover-up – of what precisely?

Walking slowly away from the hospital, Gerry weighed up

the pros and cons. It had come as a shock to learn that Dorothea Lazlo had never been admitted to St Benedict's. If not, how come that tarradiddle about the Last Rites?

Her writer's instincts at full alert, Gerry sidestepped oncoming pedestrians on her way to the car park to find her Mini. Things were beginning to come together in her mind. Had Dorothea been kidnapped? If so, had this to do with an impostor at Bagdale Manor? Had Elliot Lazlo hired an actress to cover up his wife's abduction? Had he been warned by his wife's kidnapper not to inform the police of her disappearance? Could the kidnapper possibly have been – Aubrey Sandys? Had that been the reason for Sandys' Christmas Eve visit to Bagdale Manor, to collect his ransom money?

Glancing at the time, Gerry sighed deeply, remembering that she had promised Bill faithfully to begin a new novel and to give him a roast duck dinner.

Returning to the Eyrie, Gerry rushed upstairs to her sanctum to tap out the opening sentences of her new saga, *Dead Men Don't Bleed* . . . 'The last thing Virginia Vale had envisaged on an early morning jog to Hampstead Heath was the discovery of a body. Alerted by the howling of a dog, she had entered a spinney to investigate.'

There, Gerry thought with relief, she had kept her promise to begin the book. Now, high time the duck was in the oven, duly bunged full of sage and onion stuffing – the Paxo packet variety – to peel potatoes, scrape carrots, and shave a couple of parsnips. How long the duck would take to cook, she hadn't the faintest idea. Just as long as Bill caught wind of it when he came home from work.

'Hmm, something smells good!' Entering the Eyrie, Bill sniffed the air appreciatively. 'Who's been a busy girl, then?'

'*I* have,' Gerry supplied modestly. 'The duck's almost ready. What's more, I've started a new novel, and I have a new slant on the tramp's murder. I'll tell you about it, over dinner.'

'Oh lord, here we go again,' Bill said darkly, 'I thought you'd given up sleuthing.'

'Ah well, Inspector Brambell came for a cuppa, this morning. He and Sergeant Briggs. We got talking and, next thing

I knew I was at St Ben's, disguised as an art student, making enquiries about Dorothea Lazlo. And guess what?'

'They threw you out, neck and crop?' Bill suggested hopefully.

'No. I dug up some interesting information. Well, do you want to hear about it or not?'

'Not until I've had a shower and slipped out of my wet things into a dry martini,' Bill quipped. On his way upstairs, 'What's the title of your new book, by the way? I'll look forward to reading the first chapter after dinner.'

'You'll be lucky! You'll read the first couple of sentences, and like it! I'm calling it *Dead Men Don't Bleed*. Now hop it while I see to the duck, before it starts quacking for mercy!'

Bill 'hopped it' with alacrity. Showering, he realized that the things he most loved about Gerry, her gutsy pride and determination, her unquenchable sense of humour, her loyalty towards those she loved, were as unchangeable as the moon and stars. So why even attempt to change the unchangeable? So what if she couldn't cook for toffee? What if she marched in, occasionally, where angels might fear to tread, with little or no regard for her own safety? It was this sublime innocence about her that he loved so much. From now on, he figured, far better to assume his role as her watchdog, her guardian angel, her knight in shining armour, than to risk losing her utter and sublime confidence in himself as her watchdog by virtue of his over-protectiveness towards her. If Gerry marched into danger, he would march along beside her every inch of the way, Bill decided, marching downstairs to the kitchen to partake of his roast duck dinner.

To his amazement, Gerry had cooked the duck to perfection, along with its accompanying roast potatoes, peas, parsnips, cauliflower and carrots. He said, admiringly, 'But this is simply delicious. I thought you said you couldn't cook?'

'No!' Gerry responded happily. 'When you asked me if I *could* cook, I said I could, if the need arose. Now it *has* arisen! So there!'

Uncorking a bottle of wine to accompany the meal, raising his glass to her across the table, 'Here's to you, Gerry, my love,' he said mistily. 'Now tell me all about your visit to St Benedict's.'

119

'You mean you're not against me any more?' she queried anxiously.

'No, not any more,' he responded quietly. 'And I never shall be again, believe me.'

Fourteen

Brambell had scarcely relished the prospect of his return visit to No. 14 Skinner Road, this time with WPC Viv Betts in tow, Briggs having disappeared to the archives to research the prison records of Aubrey Sandys and Alex French. Only one or two interesting and salient facts emerged from the inspector's interview with the Simpkinses and their 'lodger' Colm Carmody. They were all members of Equity, presently 'resting', apart from Carmody, a strapping Irishman with a mane of tawny hair and a brogue as thick as Irish stew, who had landed himself a small speaking role in the current episode of *The Old Bill*, on location off the Old Kent Road.

And, 'Sure,' he admitted laconically, 'I knew Rafe Barmby. Not that we were what you might call bosom pals. Not like him and Adrian Sweeting, for instance.'

'Adrian Sweeting?' Brambell enquired mildly. 'You mean the film director?'

'The self and same,' Carmody acquiesced coolly. 'Closer than two bugs in a rug, they were. As a matter of fact, I saw them together in the Nag's Head bar parlour, on the night before Rafe's murder. Or should I say on the night of Rafe's murder? Arguing like billio, they were. Well, to be honest, squire, I didn't take much notice. I left the pub well before closing time, came home, and went straight to bed. Ask Bella, if you don't believe me. I daresay she'll remember well enough, won't you, Sweetie?'

'Sweetie' blushed becomingly. 'Yes, that's so,' she murmured in agreement. 'You see, Inspector, Colm isn't just a – lodger. He's my lover.'

Carmody continued cockily, 'If it's thinking you are, Inspector, that *I* had anything to do with Barmby's murder, you're

121

barking up the wrong tree entirely. I had far more important things on my mind than putting paid to a bloke on the floor below. I mean to say, why the hell should I? I couldn't have cared less about him one way or t'other.'

'I see,' Brambell replied quietly, turning his attention to Bella's brother, Hugo Simpkins. 'So where were you at the time of the murder?'

'In my sleeping bag on the sitting-room floor,' Hugo informed him. 'I heard Colm come in around eleven o'clock, heard him go through to the bedroom, then I fell fast asleep, and stayed asleep till six o'clock next morning.'

Brambell left No. 14 Skinner Road, an hour later, little the wiser than he had been sixty minutes before, with only one possible suspect in mind, the film director, Adrian Sweeting.

About to enter the police car, suddenly Brambell swore softly beneath his breath. 'Is anything wrong, sir?' Viv Betts, his driver, dark-eyed, bushy-tailed and intelligent, asked concernedly.

'Yes, a great deal is wrong,' Brambell muttered hoarsely. 'We're going back indoors! My interview with the ménage à trois on the top landing is not over and done with quite yet! There's one vital question I neglected to ask!'

DS Briggs drew in a deep sigh of satisfaction, having discovered that French and Sandys had, indeed, come into contact in an open prison, near York, a little over two years ago. French on a charge of obtaining money by false pretences from a former employer of his. In short, of swindling the man of the sum of twenty thousand pounds via a series of forged cheques and the falsifying of the firm's accounts, to which, at his, French's trial, he had pleaded guilty, due to extenuating circumstances beyond his control.

Sandys had also pleaded guilty to a charge of obtaining money by false pretences with regard to a series of unpaid bills at various well-known hotels in the West End of London: the Grosvenor, the Ritz, and the Savoy, amounting, all told, to a sum in excess of fifteen thousand quid: squandered on champagne parties for his friends in whichever hotel he happened to be staying at the time.

And so the pair of swindlers had ended up together in

that open prison, near York, on charges far less serious than robbery with violence, for instance, manslaughter or – murder. A couple of pussycats in the eyes of the law, Briggs thought disgustedly, due for parole halfway through their original three-year sentences for fraudulent conversion, and living the life of Riley in what was tantamount to a prison without bars.

Then, York, Briggs considered cannily. A city scarcely a stone's throw away from Bretton Sandys' garden centre, a busy mainline station: the home of Arthur and June Scott and their daughter Annie. Was it remotely possible that either one of the two prisoners, or both, had known the Scotts? If so, had they been instrumental in luring Annie to London for nefarious purposes of their own devising? Both had been in London at the time of the girl's murder. Only one of them could have committed the crime. Alex French! But *why*? Why kill an innocent young girl? Briggs pondered. Unless Annie had not been as innocent as she appeared to be.

Briggs' mind went back to Gerry Frayling's far-fetched theory concerning Dorothea Lazlo's false identity, which he had taken with a large pinch of salt, bearing in mind that Miss Frayling, a writer of crime fiction, was bound to possess a vivid imagination. An over-vivid imagination, in his view.

True, she had been clever enough to suss out the identity of the late Aubrey Sandys, more by good luck than good management, he suspected, but to suggest that Dorothea Lazlo was an impostor belonged in the pages of one of her bestselling novels. Not that he disliked Gerry. He didn't. He simply wished that she had not become involved in a complex triple murder inquiry, the solution of which would depend on hard facts not – fantasy.

Gerry lost no time letting Brambell know the results of her visit to St Ben's. When the tale was told, 'But that's incredible,' he said. 'Proof positive of collusion between Sandys and Lazlo.' He paused to consider the ramifications of this startling new evidence, then pressed his desk buzzer to summon Briggs to his office. Awaiting his arrival, Brambell said, his voice betraying his excitement, 'You've done well, Gerry. Very well indeed. So you were right all along. Wait till Briggs hears about this!'

Aware of Briggs' slight antipathy towards her, Gerry got up to leave the two men alone, murmuring that she had urgent matters to attend to. Brambell wouldn't hear of it. 'Please sit down, Gerry,' he said. 'Briggs has also come up with vital information, and I want you in on the act, so to speak.' He smiled at her encouragingly. Gerry sat down obediently. Briggs entered the office.

Astutely, Brambell, also aware of the slight edge between his sergeant and his star performer, explained Gerry's findings to Briggs matter-of-factly, making no mention of Gerry's unorthodox method of detection or her student get-up, which Briggs might not find particularly amusing in one of what the inspector thought of as his 'Scotland Yard' moods.

In the event, Gerry listened intently to Briggs' detailed account of his research into the French/Sandys affair, whom she had mentally dubbed 'French and Saunders', and to his carefully considered theory of a possible connection with Arthur Scott and Annie. In short, a York connection. After all, why not? An open prison, near York, close to a mainline station and Bretton Sandys' garden centre. Food for thought. She said breathlessly, 'Yes, of course. How clever of you to have thought of that, Sergeant Briggs! So now what? A return visit to Bretton Sandys' garden centre?'

Warmed by Gerry's generous response to his efforts, Briggs supplied modestly, smiling in her direction, 'That's up to DCI Brambell to decide.' He added, by way of an olive branch, 'Frankly, Miss Frayling, I doubted, at first, your theory of the present Dorothea Lazlo as an impostor. Apparently I was wrong. In which case, I owe you an apology.'

'Oh, *fudge*!' Gerry responded happily. 'But thanks, all the same. Apology accepted!'

Brambell coughed drily. He said, 'When you two have finished handing out bouquets to one another, here's what I have in mind. Certainly a return visit to Bretton Sandys' garden centre – first thing tomorrow morning!'

'Including me?' Gerry asked hopefully.

'No, certainly not,' Brambell uttered succinctly. 'Sorry, but your further involvement in this murder inquiry is out of the question. A serial killer is still at large somewhere in the London area, possibly with yourself in mind as his next victim. No, don't smile, Gerry. I'm perfectly serious, I assure you! Please, I need your promise to be on your guard from now on!'

Gerry sighed deeply. 'Sorry, Inspector, but if, as you suggest, a serial killer is after me, the sooner he's caught, the better, wouldn't you say? I've been through all this before, if you remember?' referring to the Antiques Murders of the previous year. 'So no need to worry about me unduly, Inspector. I have an inborn sense of self-preservation, you see? And I'm not about to quit this "vale of tears" quite yet! At least not without one hell of a fight!'

Understanding Gerry's disappointment, Brambell said, 'Your efforts so far have been invaluable, but I'd rather you kept a low profile from now on. It might be a good idea to take a holiday. To quit London for a while.'

'Take a trip to Outer Mongolia, you mean? To Snowdonia or the Isle of Skye? Thanks, but no thanks, Inspector. I'm staying put, ta very much.' Getting up to leave, 'Well, like I said, I have things to do, and I'd best be on my way. So, good day to you, gentlemen. Good luck, and good hunting!' Pausing on the threshold, 'You will let me know when you have the killer behind bars, won't you?'

Brambell groaned as the office door closed behind her. Briggs said levelly, 'I'd go after her if I were you, sir. She may be a bit fanciful, a rank amateur, but she has the makings of a bloody good detective.'

'An amateur she may be, but she managed to put the Antiques Murderers behind bars,' Brambell said, going after her.

Things were beginning to fall into place a little, he thought, going through his case notes. A pattern, however bizarre, was starting to emerge, stemming from identification of Aubrey Sandys as the occupant of the grave on Hampstead Heath, and Gerry's startling discovery that Dorothea Lazlo had never crossed the threshold of St Benedict's Hospital. Furthermore, that Alex French and Aubrey Sandys had been in the same prison at the same time and had, more than likely, been acquainted with Arthur Scott, Annie Scott's father.

Rafe Barmby had, presumably, been murdered for the

contents of the missing folders. The man who knew too much? Brambell considered grimly. The question remained, too much about what, and who, precisely? His director friend, Adrian Sweeting? Colm Carmody had stated categorically that he had seen the pair of them together, arguing, in a pub, shortly before Barmby's death. Pointing the finger at Sweeting as the possible killer, Brambell thought cagily, recalling that Carmody had freely admitted to having known Barmby as a result of their working relationship on the film set of *The Old Bill*. Carmody, however, had responded far less easily on being quizzed re his relationship with a fellow actor, Aubrey Sandys. An afterthought on Brambell's part, the reason why he had returned to No. 14 Skinner Road so abruptly to catch the laid-back Irishman, off guard, so to speak. A hunch that had paid off in the long run, when Carmody had admitted, albeit reluctantly, that he'd been a frequent guest at parties, hosted by Sandys, at his penthouse flat overlooking Grosvenor Square.

'So what's wrong with that?' he'd demanded hoarsely. 'His parties were great fun. So was Sandys. Then suddenly he dropped out of sight. Don't ask me why! So what became of him? Where is he now? I'd really like to know!'

'Then I suggest a visit to the Scotland Yard mortuary,' Brambell said coolly. 'Right now, if you don't mind. You see, Mr Carmody, his mortal remains have not, so far, been identified officially.' He added grimly, 'Your friend, Aubrey Sandys' body was recently discovered in a shallow grave on Hampstead Heath. To put it bluntly, Mr Carmody, your party-loving host had been brutally murdered by a person, or persons, unknown.'

'You mean you think that *I* put paid to him?' Carmody cried out in alarm. 'But that's bloody ridiculous! For what reason? We were the best of friends.' Swallowing hard, 'Oh, I get it! You have me earmarked as a prime suspect! Well, you've got it all wrong, Inspector! I'm an actor, not a killer! And you'd better believe me!'

Curiously enough, Brambell *had* believed him. Further questioning, after Carmody had attempted to identify Sandys' body – without success – revealed facts relevant to the deceased's lifestyle preceding his spell in prison, of which Carmody knew nothing, having been in Ireland at the time.

Had there been a woman in Sandys' life? Brambell asked, to which Carmody replied sarcastically, '*One* woman? There were dozens! Women fell for him like a ton of bricks. He'd been playing matinée idol roles so long they'd rubbed off on him, so they had. That's how he saw himself, as God's gift to women. And why not? He was tall, good looking. Not that he ever played leading parts, just cads, bounders, ne'er do wells. A bit like his screen idol, George Sanders, but without the same degree of success. Not that he seemed to mind playing the villain just as long as he had his fair share of the limelight, the poor devil.'

'You knew he'd been married?' Brambell asked patiently, gently probing, assuming his Father Confessor mantle, to which question he received no satisfactory answer. Carmody merely shrugged his shoulders dismissively, replying that, if so, Sandys had never mentioned a wife. Indeed, Sandys had not seemed the marrying kind. More of a love 'em and leave 'em merchant, unlikely to commit to any one woman, in his experience.

Pursuing his notes, Brambell thought about his trip to Yorkshire the following day. Armed with fresh information, on his return visit to Sandys' Garden Centre, he'd have searching questions to put to Sandys and his cohort, Alex French, to which he'd demand truthful answers. Meanwhile, DI Clooney could make himself useful interviewing guests of the Lazlos at that ill-fated Christmas house party of theirs at Bagdale Manor: namely – apart from Sandys, French, and Sandys' wife, Carla, Lazlo's literary agent, Dumas, and his wife – they were Lazlo's sister, Mrs Coverdale, and her daughter Pippa, plus a Dr Edmund Sloane, Mrs Lazlo's personal physician.

Clooney had, so far, interviewed only one person, the literary agent, from whom he had elicited little or no information relevant to the case in hand. This time, Clooney had better pull his finger out, Brambell considered grimly, otherwise he would have no choice other than to replace him with a younger, more efficient member of his Scotland Yard team. Not without prior warning, of course, and making certain that Clooney had all the facts of the case at his fingertips beforehand. He would fax all the relevant information to the Hampstead Police Station first thing tomorrow morning, before he and Briggs set off on their long journey north. Which reminded him, they'd best pack overnight bags in anticipation of an overnight stay in strange beds in some hotel or other. Brambell groaned inwardly. He hated strange beds in strange hotels.

Arriving in the vicinity of Sandys' Garden Centre around midday, Brambell and Briggs entered a village pub offering bar-snacks and advertising accommodation, to include dinner, bed and breakfast, at reasonable prices.

'Let's sample the grub first,' Brambell suggested wryly, 'before committing ourselves to an overnight stay, shall we?' Glancing round the bar parlour, he noticed that the horse-brasses framing the counter were well polished, and a coal fire was burning brightly in an inglenook fireplace. So far, so good. Moreover, the landlord appeared to be a genial fellow, hale and hearty, obviously well liked by his coterie of regulars downing pints of Tetley's bitter.

'Good day, gentlemen,' he said cheerily. 'What can I get you? Two pints? Certainly. And a menu? My missus does all the cooking, and I can recommend her steak pie and chips – her specialité de la maison, by the way. Or if it's sandwiches you're after, there's roast beef, prawn, smoked salmon or cheese an' tomatoes, served with salad and homemade mayonnaise.'

Brambell and Briggs exchanged glances. 'We'll have the steak pie and chips,' the DCI said firmly. 'By the by, what's on tonight's dinner menu?'

'Homemade vegetable soup, roast chicken, roast pota-toes, chipolata sausages, stuffing and so forth, followed by homemade apple pie and custard,' the landlord told them engagingly. 'And if you're thinking of an overnight stay, or longer, we have a couple of nice rooms vacant on the first floor.'

'Right, then,' Brambell announced, thinking longingly of a roast chicken and homemade apple pie dinner, in what appeared to be a snug haven of repose following what was bound to be a tiring day's work on top of a long, tiring journey.

'You'd best book us in, then, for an overnight stay. What's the name of your pub, by the way?'

'The Who'd Ha' Thought It?' the landlord responded merrily.

Who, indeed? Brambell thought bemusedly, Well, ask a silly question, secretly dreading the far from silly questions he would soon be firing at Bretton Sandys and Alex French.

The door was opened by a smartly dressed, sullen-faced young woman, as charmless as a pile of wet washing in a kitchen sink. 'Yes? Who are you, and what do you want?' she demanded crossly. 'I haven't got all day! If it's my husband you're after, he's in his office, as usual!'

Brambell replied courteously, 'Then you must be Mrs Carla Sandys? I am Detective Chief Inspector Brambell of Scotland Yard, and this is my colleague, Detective Sergeant Briggs. We'd like a word with you, if you don't mind.'

'But I do mind! My God, Inspector, haven't you anything better to do than waste time asking damn-fool questions about a servant girl? My husband told me about your last visit, which upset him terribly I might add. Now, if you'll excuse me, I have a hairdressing appointment for which I am running late as it is!'

Brambell said mildly, 'This visit isn't about Miss Scott. It concerns the murder of one Aubrey Sandys whose body was discovered on Hampstead Heath shortly after your Christmas stay at Bagdale Manor. Now, may we come in to discuss the matter further, or would you prefer to make a statement at police headquarters?'

Carla's face paled perceptibly. 'Aubrey Sandys? Brett's father? But that's not possible! I thought he'd died ages ago! You can't believe that we had anything to do with his – murder?'

Briggs broke in matter-of-factly, 'Take my advice, Mrs Sandys, cancel your hair appointment and stop prevaricating. You, not we, are wasting time here. If, as you say, your husband is in his office, be kind enough to lead the way.'

Confronting Bretton Sandys, Brambell said levelly, 'The last time we met, you expressed concern that your mother, Dorothea Lazlo, might have died unexpectedly.'

Bretton said, 'Dorothea Lazlo is not my mother! My mother's name is Marguerite, not Dorothea!'

'I see.' Appearing not to have noticed Sandys' scarcely concealed hostility towards him, Brambell said equably, 'But I *am* right in thinking that Aubrey Sandys was your father, am I not?'

'Yes! So what of it?' Bretton responded edgily.

'*I* don't know! You tell *me*!'

His back to the wall, hoisted by his own petard, Bretton said defiantly, 'My parents were actors. They worked together as a team long before my father married Dorothea . . .'

'Yes, do go on, Mr Sandys,' Brambell said encouragingly.

Beginning to crumble, Bretton burst forth explosively, 'All right, so my parents had a one-night stand of which I was the result! Satisfied now, are you?'

'Not entirely,' Brambell admitted ruefully. 'Forgive me for asking, so you were born out of wedlock? Nothing to be ashamed of, but am I right in supposing that you remained close to your mother, if not to your father?'

Sandys was trembling violently now. He said shakily, 'If that swine came to a bad end, I'm glad, not sorry that he's dead!'

Carla cried out suddenly, in a high-pitched voice, 'Shut up, Brett! Can't you see what's happening? Well *I* can if you can't! Next thing you know you'll be behind bars, accused of murdering Aubrey Sandys, you bloody fool!'

'Really, Carla, that's no way to speak to your nearest and dearest.' Alex French had entered the office unnoticed. He added wickedly, 'Assuming of course that Brett is your nearest and dearest?'

Rounding on him fiercely, 'Just who the hell do you think you are,' she demanded, 'poking your nose into matters that don't concern you?'

'Ah, but they *do* concern me,' Alex reminded her. 'Ask the inspector if you don't believe me. Hardly likely he's come all this way to pass the time of day, eh, Inspector? Well, I've nothing to hide, even if Brett has. He already knows about my prison record. Now, apparently he's found out that Aubrey and I served time together in the same prison a while back, and is dying to find out more about our interesting conversations together. And they were very interesting, believe me. That is why you're here, Inspector, isn't it?' He added jauntily, 'Tell me, am I your prime suspect?'

Briggs broke in coldly; disliking the man intensely, he said, 'Coercion of a Scotland Yard detective in the course of ongoing enquiries is not in your own best interests, believe me. You will be interviewed in due course.'

French pulled a wry face. 'Coercion? Whatever gave you that idea? Right then, when you need me to spill my guts, I'll be upstairs in my flat!'

Nursing a half tumbler of whisky, 'Prison has a way of bringing blokes together,' French said easily from the depths of an armchair, treating Brambell and Briggs as fellow members at some exclusive men's club. 'One tends to gravitate towards chaps with something interesting to say, especially in an open prison, such as ours.

'I recognized the name Sandys, of course. It didn't take a *Mastermind* contestant to work out that he must be connected with my school chum, Bretton. I naturally assumed him to be the boy's father, and I was right. What I didn't know at the time was that Brett was the result of a one-night stand with an actress who happened to be a member of the cast of the play they were both performing in at the time.'

He chuckled drily. 'Some performance eh? Apparently they were both as drunk as skunks after an all-night party. So, not what you might call a meeting of true minds. More of a quick grope and fumble between two consenting adults in the actress's dressing room when the party was over. The upshot being, next day they went their separate ways. The actress carrying more excess baggage than she'd bargained for. Namely, a son. Bretton. Well, Inspector, there you have it in a nutshell.'

'But why the surname Sandys?' Brambell asked, curiously, wanting to get things straight in his mind.

'For the good and simple reason that she wanted money from him towards his son's education and upbringing. And why not? After all, Sandys *was* the child's father. However misbegotten that child may have been. Marguerite had her head screwed on the right way round, make no mistake about that! She still has, come to think of it!'

'Which begs the question,' Brambell insisted quietly yet forcibly, 'how long have you known that the present-day, so-called Dorothea Lazlo, is an impostor?'

Not one whit perturbed, French replied, 'Since I heard it, with my own two ears, from Aubrey Sandys. It's a long complicated story, but I'll do my best to explain. You see, Inspector, don't ask me why, but after his one-night stand with Marguerite, Sandys met and married a girl called Dorothea, a talented artist who bore a strong physical resemblance to Marguerite.'

'Go on, Mr French,' Brambell said darkly. 'Then what happened?'

'How the hell should *I* know?' Finding himself up to the neck in deep water, French resorted to bluster, fuelled by his intake of whisky. 'All this is hearsay. I simply gathered, from Aubrey Sandys, that he was selling his wife's paintings for a great deal of money, until one day, out of the blue, she upped and left him for another man. Elliot Lazlo!'

French added tipsily, 'Sandys was shattered, to say the least, when Dorothea divorced him and married Lazlo. And who could blame him? After all, a wealthy man in his own right, making more money, hand over fist, from his wife's paintings? But as God's my witness, I swear I had nothing to do with what followed, apart from latching on to Brett Sandys as his so-called business partner. Nothing to do with extortion or blackmail. All that was Sandys' doing.'

'Blackmail? On what grounds?' Brambell spoke grimly, abruptly. 'I warn you, Mr French, that your involvement in this affair, however seemingly innocent, will carry no weight in the eyes of the law if, as I suspect, you entered into collusion with Sandys to pervert the course of justice.'

'You're wrong, Inspector! There were times when I tried to talk him out of some of his wilder ideas. I wasn't even keen on getting in touch with Brett, but Sandys insisted. He had this jealous streak inside him. He wanted revenge against his wife and Lazlo. Wanted it so badly that he would go to any lengths to get it – and the money he'd been cheated out of. That really rankled, I can tell you. He would say over and over again that

132

he'd find a way to get his hands on what was rightly his. It's my belief that he intended to use Bretton as a means to an end. Don't ask me how. I tried to find out, but he wouldn't tell me. All he would say was, "wait and see". And that's the gospel truth.'

French was sweating profusely now, beginning to shake, to lose control. Brambell knew, from experience, that to continue the questioning would prove futile for the time being. No way was French, in his present stage of inebriation, capable of understanding, let alone answering, probing questions concerning the conversations which had taken place between himself and Sandys during their imprisonment.

Signalling to Briggs with his eyes, a nod of the head in the direction of the door, the sergeant knew at once that Brambell had decided to call it a day. Rising to his feet, Briggs said implacably to the man slumped in the armchair, 'This interview is terminated for the present. Terminated, not completed, to be continued at ten o'clock tomorrow morning at the York Police Headquarters. I strongly advise you, sir, to arrive on time and in a fit state to undergo further questioning. Failure to comply will not be tolerated. Do I make myself clear?'

French nodded foolishly. 'Yeah, yeah,' he mumbled. 'Now, piss off, the pair of you!'

'Well done, laddie,' Brambell murmured gratefully, on their way to the car. 'Ten o'clock. Hmm, that'll give us nice time for breakfast. With luck, eggs, bacon and sausages, after a good night's sleep at the Who'd Ha' Thought It. What a bloody silly name for a pub, eh?' He added mistily, 'Meanwhile we've got roast chicken to look forward to, and beer. Several pints, I shouldn't wonder.'

Briggs grinned. 'Just as long as we turn up at the York nick in a fit state to conduct an interview.' He added, 'Which reminds me, you'd best give them a ring beforehand, sir, hadn't you? To give 'em time to roll out the red carpet.'

'You do it, laddie,' Brambell advised him. 'It'll be good practice.'

Briggs frowned. 'Good practice for – what?'

'Promotion, that's what.' Brambell smiled fondly at his sergeant, whom he had often regarded as a son. 'It's high time you moved up in the world, Bert. The reason why I've written a letter to Chief Superintendent Johnson, recommending your promotion from a detective sergeant to a fully fledged detective inspector.' He paused. 'Given a modicum of good luck, you'll end up in charge of your own patch. Hopefully, the Hampstead nick. Now, let's head for the Who'd Ha, shall we? Down a couple of pints before dinner?'

At the York headquarters next morning, they were welcomed warmly by an old friend and colleague of Brambell, with whom they had discussed the reason for requesting an interview room far removed from the temptation of alcohol. They kept a watchful eye on the time, as it inched towards ten past ten, to Briggs' chagrin, not to mention his displeasure at what he considered a deliberate flouting of authority on the part of a man contemptuous of the law. Well, he'd live to regret his tardiness, Briggs thought darkly, as the hands of the clock slid inexorably towards the half hour.

As it happened, Alex French would live to regret nothing at all. For the good and sufficient reason that he'd been murdered in his bed, in the early hours of the morning, by means of a lethal injection of morphine. Administered, presumably, by someone who wanted to make certain that his visit to York Police Headquarters would not take place. Not now. Not ever.

Fifteen

Possessed of a gut feeling that something was radically wrong, seated at her typewriter, Gerry tapped out a list of case notes – a means of clearing her mind and getting her thoughts in order, a necessity when her plots became too complicated for comfort. Now here she was, trying to figure out a plot far more complicated than any contained between the covers of her bestselling novels.

She typed the name Aubrey Sandys, then 'Why and by whom was he murdered?' The reason why seemed abundantly clear. Because of his Christmas Eve visit to Bagdale Manor, presumably to extort money from Elliot Lazlo, virtually signing his own death warrant. But why two bites at the same cherry? Surely, fracturing the poor devil's skull with a blunt instrument would have seen him out of harm's way without firing a bullet into him into the bargain, *after* he was dead? Why had that been necessary? Because there must have been a reason *why* it was necessary. To point the finger of suspicion at the owner of the revolver? Gerry wondered.

If so, who had actually put paid to him? Elliot Lazlo? Bretton Sandys? Alex French? All of whom had been present at Bagdale Manor at the time of the murder. Any or all of whom might have had good and sufficient reasons for wanting rid of him.

Fair enough, but who and why would any one of them have wanted rid of Annie Scott? Lazlo had sent Annie to King's Cross Station in a taxi along with the dog, Bruno. Had he meant to kill her, surely he would have done so there and then? A mission easily accomplished, given a strong man, a frightened girl, a quick strangulation, a dark night and a walled garden in which to hide a dead body. No, it simply didn't make sense to Gerry's way of thinking, hence her gut feeling of a missing link somewhere along the line. A missing person, perhaps?

Dorothea Lazlo sprang to mind. Gerry wished she had not. Had she really visited the wrong hospital in search of her records? Had she dreamed up those Press reports of a famous artist at death's door? Some fat chance, Gerry told herself severely. Otherwise she might just as well give up writing crime fiction and start writing fairy tales.

Certainly Dorothea had gone missing. Why else would an impostor have taken her place at Bagdale Manor? Gerry typed, 'Find out the whereabouts of Dorothea Lazlo.' Easier said than done, she thought ruefully, like looking for a nut in a pecan plantation. She added to her case notes: 'Enquire at every hospital in the Greater London area.'

A chilling thought occurred. What if Dorothea had also been murdered? If so, it was up to her to find out why, and by whom. On the other hand, why not simply hand over the necessary enquiries to Inspector Brambell? As Bill had pointed out to her, she was a writer, not a detective.

Glancing at her watch, suddenly, Bill, she thought desperately, who would be home soon, tired and hungry, looking forward to a good hot dinner.

Head spinning, Gerry raced down to the kitchen to bung a shop-bought steak and kidney pie into the oven. Thank God for convenience food, she thought, opening a packet of Knorr Swiss asparagus soup along with the required amount of water to begin the reconstitution process, stirring madly the contents of the saucepan to smash out the lumps, and madly peeling potatoes at the kitchen sink to provide a mashed taters accompaniment to the steak and kidney pie. Anything, just as long as Bill didn't come home, hungry as a hunter, to sniff the air in vain.

The potatoes bubbling away in a panful of boiling water, now where the hell were the Bisto gravy granules? Gerry wondered.

Entering the Eyrie, sniffing the air appreciatively, 'Something smells good,' Bill enthused, plonking a bottle of wine on the kitchen table. 'Gerry, love, it's so good to be home for a bit of peace and quiet, a home-cooked dinner, a flask of wine and thou, singing beside me in the wilderness – with apologies to Omar – Sharif. Or do I mean Omar Khayyám? Frankly, darling, it's just been one of those days. One damn thing after another. You'll never know how much I'm looking forward to giving my brain cells a bit of a holiday! How about you?'

'Yeah, me too,' Gerry assured him, pushing aside all thoughts of murder and mayhem for the time being. After all, why burden Bill with her problems when she'd far rather succumb to the pleasure of – blowing a bugle for the boy scouts?

At the parting of their lips, Gerry asked mistily, 'Oh Bill, where did you learn to kiss like that?' To which he responded, tongue in cheek, 'I was once a spaghetti taster in an Italian restaurant.'

After supper, in the drawing room, Bill said, 'I have to be in Stuttgart for an important meeting, next week. A bit of a darned nuisance really. Just when I was getting used to home cooking.'

'Oh Bill! Do you have to go?' Gerry sighed wistfully. 'Just when I was getting used to having you around again.'

'Afraid so, love.' Bill pulled a face. 'I'm not all that struck on sauerkraut and pumpernickel. Give me your homemade steak and kidney pie any day of the week.'

'Huh?' Disarmingly honest and truthful, 'Oh, I didn't *make* the pie, I only baked it,' she said. 'I bought it at that butchers in the High Street. He does chicken and mushroom, as well.' Her mind on more important things: 'Why Stuttgart? Why next week?'

Pouring Gerry a glass of sherry from the tantalus on the sideboard, a shot of whisky for himself: 'Have you heard of a bestselling German author called Klaus Winterhalten?'

'No, can't say I have. Why, what's up with him?'

'Well, in a nutshell, he lost his German agent recently, and he needs a replacement.'

'When you say "lost" his agent, do you mean he mislaid him somewhere on an autobahn, a railway station platform, or in an all-night sauerkraut and pumpernickel caff? If so, I'd steer well clear of him, if I were you.'

Bill chuckled. 'No, the agent, having reached retirement age, decided to hop it, recommending me, of all people, as his successor.'

137

'But Bill, you don't even speak German!' Gerry reminded him.

'Oh yes I do,' he protested. 'How's this for starters? "Haben Sie eine Doppelzimmer für einen Nacht für meinen Mädchen und mich?"'

'*Dodgy!*' Gerry sniffed audibly. 'So what, if this Klaus Winterbottom asks you if you are prepared to become his new agent, and you end up asking him if he has overnight accommodation for yourself and your girlfriend?'

'For your information,' Bill responded happily, with pretended dignity, 'Klaus "Winterbottom" happens to speak perfect English.'

'Just as well,' Gerry snapped back at him, enjoying the repartee enormously. 'Otherwise you might well end up in gaol. Either that or in bed with a Rhine-Maiden!'

When their laughter had subsided, 'Listen, Bill,' Gerry said more seriously, 'have you ever come across an agent by the name of Dumas? Jeremy Dumas?'

'Yeah, sure I have. Why do you ask?' Bill responded lightheartedly. He added, in mock terror, 'Don't tell me you're thinking of ditching me in favour of that stuffed shirt? Mr "Belles Lettres" as he's known in the profession. If so, love, heed my warning! The man's a – dinosaur!'

He added, 'Sorry, love. You're serious, aren't you? So what about Jeremy Dumas? I know of him, of course, but I've never actually met him. An unsociable kind of bloke, I gather, with a small coterie of clients, mainly biographers. Successful, financially speaking, from his promotion of tomes about famous figures from the past. Florence Nightingale, Gordon of Khartoum, Robert Louis Stevenson, and Alfred, Lord Tennyson, spring to mind. But why your interest in him? Come on, Gerry, I'd really like to know!'

Gerry replied seriously, albeit uncertainly, 'Because he may well be involved, however innocently, in a murder inquiry connected with Bagdale Manor, where he happened to be staying at the time of the murder. That of Aubrey Sandys, whose body Annie Scott and I came across on Hampstead Heath. Remember?'

Of course Bill remembered. How could he possibly forget those crackling transatlantic phonecalls from Gerry which he'd scarcely made head or tail of against the background cacophony of New York traffic, restaurants, sidewalks or TV studios, through which her voice had come to him as a disembodied spirit, lacking substance, in taxi cabs, hotel dining rooms or wherever he had happened to be at the time.

He said, 'I never really caught the gist of the story. It seemed a bit garbled. All that stuff about a missing dog, a dogsbody and a bloke with a bullet in his waistcoat. Why not tell me the tale from beginning to end. Fill me in, as it were. I've never quite understood about the dog. Was dogsbody its name?'

Gerry sighed deeply. 'No, the dog's name is Bruno. Annie was the dogsbody. And the bullet was in the tramp's greatcoat, not his waistcoat, though of course he wasn't really a tramp at all, just dressed up as one.'

'Hmmm, whatever turned him on, I suppose. P'raps he'd figured he might stop a bullet and didn't fancy it landing in a good suit of clothes.'

'Oh well, if you're going to sit there and take the mickey, I might as well save my breath,' Gerry said huffily.

'Sorry, love,' Bill said contritely. 'I'm just a bit brain-fagged, that's all. Go on. So there you were on the Heath with a body, a dog and a dogsbody. Then what happened?'

'No, Bill. It's far too complicated. I'm not in the mood. Neither are you. Let's call it a day, shall we?'

Not that Gerry wanted to call it a day. Far from. Loving Bill so much, she hated the restraint, self-imposed, of saying goodnight to him, for all the world like some soppy teenager whose parents would be waiting up for her, wanting to know where she'd been all evening, who with, and if her boyfriend's intentions were honourable?

Not that Gerry's parents had ever cared tuppence about where she'd been, with whom, and for what purpose. They had certainly never waited up for her in her Clapham council-house days. The need had never arisen. She'd usually been upstairs in her room by nine thirty, after evening classes at the Tech. In bed by half past ten, when they'd come in from the pub down the road to embark on one of their nightly slanging matches.

Now, here she was, all grown up, head over heels in love with a man she was engaged to marry. So what was she waiting for? She knew, deep down, of course, that it had to do with an innate lack of confidence in her appearance, her spare-tyre waistline, the width of her backside. But as Maggie Bowler had once said to her, 'It's not size that matters so much as what's inside you. And any man worth his salt will know that.' Dear Maggie.

She said, 'I've been thinking, Bill.'

'Oh?' He looked pleased, slightly puzzled. 'So what's new?'

'You haven't asked me – about what?' she said prissily.

'What about about what?' Bill asked cagily. 'No, don't tell me, let me guess.' Pausing for inspiration. 'Don't tell me you've finished the first chapter of *Dead Men Don't Bleed*?'

'No, I haven't!' Sounding cross. A bit put-out. 'It's more – romantic than that.'

Bill looked worried. 'Ye gods! Don't tell me you're about to do a Clarinda Clarkson? You're a crime writer, for heaven's sake, not a romantic novelist.'

'Now see here, Bill Bentine, if you say "don't tell me" once more, I *won't* tell you!'

'You might at least give me a clue,' he suggested. 'I left my crystal ball in the office.'

'Right then. Think about what you want more than anything else in the world at this moment in time.' Gerry fluttered her eyelashes appealingly.

Catching her drift, Bill smiled inwardly. 'A cup of cocoa would be nice,' he said teasingly.

'Ooooh, there are times when I could . . .' Gerry began. Next thing she knew, Bill's arms were about her, and he was saying, 'Marry me, you mean? Oh, Gerry love, I thought you'd never ask! So *when*? How soon?' Gerry suggested leaving wedding plans in abeyance until Bill returned from Stuttgart. He had a lot on his plate at the moment, and it wouldn't be fair to take his mind off his work. In any case, it was up to her to fix the date and decide what to wear.

She'd like a church wedding, she thought dreamily, with lots of flowers and organ music, with Maggie Bowler as her matron of honour, and Barney's arm to cling to on her way down the aisle. What one might call a quiet wedding. Despite her fame, so-called, she had never come close to anyone apart from Maggie and Barney Bowler and her one-time neighbours

Maurice and Lisl Berenger who had figured so largely in the 'Antiques Murders'. Now Lisl was serving a ten-year prison sentence for her involvement in those murders, and Maurice was living in New York, bravely attempting to rebuild his life from the shattered fragments of the old.

Now, of course, there was Bill – presently on his way to Stuttgart – to fill her days with love and laughter, and lord, how she'd miss him. The house would seem empty without him, so she might just as well set about her sleuthing activities to occupy her mind during his absence. First of all, she must make a list of hospitals in the Greater London area, at least attempt to find out what had become of Dorothea Lazlo.

Wearing slacks, an anorak, trainers, and toting a shoulder bag containing an *A to Z Visitors' Guide to London*, a flask of coffee, several bars of nut milk chocolate, a packet of corned-beef sandwiches, a can of Scholes' footspray, her wallet, purse, a box of Anadin tablets, her driver's licence, Kleenex tissues and a telescopic umbrella, she embarked on her foot-slogging journey of the Greater London area, visiting each hospital on her list, without success, until, dead beat, close to exhaustion, about to call it a day, Gerry came across St John the Baptist's, tucked away in a cul-de-sac near the Brompton Oratory.

Entering the building, too weary to turn on the charm, she asked to speak to the registrar. 'You see, I'm in search of a missing person,' she told the receptionist. 'It really is important. A matter of life or death!'

With a worried glance at the enquirer, catching the note of desperation in her voice, the girl said quietly, 'I'll see if he's available.' Picking up the phone, she dialled a number, adding kindly, awaiting a response, 'If you'd care to take a seat. I'm sure he won't be long.' When the response came, 'Oh, Hannah here, sir,' she said briskly. 'There's a lady here to see you, on a matter of some urgency, I gather . . . You will? Oh, thank you, sir. I'll show her through to your office right away.'

Invited by the registrar, an elderly man with a charming manner, to sit down in the chair opposite his desk, Gerry smiled bleakly and slumped, rather than sat. Deeply aware of her aching feet and the hunger pain in her stomach, she said wistfully, 'It's ever so kind of you to see me. A waste of your valuable time, I daresay – Mr . . . ? Sorry, I don't know your name.'

'My name is Robert Harrison. And you are?'

'Geraldine Mudd. How do? Pleased to meet you, I'm sure,' Gerry responded gratefully. 'Not that I expect to find what I'm looking for.'

'Which is?' Harrison enquired mildly.

When Gerry had explained, he said thoughtfully, 'If you'll bear with me, I'll consult my records. Lazlo, you say? Dorothea Lazlo, the artist?'

Gerry perked up, pleased that nice Mr Harrison had heard of Dorothea, which seemed a step in the right direction. Heart in mouth, keeping her fingers tightly crossed, she watched hopefully as he uncarthed several folders, from a phalanx of filing cabinets filling the wall space on the far side of his office, which he laid on his desk for further perusal, explaining, as he did so, that these were relevant to patients whose admission to St John's had occurred over a period of the past three years.

Asked if she could be more explicit about dates, Gerry shook her head. 'Sorry,' she said regretfully, 'but it can't be more than two years ago since I read that newspaper report about Mrs Lazlo having received the Last Rites from a Catholic archbishop, from which I surmised that she must have been terminally ill. What I mean is, all that bell, book and candle stuff wouldn't apply to someone suffering from a head cold, would it?'

Suppressing a smile, liking Gerry's frankness of manner enormously, 'Hardly likely, I'd say, though I'm fairly certain I'd remember such an august ritual had it taken place here,' Mr Harrison replied, adjusting his half-moon spectacles as he ran his forefinger down a list of names.

Suddenly, 'Ah!' he exclaimed excitedly.

Agog, Gerry asked, 'Have you found her?'

'Sadly, no,' Harrison sighed. 'I thought I had, but I was mistaken. The name Dorothea caught my eye momentarily. An unusual name, belonging to a lady whose surname was not Lazlo, but Sandys.'

'*Sandys!*' Gerry's face lit up. She said breathlessly, 'Dorothea's name was Sandys before she became Mrs Lazlo. Oh, thank you,

Mr Harrison. You've been so kind, so helpful. So Dorothea is still alive and kicking, thank God. What a relief!'

'Unfortunately not,' Harrison said consolingly. 'According to my records, Mrs Dorothea Sandys died shortly after her admittance to our intensive care unit, a victim of food poisoning. I'm sorry, my dear. I can see that this has come as a shock to you. May I get you anything? A cup of tea, perhaps?'

'No, ta very much.' Tears filled Gerry's eyes. 'I'd best be on my way home now. It's been one of those days.' She rose to her feet unsteadily. 'It simply hadn't occurred to me that Dorothea was dead. I knew, of course, that she was missing, the reason why I've been trying so hard to find her.'

Harrison said firmly, 'Take my advice, Miss Mudd, sit down and have a cup of tea. Something stronger, if you'd prefer. How long since you last ate, by the way?'

'Around midday, I guess,' Gerry confessed. 'I'd made myself a couple of corned-beef sandwiches, but I ate only one of them.'

Opening a cupboard, Harrison produced a small flask of brandy and a paper cup. Pouring out a slug of brandy and handing her the cup, 'Here,' he said briskly, 'get this down you. It will do you good! Now, suppose you tell me what all this is about? Were you related to Dorothea Lazlo? The truth now, Miss Mudd.'

Nursing the cup of brandy, Gerry said tearfully, 'The truth is so fantastic, so bizarre, I scarcely believe it myself at times. It has to do with murder, you see? Not just one murder, but three so far. With a missing person, Dorothea Lazlo, previously Sandys, who may well also have been murdered for all I know, since she is no longer missing, but – dead! If so, what became of her body? She died of food poisoning, you said. But what if she was poisoned deliberately? Who was her doctor? Who signed her death certificate?'

Harrison paused awhile, considering the pros and cons. To trust or not to trust, that was the question. Here was a woman he had never seen in his life before until she had walked into his office less than an hour ago. She may be mentally unhinged for all he knew. It was up to him to decide what to do in this difficult situation, whether or not to help her. Whether or not to trust her.

The answer came in the shape of an uneaten corned-beef sandwich, fallen from Gerry's shoulder bag on to the floor while she was searching for a packet of Kleenex tissues to dry her eyes.

Adjusting his spectacles, reading from the open folder on his desk, he said, 'According to my records, Mrs Dorothea Sandys was attended by a Doctor Edmund Sloane, who signed her death certificate prior to her funeral service at the Golder's Green Crematorium.'

Gerry stared at the registrar aghast. 'You mean without an autopsy to ascertain the cause of death?'

'No,' Harrison reassured her. 'There was an inquest, of course, but there was no suspicion of foul play. The poor lady had simply eaten something that disagreed with her: musscls were held responsible for her sudden demise. One tainted mussel in particular. She had been warned against eating mussels, a favourite food of hers, one gathers, but she took no notice. She was, after all, a very determined and difficult old lady.'

Sixteen

B retton Sandys had discovered French's body. Having done so, he rang York Police Headquarters in a panic. Brambell and Briggs arrived at the garden centre to find him seated in a high-back chair near an electric fire, staring into space, trembling, deathly pale and nursing a brandy balloon drained of its contents.

Carla, who had opened the door to admit Brambell and his SOC officers, said, 'My husband's in a state of shock. I've given him brandy and sent for a doctor. He should be in bed, under sedation.'

Brambell nodded. 'Quite so. I'll speak to him later. Meanwhile, my colleagues and I have work to attend to. I take it that Mr French died in his flat?'

'Of course he did. Where else? When Alex had failed to put in an appearance by ten o'clock, Brett went upstairs to find out what was keeping him.'

'Were you aware that Mr French was due at police headquarters at ten o'clock?'

'No.' Carla frowned. 'Whatever for? I thought you'd interviewed him yesterday. You were here long enough. Frankly, Inspector, I'm fed up to the back teeth of police invading my home. So just do what you have to do as quickly as possible, then get the hell out of here.'

Brambell said blandly, 'I regret as much as you do, Mrs Sandys, the necessity of our being here at all. The fact remains that a man has died under suspicious circumstances. Your husband had the good sense to report the matter to the police, hence our presence in your home. Now, if you'll excuse me, I have a not very pleasant job of work to do.'

Turning on the threshold of the Sandyses' drawing room, he flung into Carla's melting pot of discontent, 'I shall, of

145

course, require in due course statements from yourself and your husband pertaining to your movements before and after his discovery of Mr French's body.' So saying, he went upstairs to French's flat to begin initial enquiries into the man's death, be it suicide or – murder. Bound to be one or t'other, he thought grimly. More than likely, the latter.

Returning to the Eyrie, for the first time ever Gerry felt nervous at being alone in the house, wishing she'd followed Bill's advice to stay with Maggie and Barney during his absence.

About to call Maggie on her mobile, with a frisson of fear, listening intently, she heard the sound of footsteps on the fire escape outside her room. Stealthy footsteps, coming closer and closer.

Thinking and acting quickly, first she switched on the fire-escape light. Then, switching off her bedside lamp, almost rigid with fear, she retreated to the darkness of the landing where she jabbed her forefinger three times on what she fervently hoped was the number nine button.

Having prodded 888 not 999, alone on a dark landing, aware that Brambell's warnings about her being the next victim on a serial killer's list were true, berating herself as a blithering coward, wondering what her alter ego, Virginia Vale, would do in a similar situation, Gerry knew only too well that she would go for the jugular; fling open the fire-escape door, confront the killer face to face, knee the bastard and send him spinning backwards on to the patio beneath.

Right, then. Stealthily re-entering her room, breathing heavily, plucking up her courage, unlocking and flinging open the fire-escape door, stepping on to the escape landing, prepared to do battle with a mass murderer, she dimly discerned a tall figure, dressed all in black, hurrying away from her down the fire escape, whether that of a man or a woman, she couldn't be certain. Heart pounding, she called out, 'Well, here I am! Come and get me, why don't you? As I shall get you, sooner or later, and you'd better believe it, you murdering son of a bitch!'

The figure on the fire escape paused momentarily, turned, then fired a shot from an upraised revolver, the bullet from which missed Gerry by inches. At least, Gerry thought, closing and locking the fire-escape door behind her, feeling sick, sinking down on her divan bed, had that bullet entered her heart, as it was meant to do, she'd have died heroically, a credit to Virginia Vale, Brambell and Briggs, Maggie and Barney Bowler, above all, to her beloved Bill Bentine.

But what the hell? She wasn't dead yet. Far from. Still alive and kicking. And, common sense told her that the bullet fired from a serial killer's revolver must have landed somewhere. In a tree trunk, perhaps, or an iron railing? It could not possibly have gone into orbit. And when that bullet was found, it might well match up with the bullet fired into a murder victim's greatcoat.

Brambell regarded the initial stages of a murder inquiry as the least enviable aspect of his job, invariably depressing and time-consuming as the SOC officers went about their business of fingerprinting, gathering evidence, examining in detail every facet of the crime, while the pathologist, inured to his distasteful task of dealing with the deceased, solemnly expounded his theories concerning the time and the cause of death of the corpse.

Thankfully, on this occasion, there had been no blood-let. French, apparently, had died peacefully by means of a lethal injection of morphine administered to him in his sleep in the early hours of the morning. So at least the poor devil had fallen into the deep sleep of eternity without undue stress or strain. Brambell felt pleased about that. Truth to tell, he had quite liked Alex French's gung-ho attitude to life, his underlying honesty despite his prison sentence for the exact opposite. Fair enough, so he had stolen money under false pretences, for which he had paid the penalty. But never at any time had Brambell regarded him as a potential mass murderer. In short, a serial killer. A man capable of strangling a young girl with a dog-lead, or choking the life out of a young man by means of his pony tail.

When the SOC team had completed their work and departed, taking with them the mortal remains of Alex French to a mortuary slab at York headquarters, doffing his brown felt hat as a mark of respect as the mortuary van and its attendant procession of police cars drove away from Sandys' garden centre, walking slowly towards the front door of Sandys' house, glad of the company of his stalwart Sergeant Briggs, walking beside him, Brambell said quietly, 'You know, laddie, I have a gut feeling that French meant to turn up on time, this morning. How about you?'

Briggs said thoughtfully, 'I agree with you, sir. The pity is that we shall never know now about his prison conversations with Aubrey Sandys. So where do we go from here?'

Brambell smiled grimly. 'Unfortunately, back to Sandys' house to interview him and that charming wife of his – to listen to a tissue of lies, I shouldn't wonder. More than likely to find Sandys in bed, under sedation, his wife, up in arms as usual, inviting us to get lost.'

Briggs said, frowning, 'Has it occurred to you, sir, that she might have something to hide? That she and Alex French might have been – lovers?'

'Well yes, the thought had crossed my mind,' Brambell admitted. 'But why French? Why a poor man? Why not a rich one? Remember her fondness for the good things in life. Shopping, for instance. Lots of new clothes, expensive beauty treatments, and so on, beyond the capabilities of either her husband or Alex French to afford. No, laddie. My guess is that Mrs Sandys' lover is a man of substance. Someone with a healthy fear of blackmail, should their affair come to light. A married man, well heeled, a proud man. A public figure, perhaps. A politician or – a writer.'

Light dawned. Briggs said hoarsely, 'You mean – Elliot Lazlo? Yes, of course, it has to be Lazlo. Why didn't I think of that?'

Brambell smiled obliquely. 'You just did, laddie! Well done! Lazlo had never entered my mind.'

As he had anticipated, eliciting information from Sandys and his missus was comparable with extracting hen's teeth. Frankly, Brambell was sick and tired of the pair of them. Difficult to discern whether or not Bretton had been sedated since he bore his customary expression of glassy-eyed bemusement. As for Carla, the inspector felt inclined to remind her that severe penalties could result from the withholding of evidence in a police inquiry and wasting police time.

In the event, Briggs saved him the trouble. 'Please sit down,

Mrs Sandys,' he said coldly. 'Questions put to you and your husband must be asked, and answered satisfactorily. Unless, of course, you'd prefer a spell in custody on a charge of perverting the course of justice? In short, you can either answer the questions put to you by Inspector Brambell and myself, here and now, or in an interview room at York Police Headquarters. Is that perfectly clear?'

Carla said defiantly, 'I prefer to stand! So what is it you want to know, precisely?'

'Apart from your own and your husband's movements before and after his discovery of Mr French's body, the nature of your relationship with the deceased. Were you and he – lovers?'

Standing her ground, 'No, we were *not*! How dare you even suggest such a thing? Alex was my husband's business partner, nothing more! Indeed, I disliked and mistrusted him intensely at times. Ask Brett if you don't believe me! Well, don't just sit there saying nothing, Bretton! Tell them, why don't you, that I warned you, time and time again, to get rid of him?'

Turning his fire on the man seated in a high-back chair near the fireplace, Briggs demanded coolly, 'And did you "get rid" of Alex French, Mr Sandys, by means of a morphine injection, in the early hours of this morning?'

Springing to her husband's defence, Carla uttered scathingly, 'No, of course he didn't! Why should he? He thought the world of Alex!'

'Which you, Mrs Sandys, apparently did not,' Briggs reminded her quietly.

Carla sat down abruptly. 'Well, no. But I didn't kill Alex, if that's what you're driving at.' Then came a startling admission: 'I was elsewhere, you see, in the early hours of this morning, with a – close friend of mine, with whom I had spent the night in the York Station Hotel.'

Entering the conversation, Brambell suggested mildly, 'A London friend of yours, I take it? A gentleman fully conversant with railway timetables? The time of the last train from King's Cross Station to York, I imagine, and that of the departure of the early morning train from York to King's Cross?'

'If it pleases you to think so, Inspector, but you're wrong as it happens. I spent that night with a woman friend of mine, not a man. Someone known to you as a matter of fact. Mrs June Scott, the murdered girl's mother.'

Brambell and Briggs exchanged glances. Neither of them doubted that Carla was telling the truth. Her statement could be easily verified and she knew it.

Brambell tried a different tack. He said, 'Now, I want to know about your visit to Bagdale Manor.'

She continued, speaking jerkily, 'Frankly, the invitation to spend Christmas at Bagdale Manor came as a surprise to me – if not to my husband. Never forthcoming at the best of times, when I asked him about the invitation, all he said was that his mother, an actress by profession, had embarked on a part-time role as a stand in for Elliot Lazlo's artist wife, Dorothea, who was non compos mentis at the time.

'To cut a long story short, Brett, ever a "Mummy's boy", was overjoyed at the prospect of their reunion. As for me, I was more than anxious to clap eyes on his birth mother, one Marguerite Lascelles according to Alex French, who had also been included in the Bagdale Manor invitation and who appeared to know all about the substitution of Dorothea Lazlo for a lookalike impostor. As, indeed, so did the rest of the guests at that bloody awful house party.'

Carla stopped speaking abruptly. Brambell said kindly, 'Thank you so much, Mrs Sandys, for your help in this inquiry. Even so, I shall require your own and your husband's attendance at York Police Headquarters pending further enquiries into the death of Alex French.'

Later, at The Who'd Ha' Thought It, squaring up to sizeable portions of steak and kidney pudding, 'I thought we'd be spending tonight in our own beds,' Brambell said dolefully. 'The way things are going, we might well be holed up here for the foreseeable future.'

Briggs grinned across the table at his senior officer. 'At least the food's good, sir. This steak and kidney pudding is the best I've ever tasted!' He added anxiously, 'Just don't ever tell my missus I said so. Which reminds me, I'd best give her a ring, after dinner; tell her I've been unavoidably detained in the wilds of north Yorkshire, on the trail of a serial killer.'

Brambell's mobile phone rang suddenly. Gerry's voice came

on the line. Brambell listened intently. All he said was, 'Yes, I see. Thanks for telling me!'

Frowning, 'Anything wrong, sir?' Briggs asked briefly.

'A great deal,' Brambell assured him. 'Our serial killer has just made an attempt to murder Geraldine Frayling. Now it's up to DCI Dancey to deal with the Sandyses' interviews, and to pay Mrs June Scott a visit!'

'I take it, then, that we shall not be staying on here for the foreseeable future?' Briggs ventured.

'No. We'll have an early breakfast, then head for home. Dancey's a first-class officer. He'll make a thorough job of the Sandyses' interviews once he has the facts at his fingertips.' Brambell added wryly, 'Presenting those facts in some semblance of order won't be a doddle.' He sighed deeply. 'I've come across some complicated cases in my time, but this takes the biscuit! Darned if I can make head or tail of it. Four murders, an impostor, conversations between prison inmates, both of whom were linked in some way with a house in Hampstead. A houseful of guests at a Christmas get-together who, presumably, knew damn fine well that their hostess was an impostor. So why the veil of secrecy?'

Briggs coughed discreetly. 'With your permission, sir, wouldn't it be quicker, and simpler, to speak to DCI Dancey directly? Tell him the whole story from beginning to end?' Glancing at his watch, 'He might well be still on duty. I could give him a call, if you like; tell him we're on our way.'

'Now, why didn't *I* think of that?' Brambell fairly beamed at Briggs. 'Yes, of course! Here, use my mobile!'

Detective Chief Inspector Dancey listened intently to the tale, as it unfolded; breaking in, now and then, to get events clear in his mind. Frankly, Briggs felt sorry for the man, at the same time filled with admiration for his grasp of the salient facts of the case, presented so ably and precisely by DCI Brambell – off the cuff, as it were, without recourse to his notebook, without hesitation or prevarication, indicative of a shrewd, analytical mind ticking away relentlessly beneath that battered brown trilby hat of his, and his oft-times assumed persona of a woolly-inded medico, clergyman or an absent-minded professor when, in reality, he was nothing of the kind, Briggs thought affectionately.

The meeting between Dancey, Brambell and himself had taken place in Dancey's office. A long drawn out affair of two and a half hours' duration, after which the two senior officers had parted company on the best of terms, and Briggs and Brambell had returned to The Who'd Ha' Thought It, for a nightcap of whisky before bidding each other goodnight and making their way upstairs to their rooms to enjoy a much-needed, peaceful night's sleep.

Switching off his bedside lamp, this had been a bloody long, difficult day, Briggs thought. Moreover, he had forgotten to ring his missus.

In the event, neither of the two men enjoyed a good night's sleep. Briggs dozed fitfully at first, then woke in the early hours niggling over not having rung his wife, and with a hunger pain in the pit of his stomach, wishing like hell he'd ordered a plate of sandwiches to accompany his nightcap: wondering how soon he could conveniently nip downstairs to the dining room for a nosh-up of ham and eggs.

Meanwhile, in his room along the landing, Brambell had lain awake till the early hours worrying about the attempt on Gerry's life: pondering the identity of her attacker, with Elliot Lazlo uppermost in his mind. At least his list of suspects had been whittled down somewhat, since Bretton Sandys, his wife Carla, and now Alex French were out of the running, so far as the attempt on Geraldine Frayling's life was concerned. And yet he had a gut feeling that the murder of Alex French had been perpetrated by the person responsible for the deaths of Aubrey Sandys, Annie Scott and Rafe Barmby, and the attempted murder of Geraldine Frayling. That person au fait with railway timetables, he shouldn't wonder.

Detective Inspector Clooney was not a happy man. Not that he had ever been what could be described as a ray of sunshine. Of a naturally sombre disposition, his personal life had been complicated recently by his wife's divorce proceedings against him on the grounds of an irreparable breakdown of their marriage, which he regarded as an affront to a man of his age and integrity, a slur on his reputation as a high-ranking police officer.

Now, having conducted a series of abortive interviews with members of the Lazlos' Christmas house party, namely Lazlo's sister Marianne Coverdale, his niece, Pippa Coverdale, and Dorothea Lazlo's personal physician, none of whom had furthered his enquiries to the nth degree, Clooney felt inclined to 'throw in the towel', admit defeat, and bugger off to the Bahamas.

After breakfast at The Who'd Ha' Thought It?, a satisfying meal consisting of bacon, eggs, sausages, mushrooms, tomatoes, coffee, toast and marmalade, Brambell and Briggs set forth on their journey back to London, replete, if not entirely happy; discussing puzzling facets of the case, en route.

Brambell said thoughtfully, 'What beats me is the acceptance of an impostor as the real McCoy! Carla Sandys knew about the substitution, as did the rest of the party. I wonder if Lazlo was really being blackmailed by Carla? Frankly, I have my doubts about that now, in view of her friendship with June Scott.'

Sighing deeply, Brambell pushed back his trilby in order to scratch his forehead. He said, 'Tomorrow, first thing, we must pay Elliot Lazlo a visit. But first, I think we had better talk to Gerry Frayling: find out more about the attempt on her life. Meanwhile, I could do with a cup of coffee. How about you?'

Seventeen

B rambell and Briggs discovered Gerry at Barney's Hamburger Joint in the Old Kent Road when they arrived in London after their long journey south.

'My dear girl, are you all right?' Brambell asked warmly, relieved at having discovered her whereabouts following a fruitless visit to Hampstead.

'Yeah, I'm fine,' Gerry replied. 'All the better for seeing you! Please, sit down and have a cup of coffee. But first I'd like you to meet my friends, Maggie and Barney Bowler, my surrogate parents. Maggie, Barney, this is Detective Chief Inspector Brambell, and this, Detective Sergeant Briggs, of Scotland Yard.'

'Well, I never. Just fancy that,' Maggie murmured, overcome by the presence of Scotland Yard in the caff, feeling inclined to curtsey. 'Pleased to meet you, I'm sure.'

'Likewise,' Barney uttered, equally impressed, though he wasn't sure why. They looked quite ordinary, come to think of it: somehow he'd imagined Scotland Yard officers would appear in full dress uniform, wearing caps and carrying handcuffs and batons. But these were detectives, not common-or-garden bobbies, he reminded himself sharply, making the coffee, which he handed across the counter to Maggie, who said mistily, conveying the mugs to the formica-topped table at which they were seated opposite Gerry, 'On the house, gentlemen. An' if there's owt else you fancy, just ask.'

Brambell beamed at her. 'How kind of you, Mrs Bowler. My sergeant and I are most grateful. We've had a long day, and the coffee is more than welcome, I assure you.' He added, 'You and your husband also have our heartfelt thanks for looking after Gerry so well. Not for the first time, if memory serves me correctly?'

Maggie frowned bemusedly, then, light dawning suddenly, she said, 'Oh you mean those "Antiques Murders" last year? Well, we did our best, but Gerry takes some looking after. She has a mind of her own, that 'un. Huh, a death wish, if you ask me! She should have come to us as soon as Bill left for Stuttgart, not stayed alone in that house for someone to take a pop at!'

Brambell asked quickly, 'Mr Bentine has gone to Stuttgart? Tell me, who knew about his absence?' Speaking directly to Gerry.

'No one, apart from myself, Maggie and Barney.' Hands clasped, looking stricken, 'Why? You don't think he's been – man-napped – do you?'

'I hardly think so,' Brambell said consolingly, 'it simply occurred to me that Bill's movements might have been known to our killer, who, seizing his opportunity, thinking you'd be alone in the house, took a potshot at you.'

'You mean Dumas might have got wind of it and told one of the Bagdale Manor fraternity?'

'Why Dumas and Bagdale Manor in particular?' Brambell asked.

''Cos Dumas's a literary agent, and there's summat mighty peculiar going on at Bagdale Manor,' Gerry explained. 'Why a lookalike Dorothea Lazlo, for instance? Well, I've been doing a bit of snooping on the QT, and something interesting has turned up. I wanted to find out what had happened to the real Dorothea.'

'And did you?'

'I'm not sure. All I know is that a woman by the name of Dorothea Sandys was admitted to St John the Baptist's Hospital around the time of Mrs Lazlo's disappearance, and died of food poisoning.'

'Ye gods!' Brambell frowned. 'Did you hear that, Briggs?'

'The plot thickens,' Briggs remarked wickedly.

'It was thick enough to begin with.' Brambell sighed deeply. 'Go on, Gerry. What else did you find out?'

Warming to her theme, 'It struck me as significant that the name of Dorothea Sandys' doctor was Edmund Sloane.'

'Was it, by gum?' Brambell smiled grimly. 'An exhumation order springs to mind.'

155

Gerry said bleakly, 'Not possible, I'm afraid. Dorothea Sandys' body was cremated.' She added thoughtfully, 'If the woman who died *was* Dorothea Lazlo. The registrar at St John's described her as a "very determined and difficult old lady", you see? And Dorothea Lazlo certainly doesn't fit that description. She's only in her fifties, for Pete's sake!'

'So what you're saying, Gerry,' Brambell probed gently, 'is that you believe the real Dorothea to be still alive and kicking?'

'Yeah,' Gerry admitted, 'I guess so. I just have the gut feeling that she's been abducted, for whatever reason, possibly against her will. Why else the bogus Mrs Lazlo at Bagdale Manor? Why Doctor Sloane's finger in the pie? How come a conveniently named Dorothea Sandys, suffering from a surfeit of tainted mussels? Darned if *I* know. Do *you*, Inspector?'

'No, Gerry, I don't,' Brambell confessed, 'but it's just a matter of time. Now, how do you feel about a trip to Scotland Yard to make a statement? I need every scrap of information you can give me about your visit to St John's Hospital and the attempt on your life. That bullet the killer fired at you has to be somewhere, and I want it found.

'Briggs, alert the search team! I want them on the job first thing in the morning, and they'd best not return empty-handed, or I'll have their guts for garters. Understood?'

'Sir!' Briggs smiled happily. Things were beginning to hot up, and he was ready for action.

On their way to the Yard, a thought occurred to Gerry. She said, 'That bag of files I gave you. I never really studied them. When Rafe Barmby mentioned Aubrey Sandys' name, I just thought, that's it! Now I'm not so sure. Could there be something in those files that's been overlooked? I've never understood why Rafe was killed. What I mean to say is, the murderer had already found the files; why, then, didn't he just beat it back down the fire escape? Why risk being seen? And why take a shot at me? What did he imagine? That I knew more than was good for me? But that adds up, I suppose. He couldn't have known that I hadn't even looked at the damn things.'

'Not to worry,' Brambell said kindly, 'Briggs will go through them with a fine-tooth comb, won't you Sergeant?'

* * *

Brambell drove Gerry back to the Old Kent Road. He said firmly, 'Promise me you'll keep a low profile from now on. There's a killer on the loose, so no more heroics.'

Walking with her to the caff, 'By the way,' he added, 'some good news for a change. Annie Scott's dog is up for adoption. Your name's top of the list. He's yours, if you still want him.'

'*Want* him? Of course I do. Thank you, Inspector. Where is he? How soon can I collect him?'

'He's at Battersea. But why not wait till Bill gets back from Stuttgart? I dare say he'll want to decorate the – nursery.' He chuckled. 'Well, 'bye for now m'dear. And if you notice a strange man hanging around outside, don't ring the police. You see, Gerry love, he'll *be* the police.'

'You mean I'm to have a *bodyguard*?' Gerry's face lit up. 'Does he look like Kevin Costner?'

Brambell laughed, 'Not really. More like Victor Meldrew. Kevin Costner will be in the back lane, guarding the rear entrance!'

Lazlo greeted Brambell and Briggs coldly. 'Oh, not *again!*' he snapped. 'Frankly, Inspector, I deeply resent your invasion of my privacy. I'm a busy man. Furthermore, I have already made a statement to the effect that the tramp who appeared on my doorstep last Christmas Eve was unknown to me. I further resent that my wife has been drawn into this unfortunate affair!'

Brambell said mildly, 'Ah yes, your wife, Dorothea Lazlo. May we come in, by the way? Unless, of course, you'd rather discuss your private affairs in public?'

'Very well, then. You'd best come through to my study. Though what there is left to discuss is beyond my comprehension.'

Entering Lazlo's book-lined sanctum, Briggs beside him, Brambell said quietly, 'I take it, then, that you have not yet learned of the death of a member of your Christmas house party? Namely, that of a Mr Alex French, who was, to the best of my knowledge and belief, the business associate of your present partner's son, Bretton Sandys.'

Those words had a profound effect on Lazlo, Briggs noted,

as if the wind had gone out of his sails, leaving them at half mast. Possibly he knew nothing about the death of Alex French. He must have known, however, by Brambell's reference to Bretton Sandys as the son of his present partner, that disturbing elements of his past had come to light. And yet, apart from his temporary loss of control, dwelling on the demise of Alex French, 'This has come as a shock,' he said stiffly. 'I had no idea that French was ill. A charming young fellow: great company. Always a welcome guest of ours. My wife will be devastated. Even so, Inspector, I fail to see why you felt it necessary to impart the news to me personally.'

'Ah well, Mr Lazlo,' Brambell replied, assuming his country doctor persona, speaking regretfully as though informing a grieving relative of the death of a nearest and dearest, 'I should not have done so had Mr French died of natural causes. Unfortunately he did not. He was – murdered.'

'*Murdered*! But *why*? How? *Where?*'

Was Lazlo as shocked as he pretended to be, or merely play-acting? Briggs wondered. And why his insistence on referring to Marguerite Lascelles as his wife, when she was obviously nowt of the sort? His mistress, his bit on the side, more likely. So what the hell were *they* supposed to call the woman? Darned if he knew. Thankfully, Brambell had no such inhibition.

He said clearly, refusing to indulge in a game of make-believe, 'I should like Miss Lascelles to be present at this interview. I take it she's at home? If so, would you be kind enough to send for her?'

'But *why*?' Lazlo blustered. 'This lamentable affair has nothing to do with her. May I remind you, Inspector, that my wife is of a nervous disposition: highly strung, in need of rest and quiet following a recent breakdown in health. So no, Inspector, I shall certainly not send for her, as you suggest. I might add that I deeply deplore your lack of consideration and good manners, and I shall lodge a complaint against your high-handedness at the highest level. Do I make myself clear?'

Briggs said coolly, 'May I remind you, sir, that in a murder inquiry it is a senior police officer's duty to establish the facts of the case. Of course, if you'd prefer to be interviewed at Scotland Yard, that could be easily arranged.'

Lazlo's lips narrowed. Making no reply, he tugged the bell-pull near the fireplace. When the housekeeper appeared, he said brusquely, 'Ask madam to come down to the study. And bring coffee at eleven.'

When she had gone, Lazlo said scathingly, 'I see no reason to interrupt my normal routine on your account. I have agreed, under duress, to request my wife's presence here. I warn you, however, that I shall not agree to having her intimidated. If that happens, I shall make it my business to show you the door!'

Pompous sod, Briggs thought. Consideration and good manners indeed? So far he hadn't had the good manners to ask Inspector Brambell to sit down.

When Marguerite entered the room, looking pale and fragile, 'Sit down, my dear,' Lazlo said unctuously, guiding her to a high-backed chair near the fire. 'There's unpleasant news, I'm afraid, but try not to get too upset.'

'News? What news?' Marguerite wrinkled her forehead, then, 'Not to do with Brett? Oh God, he hasn't met with an accident, has he?'

This time she wasn't play-acting, Brambell thought. Her concern was genuine. He said quietly, 'No, madam, your son is quite safe. Mr Lazlo was referring to the death of Alex French, your son's business partner.'

'Alex? But that's not possible! A fit young man in the prime of life!' A flush of colour appeared beneath her thickly applied beige make-up. 'But this means that Brett will be left alone to run things! I must get in touch with him at once. The poor boy will be devastated!'

About to spring from her chair, her air of frailty forgotten, for all the world like a tigress in defence of its cub, Lazlo said warningly, 'Remember you are under doctor's orders to stay calm. Undue exertion is bad for your heart!'

Heeding the warning, 'Yes, of course,' she murmured, sinking back against the cushions, 'I forget, at times, that I'm not as strong as I used to be. News of Alex's death came as a shock to me, that's all. Tell me, did he have a heart attack?'

'No, ma'am,' Brambell said mildly, 'Mr French died of a morphine injection administered to him by a person or persons unknown. In short, he was – murdered. His body was discovered by Mr Bretton Sandys at ten o'clock yesterday morning.'

As the carriage clock on the mantelpiece chimed eleven, a knock came at the door and the housekeeper entered the room with coffee things on a silver tray, which she set down on a low table in front of the fireplace.

'Do you wish me to pour, sir?' she asked loftily. To which Lazlo replied testily, 'No need. I'll see to it myself!' Not that he made any attempt to do so, Briggs noted. Just as well perhaps. He for one didn't fancy coffee, drunk from a standing position, balancing a bloody cup and saucer in one hand, a plate with a shortbread biscuit in the other. This, after all, was a serious murder inquiry, not a social gathering.

When the housekeeper had gone, Marguerite said hoarsely, 'But surely, Inspector, you cannot possibly believe that Brett was involved in the murder of Alex French? Alex was his best friend, for God's sake! They'd been at school together! Brett wouldn't hurt a fly! More than likely my son's wife was involved! So why come here asking questions? Why not ask *her*?'

Briggs broke in, 'Chief Inspector Dancey, of the North Yorkshire Police, has that matter in hand, ma'am. Your son and his wife are presently at York Headquarters, helping the police with their enquiries.'

'You mean to tell me that my son is being treated as a common criminal?' Marguerite was on her feet now, shaking like a leaf. Thrusting aside Lazlo's restraining hand on her arm, 'No, Elliot,' she blazed at him, 'I shall not sit down! I must go to him at once! At once, do you hear?'

Ignoring the histrionics, Brambell said calmly, 'I am right in thinking, am I not, that Aubrey Sandys was your son's father?'

Disbelief registered strongly on Marguerite's face. Lazlo also appeared startled by the unexpected shot from Brambell's locker. Briggs smiled grimly. Typical of Brambell, he thought admiringly, the firing of a question to which he obviously knew the answer, albeit pleasantly, conversationally, as if he were asking Marguerite if she'd read any good books lately.

'Yes. What of it?' she replied sullenly. 'Though I fail to see what bearing it has on the death of Alex French. Sandys and I were members of the same repertory company some years ago. We were—'

'Lovers?' Brambell suggested artlessly, since Marguerite had stopped speaking abruptly. 'You had an affair with him?'

'*No!*' Marguerite snapped back at him. 'Not an – affair – as such, if it's any of your damned business! When the company we were in split up, he went his way, I went mine. I've neither seen nor heard of him from that day to this! What became of him, I haven't the faintest idea!'

Sighing deeply, 'Then I'd best enlighten you,' Brambell said levelly. 'Cast your mind back to last Christmas Eve, when a man, in tramp's clothing, appeared on your kitchen doorstep.'

'I never even *saw* the man,' Marguerite protested hoarsely. 'I was with my house guests, at the time!'

Turning his fire on Elliot Lazlo: 'Possibly not. But *you* did, didn't you, Mr Lazlo? And recognized him at once as the former husband of your wife, Dorothea? And yet you continued to deny all knowledge of him, to the extent of failing to identify the remains of a man you knew full well, whose body had been discovered, dressed as a tramp, in a hastily dug grave on Hampstead Heath, whose death had occurred around the time of his visit to Bagdale Manor.'

Drawing in a deep breath, drawing a bow at a venture: 'Come now, Mr Lazlo, why not admit that Aubrey Sandys came to this house, last Christmas Eve, to extort money from you? That, in a fit of anger, when he later came back to the house to threaten you with blackmail if you refused to write a cheque for the sum of money requested, you cracked his skull with a blunt instrument, dragged his body to the boot of your car, drove to Hampstead Heath, scooped out a grave for him, then fired a shot into him to make certain he was dead?'

'Because it simply isn't true!' Lazlo was sweating profusely now, mopping his forehead with a crisply ironed hanky from his top pocket.

At which moment, Marguerite uttered faintly, sinking back into her chair, 'I need a doctor! It's my – heart!' Closing her eyes, she held a fluttering, be-ringed hand to her chest.

'There! Now see what you've done,' Lazlo exclaimed angrily. 'I warned you what would happen in the event of intimidation! I meant what I said. Now, if you are not out of my house in the next few minutes, I shall make it my business to eject you forcibly, if necessary!'

'Come on, Sergeant,' Brambell said quietly. 'There's nothing more to be done here, for the time being at least,' exerting a calming influence on Briggs, noting his tightly clenched fists, one of which might well land squarely on Lazlo's out-thrust jaw if nothing was done to prevent a punch-up between the pair of them, thus ruining Briggs' chance of promotion.

He added urbanely, 'Not to worry, Mr Lazlo, we can find our own way out. It is, however, my duty to remind you that the matter of your involvement in the murder of Aubrey Sandys doesn't end here. This is merely a postponement.' He smiled grimly. 'Do *I* make myself clear, Mr Lazlo?'

On their way to the car, Briggs said angrily, 'Just who the hell does he think he is?' Fists still clenched, his knuckles white with tension. 'Very convenient, don't you think, his fancy woman's sudden heart attack? A put-up job, in my opinion, to get rid of us in a hurry!'

'I *had* noticed,' Brambell said mildly. 'And your self-restraint was admirable. But, as I reminded Mr Lazlo, his involvement in the murder of Aubrey Sandys doesn't end here. Patience, laddie! He'll be brought to book sooner or later! Now, what I need is a good strong cup of coffee. How about you?'

Eighteen

Over their second cups of coffee, plus jam doughnuts, in a cafeteria round the corner from Scotland Yard – a decent, clean little caff often frequented by off-duty coppers in need of nicotine, sugary snacks, sandwiches, jacket potatoes, or chips with eggs, sausages, bacon or baked beans, an amalgamation of the latter listed on the menu as an all-day breakfast – Brambell and Briggs talked turkey.

'So where do we go from here, sir?' Briggs asked, removing a morsel of raspberry jam from his top lip with a paper serviette.

'I rather think we'd better have a word with Doctor Sloane,' Brambell mused thoughtfully. 'I can't quite get my head round the disappearance of Dorothea Lazlo, the coincidental death of a woman called Dorothea Sandys. Too much of a coincidence to my way of thinking. Fortuitous to say the least, if, for instance, Lazlo wanted rid of his wife and planned a convenient cremation as the best way of doing so once and for all, aided and abetted by Doctor Edmund Sloane.'

Briggs frowned concernedly, weighing up the pros and cons. 'You mean you think that Sloane's a wrong 'un?'

'By no means. He could be as white as newly fallen snow, but something's wrong somewhere, and I want to know what it is. The awkward part of it is, officially Dorothea Lazlo is not a missing person. No one has come forward to report her as such, therefore I'm sticking my neck out in attempting to solve a crime which might not have been committed in the first place.' Brambell sighed deeply.

'Then what do you hope to learn from Doctor Sloane?' Briggs asked. 'What I mean is, how will you set about finding out about Dorothea Lazlo's disappearance without landing yourself in hot water?'

'Frankly, laddie, I haven't a clue,' Brambell admitted, swallowing his last mouthful of coffee. 'I'll cross that bridge when I come to it.'

Bill appeared to be having a 'Snowball' in 'Winterhalten's Wonderland', Gerry surmised from his phonecalls.

So far, pumpernickel, sauerkraut and liver sausages had not appeared on the menus, Winterhalten being an oysters, caviar and champagne aficionado with a penchant for imported Scottish beef, venison, food hampers from Fortnum and Mason, containing goose liver pâté, York hams, Cumberland sausages, Kendal Mint Cake, and Liquorice Allsorts.

A Citizen Kane lookalike with a Xanadu complex, he spoke English with an American accent, smoked Churchillian cigars, treated his servants like dirt, and utterly refused to discuss business matters until the early hours of the morning, by which time, befuddled by booze, he needed an air lift to his bedroom. The reason why, Bill explained, sounding fed up to the back teeth, he couldn't see his way clear to returning home just yet. Not until he'd persuaded Winterhalten to sign a contract designating himself as his new agent. Otherwise, he pointed out, his visit to Stuttgart would be a complete waste of time.

'Huh!' Gerry commented drily. 'Take my advice, Bill, tell him to go to hell and pump thunder! Do you really need all this hassle? I certainly don't. All I need is you!'

'I know, love. But my reputation as a literary agent is at stake here! I'm not leaving until Winterhalten has signed on the dotted line.' He added darkly, 'Which, once that contract has been signed, I shall, with the greatest pleasure, tear up, clause by clause, telling him, at the same time, precisely what I think of his inflated ego, his disgusting habit of smoking cigars at table; stubbing his dog ends into the pâté de foie gras: give him the "up yours" sign; pack my duds, take a taxi to the nearest airport and catch the first available flight to Heathrow. OK?'

'Yeah, Bill, I guess so,' Gerry replied mistily, 'just let me know when you're coming and I'll nip down to the village for a chicken and mushroom pie and a bottle of vin de plonk.'

Doctor Sloane, thin, greying, bespectacled, short in height

and lofty in manner, obviously regarded the appearance of the police on his premises as an affront to his reputation.

'Really, Inspector,' he said when they had been shown into his surgery, 'I fail to understand the reason for this visit. I have already been interviewed by a Detective Inspector Clooney, to whom I made it abundantly clear that I knew nothing whatever pertaining to the unfortunate events at Bagdale Manor, last Christmas.'

Brambell said affably, removing his trilby and placing it on Sloane's desk preparatory to seating himself in a chair opposite, 'What unfortunate events would they be, I wonder?'

'You mean you – don't know?'

'Not in precise detail. Would you care to enlighten me?'

Briggs swallowed a smile. Brambell was leading the witness by the nose, a favourite ploy of his when uncertain of his ground. A bit like a game of follow my leader. Few witnesses could resist being invited to enlighten a senior-ranking police officer, he'd discovered. Sloane was no exception.

He said, self-importantly, 'One knew, of course, that there had been some unpleasantness about a tramp who had come to the house in search of a handout.'

'Really?' Brambell nodded like a mandarin. 'And did he get one?'

'Certainly. Lazlo gave him a ten-pound note and pointed him in the direction of a Salvation Army shelter in Hampstead Village. A generous gesture, in my opinion, typical of Elliot Lazlo, I might add.'

'So you witnessed the transaction?' Brambell asked pleasantly.

'No. No, I didn't. I was upstairs at the time with my fellow guests and Mrs Lazlo, enjoying an aperitif before dinner was served. We were in the drawing room at the time, awaiting our summons to the dining room. Looking forward enormously to a happy, carefree Christmas.'

'Ah yes,' Brambell sighed reflectively, 'I'm fond of Christmas myself. A time of goodwill to all men. My wife and I had friends and relatives to spend Christmas Day with us. A heartwarming occasion, though I couldn't help thinking afterwards that all the preparation beforehand, and cooking lunch for seven people, plus the clearing up afterwards, had perhaps placed too great a strain on my wife, who spent Boxing

Day in bed, as I recall. And she, bless her, was not recovering from a life-threatening illness. Unlike your Christmas house party hostess, Dorothea Lazlo.'

He continued vaguely, 'I am right in thinking that Mrs Lazlo had been desperately ill recently, am I not? As her personal physician, a long standing friend of the Lazlos, didn't it strike you as odd that she was now capable of entertaining, not merely a handful of guests at a Christmas luncheon party, but a houseful of guests at a three-day event? Unless, of course, Doctor Sloane, you knew all along that your Christmas house party hostess was not Dorothea Lazlo, but an impostor?'

Sloane's mouth sagged open momentarily. 'Are you implying,' he demanded hoarsely, 'that I am being accused of misconduct of some kind?'

'Not at all,' Brambell supplied serenely, 'misconduct of "some kind" doesn't enter into it. The misconduct I have in mind is far more specific. I have reason to believe that you were deeply involved in a plot to supplant the bona-fide Dorothea Lazlo with a bogus lookalike version of the real McCoy. Moreover, I have proof positive that a patient of yours, a Mrs Dorothea Sandys, suffering the effects of food poisoning, died in St John the Baptist's Hospital around the time of Dorothea Lazlo's disappearance. All I require from you, Doctor Sloane, is a satisfactory explanation of those events. Well, Doctor, I'm waiting.'

'I haven't the faintest idea what you are talking about,' Sloane blustered. 'I'd have you know that I have been a well-respected member of the medical fraternity for nigh on thirty years! By what right do you question my integrity? How dare you come here to accuse me of malpractice?'

'It's my job,' Brambell reminded him, 'to ask questions. Hopefully to receive satisfactory answers. I also have been a respected member of my profession for nigh on thirty years.' He continued patiently, 'So far as I'm aware, the word "malpractice" has never entered the conversation.' He paused momentarily, then, 'Come now, Doctor Sloane, you're an intelligent man, so am I, so, if you've nothing to hide, simply tell me the truth. I have an open mind at the moment, so let's begin with the well-documented death of the so-called Dorothea Sandys, shall we? Was that really her name? If so didn't it strike you as odd, at the time, that Dorothea Lazlo's former surname was Sandys?'

'Well no! Not really! I regarded it as a mere coincidence!'

Sloane was sweating profusely now, Briggs noted with a kind of grim satisfaction. Obviously the man was lying through his teeth. But Brambell had the measure of him right enough, Briggs realized, anxiously awaiting his senior officer's next move in this fraught situation, correctly anticipating Brambell's decision to remove Sloane to the Yard for further questioning, despite the poor devil's protestations of innocence and his heartfelt plea not to be escorted from his premises by the front door, thus running the gauntlet of a waiting room filled with his patients.

Briggs had never admired Brambell more than when he said quietly, 'Let's use the rear exit, shall we? No use making a public spectacle of a man's humiliation.'

All he said was, 'Don't forget your hat, sir.'

Brambell smiled. 'Thanks, Sergeant,' he replied.

In an interview room at Scotland Yard, Sloane admitted that he had known his Christmas Eve hostess at Bagdale Manor to be an impostor.

'What puzzles me,' Brambell said levelly, 'is the reason why you, a respected member of the medical profession, felt it necessary to go along with the deception.'

'From a sense of loyalty towards old and dear friends of mine,' Sloane replied proudly, 'Dorothea and Elliot Lazlo. Elliot had been worried about his wife's state of health.'

'Why was that?' Brambell enquired mildly.

'She had been complaining of persistent headaches, nausea and loss of balance; symptoms cognizant with those of a brain tumour. As her personal physician, I suggested a brain scan, to which she reluctantly agreed.'

'And the outcome?' Brambell asked.

'Thankfully, the scan proved negative.'

'Then what?'

'I prescribed suitable medication; painkillers, sleeping capsules and so on. She was in a highly strung condition at the time. Her blood-pressure was dangerously high, hence her loss of equilibrium. In short, she was on the verge of a complete physical and mental breakdown, hence my suggestion that she might well benefit from a period of complete rest and quiet at my nursing home in Berkshire.'

'I see,' Brambell nodded. 'Now tell me, Doctor Sloane, what in your opinion was the root cause of Mrs Lazlo's breakdown? Had she for instance got wind of her husband's affair with another woman?'

Sloane stiffened. 'That is uncalled for! Lazlo is devoted to his wife. His one thought was to see her fully restored to health, to have her back home at Bagdale Manor.'

Brambell frowned, 'Meanwhile, he engaged an actress, a lookalike Dorothea, to take her place? An odd thing to do, wouldn't you agree?'

'Not at all, Inspector. Dorothea is a well-known public figure, also a very private person. Lazlo decided, quite correctly in my opinion, to keep news of her illness from the – gutter press. The reason why he agreed to her admission to my sanatorium for the time being.'

'Sanatorium?' Brambell queried. 'A moment ago you referred to your retreat as a nursing home. Do you also treat chronically sick patients: infectious diseases?'

Sloane said uneasily, 'We have a special unit for isolation cases. The grounds are extensive. Why? What's wrong with that?'

Brambell wasn't entirely sure. Perhaps Sloane's uneasiness had rubbed off on to him? He'd pictured a cosy rest home with nurses dispensing cups of bedtime cocoa, plumping pillows, pampering wealthy women temporarily removed from the stress of everday life. Now a different picture entered his mind. Sloane's mention of a special unit, a sanatorium, smacked of something more sinister.

He said, 'Tell me, doctor, do you also have a geriatric unit tucked away in the grounds?'

'Well yes. What of it?' Sloane was up in arms now. 'The units are quite separate from one another, and I have a splendid team of doctors and nurses, well trained and qualified, under my supervision.'

'And was Dorothea Sandys a patient in the geriatric unit?'

'Yes, she was!'

*　　*　　*

168

During a break in the recording, Brambell detailed Briggs to find out about Sloane's set-up in Berkshire, which he had mentally dubbed 'Rancho Notorious'.

'Have a scout round, laddie,' he said, 'paying particular attention to that geriatric unit. Find out the names of the inmates, including any who have popped off recently.'

'Shall I need a search warrant?' Briggs asked.

'Not at this stage,' Brambell told him. 'Just flash your warrant card, and take someone with you. A constable or a WPC. Charm the receptionist. Bound to be a woman. All you're after is information. Find out about a patient called Dorothea Sandys.'

'If she ever existed,' Briggs replied, latching unerringly on to the inspector's train of thought. 'Right, sir, the sooner I get started, the better.'

Brambell grinned. 'If a patient called Dorothea Sandys ever existed, I'll eat my hat!'

On his return to the interview room, Sloane demanded petulantly, 'How much longer am I to be kept here, Inspector Brambell? Am I under arrest? If so, why? On what charge? I've told you everthing I know about Dorothea Lazlo's illness.'

'No, Doctor Sloane,' Brambell assured him calmly, 'you are not under arrest, merely helping the police in their enquiries.' He added patiently, 'I'm prepared to accept that Mrs Lazlo is now receiving the best of care and attention in your Berkshire nursing home. What I cannot fully accept is the sudden death of a geriatric patient of yours, Dorothea Sandys. Tell me, doctor, was that really her name?'

Deeply shaken, Sloane blustered, 'Are you implying that it was not? That I issued a bogus death certificate?'

'That remains to be seen,' Brambell said levelly. 'I hope not, for your sake.'

'But that is a monstrous suggestion!' Sloane was perspiring now, wiping his forehead with a silk hanky from his breastpocket. 'Why should I have done such a thing? For what possible motive?'

Several reasons sprang to Brambell's mind. Coercion, money, a misplaced sense of loyalty, blackmail? Some incident, some misdemeanour in Sloane's past that he wished to keep hidden? But he said nothing. Much depended on Briggs' visit to Berkshire.

The receptionist at the geriatric unit of 'Rancho Notorious' was, as Brambell had predicted, a woman – a veritable Amazon with powerful arm muscles, cropped hair, heavy jowls and teeth like tombstones, who regarded Briggs suspiciously at first until, taking in his tall, broad-shouldered frame, handsome features and abundant dark-brown hair, she gave him the benefit of her 100-watt smile, putting the fear of God into Briggs, who preferred petite women with long curly hair – and fewer teeth.

'My name is Cassidy,' she beamed, 'Miss Constance Cassidy, referred to as "Butch", though I can't think why, can you?'

'No, not off-hand,' Briggs responded kindly. 'Now, the reason I'm here . . .'

Twenty minutes later, having trolled through her computer records, she came up with the information that a patient by the name of Emily Fothergill had died recently of food poisoning. A crabby old creature with a fondness for whelks, mussels, shell fish in general, which figured.

Briggs said desperately, 'But it's a lady named Dorothea Sandys I came to enquire about.'

'Oh, *her*?' Butch shrugged her shoulders dismissively. 'Then you've come to the wrong department. 'She's up yonder in the nursing home. Leastways she was, till she went missing a while back.'

'*Missing?*' Briggs' pulse rate quickened. 'Under what circumstances?'

'How should *I* know? You'd best ask the nursing home staff.' Butch's smile faded along with her hope of a brief physical encounter with the handsome detective sergeant over a cup of coffee in the kitchen behind the desk – always a bit of a tight squeeze. Some fat chance! Now he and his constable sidekick were halfway out of the building.

The nursing home receptionist, self-contained, flat-chested and wearing a wedding ring, to Briggs' relief, confirmed that Mrs Dorothea Sandys had indeed gone missing, inasmuch as she had simply packed her personal belongings and 'done a flit', leaving no forwarding address and without notifying anyone of her intention to vacate her room. Not a very nice thing to do in the receptionist's opinion.

'We were naturally concerned about her disappearance,' the woman continued prissily. 'Nurse Phillips was very upset, when she took in the early morning tea, to find the room empty, the bed unslept in, Mrs Sandys' clothing and toiletries missing.'

'Had you reason to suspect foul play?' Briggs asked intently.

'*Foul play?* No, of course not!' The receptionist appeared shocked. 'This is a nursing home, for heaven's sake, not a prison! Patients are free to come and go as they please!' Curiosity getting the better of her, 'Why? You don't think she was – abducted – do you?'

'Hardly likely,' Briggs assured her. 'We, Constable Green and I, are simply here to enquire into the date of her disappearance and to discover her present whereabouts. The lady may well be suffering from amnesia.' He added charmingly, 'Now, if you'd care to check your records . . .'

Alone in his office later that afternoon, Brambell considered the case so far. Weighing up the pros and cons, thanks to Bert Briggs' discoveries at 'Rancho Notorious' he had formally charged Doctor Sloane with the falsification of a death certificate issued in the name of Dorothea Sandys, not that of Emily Fothergill, a geriatric patient of his who had died of food poisoning in St John's Hospital prior to her hastily arranged funeral and cremation at the Golder's Green Crematorium.

Initially, Sloane had hotly denied the charges levelled against him: perversion of the course of justice; signing a bogus death certificate; implication of his culpability in the disappearance of Dorothea Lazlo from his Berkshire nursing home: booked in there under a false name. That of Dorothea Sandys, not Lazlo.

Then, suddenly, painfully, aware of the weight of evidence stacked against him, overcome with heat and emotion, sweating profusely, the poor devil had broken down and admitted his wrongdoing. Almost, Brambell thought, as if resigning himself to the thought that the strong arm of the law would at least bring relief from the torment of interrogation, a modicum of peace of mind, an acceptance of his fate at the hands of a jury: possibly a prison sentence? Almost certainly an end to his career as a well-respected member of the medical profession. Brambell couldn't help feeling sorry for the man. More sinned against than sinning, in his opinion.

Pursuing his case notes, at least his SOC team had discovered the whereabouts of the bullet fired at Geraldine Frayling that night on her fire-escape landing, he mused gratefully, which, to his satisfaction, had matched the bullet fired into Aubrey Sandys' greatcoat. But who had fired those bullets, and where was the revolver?

A knock came at the door. Briggs poked his head round. 'Still here, sir?' he asked concernedly. 'Anything I can do to help?'

'Since you're here,' Brambell said gratefully, 'sit down, and tell me what you make of this case. Darned if I can make head or tail of it. I still can't figure out why Doc Sloane should have put his career in jeopardy for the sake of a bogus death certificate in respect of Dorothea Sandys, not Lazlo. Why *Sandys*, for Pete's sake?'

Briggs said thoughtfully, 'For what it's worth, I believe that Elliot Lazlo wanted rid of his wife all along, and coerced Doc Sloane into issuing that certificate as a kind of – stop gap.' Warming to his theory, 'After all, the body of Emily Fothergill had been cremated, and if awkward questions were asked of Lazlo re his wife's disappearance, he'd come up smelling of roses, able to prove, beyond a shadow of doubt, that she was merely taking a rest in Sloane's nursing home, under an assumed name.'

'So you see Lazlo as our killer, do you?' Brambell asked doubtfully. 'Well, you could be right. He could have murdered Aubrey Sandys and Annie Scott, but why Rafe Barmby and Alex French? And why the attempted murder of Geraldine Frayling? I'm not even certain that he was in London at that time. He accompanied Marguerite to York, remember, to help wet-nurse that precious son of hers following the murder of Alex French, and they're still there, under surveillance of

172

course. Dancey's keeping a wary eye on the pair of them, as per request I might add.' Brambell tapped his nose and chuckled. 'Old I may be, but I'm not daft. Well, not yet at any rate.'

Briggs said seriously, 'Just a thought, sir, but mightn't this be a good time for a look-see at Bagdale Manor? That missing revolver has to be somewhere, and I'd bet my bottom dollar it belongs to Elliot Lazlo.'

'Good thinking, laddie. I'll request a search warrant right away,' Brambell said, picking up the phone, glad of his sergeant's support and clear-sightedness at the end of what had been a long and difficult day.

'And have you thought, sir,' Briggs continued when the call had been made, 'of the York connection in this case? It struck me as significant that Sandys and French were together in that open prison near York, that Bretton Sandys' garden centre is within spitting distance, Annie Scott's father a signalman at York Station—'

Latching on to Briggs' train of thought, 'Yes, of course,' Brambell interrupted eagerly. 'Moreover, we have proof of a liaison between Carla Sandys and June Scott, the murdered girl's mother. And the murder of Alex French occurred at Sandys' garden centre. But I don't quite see how all this ties in with Elliot Lazlo.'

'You're tired, sir, and hungry I dare say,' Briggs suggested kindly. 'I know I am, so why not call it a day? By the way, I'm taking those folders home with me, just in case there's something we've overlooked so far.'

Briggs was right, Brambell thought, driving homeward, he *was* tired and hungry, in need of tender loving care and the beef stew and dumplings his wife, Jenny, had promised for his supper. Baked dumplings, crisp on top, not flaccid and flabby, drowned in gravy, but standing proud and tall, crowned with Cheddar cheese, all hot and bubbling, served to him on a table in front of the telly, so he could eat and watch *EastEnders* at one and the same time.

Bert Briggs' wife, Polly, had made a shepherd's pie for supper – more taters than meat, she thought wistfully – due to their straitened finances with the kids growing up so fast, in need of new clothes, money for school outings, football gear and so on. They were upstairs in their rooms now, doing their homework. Good kids, nice kids; Billy the spit and image of his dad, Grace a small facsimile of herself. If only she could afford to surprise Bert with a rump steak and chips supper once in a while, plus a bottle of wine, not that he'd care one way or t'other. Far too wrapped up in his job, that was Bert's trouble. And if he didn't soon come home to eat his supper, the shepherd's pie would be ruined, burned to a cinder, the gravy all dried up, and serve him right. Then, ah, there was his key in the lock. Joyously, she hurried into the hall to greet him.

Not that Polly wore her heart on her sleeve, far from. 'Huh,' she said chirpily, 'so you've made it home at last, have you? And what, may I ask, is that rubbish you've brought in with you?' Glaring at the carrier bags he'd dumped at the foot of the stairs.

'Oh that? Just some folders I promised to take a look at later, after supper,' he said amiably. Sniffing the air, 'Hmm, something smells good. What is it? I'm starving.'

'Anyone would think they don't feed you in that canteen of yours,' Polly said reprovingly, leading the way to the kitchen.

'They don't always get the chance. Take today, for instance. All I had time for was a sandwich and a cup of coffee, the reason why I brought the bags with me. The old boy asked me to take a squint at them. He thinks they might contain something we've overlooked, which I very much doubt, to be honest.'

But he was wrong. Glancing through the folders after supper, when Polly had done the washing-up and he'd been upstairs to say goodnight to the kids, suddenly, 'Well, I'll be blowed,' he uttered excitedly, 'I think I've found something important! I'll ring Brambell right away!'

'That you won't,' Polly protested reasonably. 'The poor man's probably fast asleep in bed. And that's where we should be right now. Talk about being married to a job! Well, you're married to me, Bert Briggs, and don't you forget it!'

'As if,' Bert murmured contentedly, switching off the landing light and following his wife to their bedroom.

Nineteen

B rambell rang Gerry early next morning, at Barney's Hamburger Joint.

'Everything all right with you?' he enquired anxiously.

'Well, so far nobody had tried shinning up the fire escape again,' she said resignedly. 'I'm still in one piece, but Bill's stuck in Stuttgart and, quite frankly, Inspector, I'd like to go home, to get on with my work. I need something to occupy my mind, not to mention my – carcase!'

Brambell chuckled, 'In which case, why not head in the direction of my office? I have news for you! Before ten o'clock, if possible.'

'I'll be there at nine,' Gerry assured him. 'Thanks, Inspector!'

Rising to his feet when Gerry entered his office, extending his hand in greeting, Brambell said warmly, 'It's good to see you again, m'dear. Thanks for coming. Please, sit down. Now, where was I? Ah yes, the good news is that you were right about Rafe Barmby's folders, one of which contained the – massing link – so to speak. The name of someone closely connected with our investigations, which has proved quite an eye-opener to say the least.'

'Oh? *Whose* name?' Gerry asked eagerly. When Brambell told her, 'But that's ridiculous!' Gerry exclaimed fervently. 'June Scott wouldn't hurt a fly! Arthur Scott, yes, but not his wife! You must be mistaken, Inspector!'

Brambell said gently, 'I'm not for one moment suggesting that Mrs Scott was involved in the murder of her own daughter, or that of Aubrey Sandys. It does seem significant, however, that Mrs Scott's maiden name was Barmby, that Rafe Barmby was, in fact, her brother. Let's just say that the relationship between them warrants further investigation, and leave it at that for the time being, shall we?'

'And to think that *I* suggested taking a closer look at those folders,' Gerry uttered bleakly. 'Poor June Scott! Such a downtrodden woman with that beast of a husband to contend with!' She added vehemently, 'If *his* name had cropped up in those damned folders, I shouldn't have been the least bit surprised! The man's a – *monster*!'

Briggs entered the office at that moment, knocking briefly beforehand. 'Ah, good morning, Miss Frayling,' he said cheerfully, then, 'Ready when you are, sir. The search warrant's in order and the search team's foregathered on the car park, awaiting the word go.'

'Thanks, Briggs, I'll be with you directly.' Brambell put on his hat and coat. Gerry stood up. 'Where are we going?' she asked eagerly. 'I had my garden shed searched last year, though I don't suppose Inspector Clooney needed a search warrant for a shed, since he didn't know it had been vandalized at the time. He'd come to find out who had tried to smother me the night before, and he didn't need a search warrant for that neither.'

Aware that she was babbling, she added dejectedly, 'Me and my big mouth! You don't want me to go with you, I guess, to wherever you're going. Where *are* you going to, by the way? A – vice den in Soho?'

'Nothing so bizarre,' Brambell admitted. 'To Bagdale Manor, as a matter of fact, in search of a missing revolver for one thing. In short, hard evidence of any kind to tie in Elliot Lazlo with the murder of Aubrey Sandys, Annie Scott and possibly his wife, Dorothea. You see, Gerry, the bullet fired at you that night on the fire escape matched the one found in the body of Aubrey Sandys. Now, Dorothea Lazlo has gone missing, and – well, need I say more?'

'Just one thing, Inspector,' Gerry responded urgently. 'Please say you'll let me go with you to Bagdale Manor. What I mean is, I *do* have a vested interest in this case. I want that revolver found as much as you do. Maybe even more. And I promise faithfully to keep my mouth shut and my eyes open, if only—'

'All right, Gerry, you win,' Brambell conceded, against his better judgement. 'But no heroics, no outbursts, remember. No meddling, no interference with the men on duty.'

'As if!' Gerry smiled broadly. 'After all, I *am* an engaged woman!'

Walking across the car park with Gerry beside him, Brambell suddenly felt more confident, more relaxed in the company of a shrewd, sharp-eyed, sharp-witted young woman with the heart of a lion, capable of instilling a sense of fun and excitement into an otherwise mundane job of work. A policeman's lot was not always a happy one, in his experience, but it seemed so today, despite the wind, rain and snow flurries gusting across the car park.

Mrs Brook, the Lazlos' housekeeper, reacted furiously to the incursion of Brambell's search team in the absence of her employers. 'This is monstrous,' she protested violently. 'By what right—?'

'By right of this search warrant, ma'am,' Briggs reminded her, producing the document for her perusal. 'Now, tell me, who else, apart from yourself, is resident here at the moment?'

'The cook and a parlourmaid,' Mrs Brook supplied unwillingly. 'The master and mistress are away at the moment. Even so, there's work to be done, mouths to be fed, the house to keep clean, and it's my duty to attend to such matters in their absence. I'd risk losing my job otherwise.'

Her glance falling suddenly on Gerry, 'What's *she* doing here?' the woman demanded hoarsely. 'She's been here before, stirring up trouble, poking her nose in where it wasn't wanted. Actually pushing her way past me when I tried to stop her, the cheeky young madam!'

Keeping her lips firmly buttoned, recalling her promise to keep her eyes open, her mouth shut, Gerry made no reply. She simply stared, momentarily, at the housekeeper, then solemnly closing one eye, and keeping it closed in a travesty of a wink, feeling a bit like Admiral Lord Nelson without his eye patch, she slid past Mrs Brook with a murmured, 'Excuse me,' resisting a strong desire to kick the woman's shins, en passant, relying on the wink to reduce the housekeeper to a nervous wreck.

This was a big rambling house, Gerry thought, trying hard not to meddle. The housekeeper and her minions had elected to

177

stay in the kitchen. Perhaps they were brewing up cauldrons of coffee, she thought wistfully, and baking gingerbread men for the search team. It must be a devil of a job, searching for evidence, and not knowing what exactly and whether or not you'd found it, not knowing what you were looking for in the first place. Except, of course, a revolver, a gun licence or a dead body.

Shivering slightly, recalling her alter ego Virginia Vale, her imagination going into overdrive, called upon to hide a revolver, where would *she* have put it? Gerry wondered. Certainly not in a drawer or a wall-safe. A shrewd cookie like Virginia would, more than likely, have stuffed it inside a chicken, duck or turkey destined for a deep-freeze unit.

Feeling like a spare tyre in a man-size white overall, SOC boots, and a pair of rubber gloves, the obligatory apparel of a research team, glancing out of Lazlo's study window at the walled garden beyond, Gerry saw members of the team moving slowly, concertedly, examining every inch of the ground as they wended their way through the barriers of overgrown bushes, tangled briars and the various other obstacles impeding their progress. And, ye gods, she thought bemusedly, how come any garden, much less that of Elliot Lazlo, had fallen into such a state of neglect? She'd heard of wildlife sanctuaries before, but this was nothing short of ridiculous. A breeding ground for rats and mice, more like! But *why*? Unless Lazlo was less well off than he cared to admit? A – serial killer to boot? Gerry wondered. Frankly, she wouldn't be in the least surprised if he were, a towering bully of a man, bad-tempered, egotistical and brutal to the nth degree, recalling her brief encounter with the man, in his study, when she, Gerry, had believed for one awful moment that he was about to drive a clenched fist into her fizzog! Had he done so, she might well have landed up in hospital. Worse still, in a shallow grave in a spinney on Hampstead Heath, with a black eye and a bullet hole in her anorak.

Turning away from the window, she encountered Inspector Brambell. 'A penny for your thoughts,' he said.

'What? *All* of them? I wouldn't know where to begin!' Gerry smiled wanly. 'Right, well since you ask, that garden for starters, if you could call it a garden. It looks more like a – rubbish dump. As for this house, I wouldn't live in it for all the tea in China!' She shivered involuntarily. 'There's something sinister about it, an evil atmosphere. All those long creaking corridors, empty rooms. Oh, I know I write about such things, and I shan't forget in a hurry "Black Gull House" in Robin Hood's Bay, where I damn near met my Maker, last October, during the 'Antiques Murder' case, but it couldn't hold a candle to Bagdale Manor.' She paused momentarily, then, 'Sorry, Inspector,' she said apologetically, 'there I go again, letting my imagination run riot, as usual.'

Brambell said persuasively, 'Sit down, m'dear. High time I filled you in on details of our present inquiry from beginning to end. Not that I'm fully congnizant with all of them myself, so far. Frankly, this is the most complicated case I've come across in my entire career. So many dead ends, nothing by way of substantial evidence apart from a forged death certificate, the bizarre business of the Dorothea impostor, the seemingly motiveless murder of Rafe Barmby. Now, to crown all, the disappearance of Dorothea Lazlo.' He sighed deeply.

'Forged death certificate?' Gerry frowned. 'I didn't know about that. Whose death certificate?'

When the tale had been told, 'But surely,' she said eagerly, 'doesn't that prove Lazlo's complicity in the murder of Aubrey Sandys?'

'Up to a point, but not conclusively,' Brambell said dejectedly. 'True enough, I could arrest him on a perversion of justice charge, but that's not what I'm after. I need hard, irrefutible evidence against him to nail him to the murder of Aubrey Sandys, hence my decision to issue a search warrant in respect of Bagdale Manor, hoping against hope that the evidence needed would come to light.' He added wearily, 'Another dead end. No sign of a revolver, a gun licence. No incriminating letters, no overdrawn bank statements, just overdue bills. No secret diaries. In fact, sweet damn all!'

'Bills? What kind of bills?' Gerry asked intently.

'Well, just household bills. You know, bills for gas and electricity; phone bills, butchers' and grocers' bills; repair bills; Income Tax, Council Tax. Why do you ask?'

'Dunno really, just an idea! I'd like to take a gander at the butcher's bill, if possible.' Gerry smiled disarmingly. 'Not that

I want to meddle, Inspector. God forbid! But there's no harm in *looking*, is there?'

'None at all.' Brambell chuckled. 'Lazlo's bills are over yonder, in the top left-hand drawer of his desk. I just wish I knew what you're up to, that's all. Here, let me help.' Spreading out Lazlo's household bills on his desk top for Gerry's perusal, Brambell stood aside and waited. For what exactly, he wasn't entirely certain. Possibly his honorary SOC assistant had spotted something his bona-fide SOC associates had overlooked?

Eventually, straightening up from her scrutiny of Lazlo's current butcher's account, 'Yeah, just as I thought,' Gerry nodded. 'A fourteen-pound turkey, a couple of Aylesbury ducks, lamb chops, smoked bacon, liver, Cumberland sausages, steak, eggs and a rib of beef. We can discount the latter, destined for the refrigerator. I'd go for the turkey if I were you, Inspector, or the Aylesbury ducks. How long is a revolver, by the way? Nine, ten inches? Well, whatever, I'd have them defrosted right away, if I were you.' She grinned. 'Ten to one you'll find the missing revolver in the turkey. I mean to say, who, in their right mind, would order a fourteen-pound turkey in the middle of February? Unless, of course, they had something to hide? A nine-inch-long revolver, for instance? Give or take a couple of inches!

'Hm, wonder who does the ordering? The housekeeper said there were mouths to be fed, but they must be pretty big mouths. No wonder Lazlo can't afford to have his grass cut. I wonder how long Mrs Brook has been here? I'll bet any money that she, the cook and the parlourmaid all fetched up here around the same time as Annie Scott, or just before.'

Thinking aloud, 'Could they be pals of the impostor? Out-of-work actors? Perhaps they'd all been together in Agatha Christie's *A Pocketful of Rye* or *Murder on the Orient Express*. Hey, now what have I done wrong, Inspector? Why the funny look? Where are you going?'

'To the kitchen,' Brambell said hoarsely. 'How long does it take to defrost a turkey?'

'Why? Are you feeling peckish?' Gerry asked, tongue in cheek.

As Brambell headed for the door, 'Hey, wait for me!'

Hurrying after him, the kitchen would be a darn sight warmer, she figured. Besides, she wanted to see the housekeeper's reaction to the defrosting of the turkey. Presumably there'd be a microwave? Whether or not a turkey would fit into it, she wasn't quite sure. If not, the SOC team would have to use a blow torch or a chainsaw. Failing that, they could always stuff it in a hot oven and await results. And if the missing revolver wasn't there? What then?

Me and my big mouth, she thought despondently, when will I ever learn to keep it shut? Imagining the expression of contempt on Mrs Brook's face when giblets, not a revolver, was discovered in the turkey's innards, she felt inclined to 'fold her tents, like the Arabs, and as silently steal away', before the final denouement of herself as an all-fired idiot. And yet, being Gerry, with curiosity getting the better of her, she just had to stay and watch the defrosting of the wretched bird, in the kitchen microwave, by her SOC associates. To her infinite relief, when the turkey was thawed out enough to handle, sticking a hand into its gizzards, Inspector Brambell withdrew, not giblets, but a deadly weapon. Elliot Lazlo's revolver, in a plastic bag, along with his missing gun licence.

To Gerry's amazement, a ripple of applause from the SOC team, directed towards herself, ran round the room. And, 'Well done, Gerry,' Brambell was saying, sounding as pleased as Punch. 'Now, thanks to you, I have the evidence I needed to tie in Elliot Lazlo with the murder of Aubrey Sandys. Many congratulations, m'dear.'

Frowning slightly, deep in thought, Gerry replied, hesitantly, bugged by a gut feeling that something, somewhere along the line, was badly wrong, 'I'm sorry, Inspector, but I think you're barking up the wrong tree. What if someone else's fingerprints are on that revolver?'

'Go on, Gerry, enlighten me. Whose fingerprints have you in mind?' Brambell asked quietly.

'Marguerite Lascelles's,' Gerry said. 'I could be wrong, of course, but my belief is that she had far more reason to kill Aubrey Sandys than he had. After all, Sandys had, presumably, come to Bagdale Manor last Christmas Eve to demand money. Marguerite would have been angry, goaded past bearing by his demands, seeing his presence as a threat to her own and

Lazlo's security, especially since they had a great deal to hide. The likelihood is that she picked up a weapon of some kind, a poker perhaps, and cracked Sandys on the head with it. He fell to the floor, groaning, as well he might, the poor devil, at which point, she helped Lazlo to carry Sandys to the boot of his car. Together, they scooped out a grave for him on Hampstead Heath, then Marguerite, who had taken the revolver from a drawer in Lazlo's desk, fired a bullet into Sandys' heart to make certain he was dead.

'A consummate professional actress, Marguerite would experience little or no difficulty whatever in assuming her role as the calm, somewhat forgetful mistress of the house. Not so Elliot Lazlo, with a guilt complex a mile wide, fearing the discovery of Sandys' body. When that happened, and Detective Inspector Clooney turned up on the doorstep asking questions about his ownership of a gun, and the tramp who'd appeared on the kitchen doorstep on Christmas Eve, naturally he denied all knowledge of the tramp, and the ownership of a revolver, to the extent of a signed statement to that effect. I know because he told me so himself, the day I came here to quiz him about Annie Scott's disappearance.'

Tears filled Gerry's eyes, her voice faltered. She said haltingly, 'I'm sorry, Inspector. If you don't mind, I'd like to go home now. And I do mean home, back to my eyrie in Hampstead. Maggie and Barney will understand why. You see, I need to be alone for a while, to ring Bill, to sleep in my own bed, to think my own thoughts – to cry if I want to!'

'Then you do just that,' Brambell nodded his approval. 'I'll get Briggs to drive you home. Meanwhile, I'll be wanting a word or two with the servants, especially the cook and the housekeeper. An interesting theory of yours, Gerry, their being associated with acting, I mean. Food for thought! A possible link between Aubrey Sandys, Marguerite, Rafe Barmby, Colm Carmody, the Simpkins and the film director, Adrian Sweeting, I shouldn't wonder.'

He smiled warmly at his SOC team associate, then, 'Now, off home with you,' he adjured her briskly, realizing that the poor kid was all in, for the time being, in need of direction, not praise for a job well done. 'Have a good hot bath, a boiled egg, a couple of slices of toast, a nice cup of tea, then snuggle down in bed and have a good night's sleep. Promise?'

'Yeah,' Gerry smiled, blinking away her tears. 'Thanks, Inspector. I promise!'

Tiredness had struck Gerry suddenly, amidships. If only Bill were here now, she thought, to take care of her. Her present mood, she realized, had to do with the evil atmosphere of Bagdale Manor, that sinister walled garden which might well contain the mortal remains of Dorothea Lazlo.

At home in her eyrie, wandering the rooms like a lost soul, she went over and over in her mind the events of the past few hours, restless and alone, recalling those SOC figures prodding their way through the undergrowth of the walled garden in search of the rotting corpse of a once beautiful woman, an artist, par excellence, whose exquisite paintings could never be reprised or surpassed by anyone else, save, perhaps, by those paintings of moonlight by John Atkinson Grimshaw. Not that Dorothea Lazlo had painted moonlight, but rain on windowpanes; rain falling on cobblestones, by night; effulgent lamplight on rain-soaked lilacs; had done so exquisitely, a consummate mistress of her art, revealing a gentleness of spirit somehow captured on canvas. A rare talent, an innate understanding of nature and the simple beauty of the quiet, ordinary values of everyday life.

Looking out of Lazlo's study window, earlier that day, seeing the outline of Dorothea's studio through flurries of windswept rain and sleet, Gerry had longed to enter that building to bask in the warmth of Dorothea's shadowy presence in that spiritual home of hers. Not in the company of a search team, but alone – as she was alone now, in her eyrie, aware of the rising wind rattling the windows, and pouring rain driving against the panes.

She had, at least, the consolation of knowing that Lazlo's revolver was now in the hands of forensic experts at Scotland Yard, being examined for fingerprints, no longer a threat to her peace of mind so far as her own security was concerned. And yet . . . Impossible to feel entirely secure on a night like this, with the wind prowling about the house liked a lost soul in torment. Unlike herself to feel so nervous, so jittery, Gerry berated herself sharply, remembering her promise to Inspector Brambell to make herself a nice cup of tea, boil herself an egg, and have a good night's sleep. So why the hell didn't she do just that?

Knowing damn well why not, because, despite her physical tiredness, she couldn't help wondering what had become of Dorothea Lazlo. If she were alive or dead? And she was worrying about Bill, in the wilds of Stuttgart with a megalomaniac author with a penchant for Liquorice Allsorts for company, while trying to piece together the complexities of the case facing Inspector Brambell, without success.

How June Scott fitted into the picture, Gerry couldn't begin to imagine, curious that she had never mentioned a brother living in the London area. Presumably they hadn't been close? Families often weren't, and she should know, having lost touch with her own immediate family some time ago, with whom she had never seen eye to eye, nor they with her. Of course June's brother, Rafe, had been alive and well at the time of the Scotts' visit to London to arrange Annie's funeral. Possibly the poor woman had been too upset about her daughter to spare a thought for her brother?

Equally curious, Gerry considered, placing a pan of water on the cooker to boil in readiness for her suppertime egg, the strong theatre connections with the impostor, Marguerite Lascelles, a former actress closely associated with Aubrey Sandys, by whom she had borne an illegitimate child, Bretton Sandys, the apple of her eye, according to Inspector Brambell, who had acquainted Gerry with the facts of the case so far in Lazlo's study, prior to the discovery of the revolver in a thawed-out turkey, and her own – from the top of her head suggestion – that the housekeeper, the cook and the parlourmaid might be members of Equity, filling in time between one engagement and the next.

Lord, she thought, what a cast list of suspects, popping an egg into boiling water: Elliot Lazlo; his mistress Marguerite; Adrian Sweeting, the film director; a pile of actors whose names were unfamiliar to her, the Simpkins and Colm Carmody, until Brambell had identified them during his explanatory dissertation in Lazlo's study as the top-floor tenants of the house in which Rafe Barmby had met his end; not to mention the nefarious Doctor Sloane and his faked death certificate, Bretton Sandys and his wife, Carla, at present under suspicion of having murdered Sandys' business partner, Alex French. Last but not least, June Scott, and more than likely, three female members of Agatha Christie's *A Pocketful of Rye*.

Poor Inspector Brambell, Gerry thought compassionately, as the egg described circles in the rapidly boiling water, as if begging to be lifted out of the pan.

Suddenly the phone rang! Bill's voice invaded her solitude. 'Where are you?' she asked shakily. 'At Heathrow? You'll be home in half an hour? Oh, Bill, how wonderful! What's for supper? At a rough guess, hard-boiled-egg sandwiches!'

Twenty

H e'd walked into the house, lean, handsome and glowing, with wet hair, a smile like a sunburst, carrying his travel bag in one hand, a bottle of champagne and a bouquet of red roses in the other.

'For me? Oh, how lovely! What are we celebrating?' Gerry asked.

'Hard-boiled egg sandwiches?' He laughed. Kissing her soundly, 'What happened to the chicken and mushroom pie you promised me? In any case, why are you here? I thought you'd be at Barney's. I rang there first. Maggie said you'd gone out early to Scotland Yard: had rung up to say you'd come home.' Regarding Gerry intently, 'Is everything all right?'

'It is now,' she said. 'Why? Don't I look all right?'

'Frankly, no, love. You look – worried. What's wrong, Gerry? You can tell me.'

'I'm just a bit tired, that's all,' she confessed. 'I've had a strange kind of day, helping the police with their enquiries.'

'Ye gods!' Bill asked, tongue in cheek. 'On what charge? Breaking and entering? Manslaughter? Parking on double yellow lines? Loitering with intent? Balling up traffic in the Old Kent Road?'

'No, of course not! This isn't a joke, Bill! I've been at Bagdale Manor all day, as part of a search team to discover the whereabouts of a missing revolver and – a dead body. We found the revolver. I just pray to God that the team will prove unsuccessful in finding the body of Dorothea Lazlo.'

'Oh, Gerry love, I'm so sorry. I had no idea! Please, forgive me? Give me a few minutes to slip out of these wet things and dry my hair, then you can tell me all about it.'

'Thanks, Bill.' Gerry's world had steadied suddenly on its axis. Putting the roses in water, the champagne in the fridge, what a homecoming for the poor darling, she thought: hard-boiled egg sandwiches! Surely she could do better than that? Risking frostbite, she rummaged through the freezer compartment to find a pack of smoked salmon, a bag of prawns and a carton of cod fillets.

When Bill came down thirty minutes later, she was standing self-consciously, near the kitchen table with its centrepiece of roses, presiding over plates of quickly defrosted smoked salmon, melba glasses containing prawns in Hellman's Mayonnaise, with a smidgin of hard-boiled egg, and the cod pieces, which did not need defrosting, serving their sentence in a hot oven alongside goodly portions of oven chips. There were also crusty bread rolls, warm from the oven, on the table, a slab of butter, a carton of Philadelphia cheese spread, gleaming cutlery, pristine damask napkins, and champagne glasses.

Deeply touched, crossing the threshold, taking Gerry in his arms, Bill said mistily, 'Know what? You'll make some lucky man a damn fine wife, one of these days!'

Realizing exactly what he meant, Gerry said huskily, 'So what will you be doing a month from today? Apart from getting married, I mean?'

Holding her close, 'Me in a flat cap and braces?' he asked teasingly.

'Whatever turns you on!' Gerry responded happily. 'So you'd best book that honeymoon in Budleigh Salterton, hadn't you? Unless, of course, you've Wigan in mind? Bridlington, Halifax or Nether Wallop?'

'Wherever,' Bill replied merrily, 'just as long as I'm with you! Now, let's pop the cork of the champagne, shall we? This really calls for a celebration!' Then, sniffing the air, 'Is something burning, by the way?'

'Oh God, the cod!' Making a dash for the oven, 'I'd forgotten all about it!' Gerry wailed. Opening the oven door to reveal the kizzened cod fillets and the blackened oven chips: 'I'm sorry, Bill, I really meant to give you a meal to remember.'

Bill laughed. Pouring the champagne, he said lightheartedly, 'You've certainly done that, my love! Oh, forget about the fish! Let's just raise a toast to the future, shall we? Yours and mine? To our being together always, from here to eternity!

Come hell or high water. Till hell freezes over. Till "All the seas gang dry"?' He added drily, tongue in cheek, 'Where is Nether Wallop, by the way? I've never heard of it before!'

'Oh, never mind, I couldn't care less where we go, just as long as I can sign the hotel register "Mrs William Bentine", and flash my wedding ring in the face of the receptionist,' Gerry said blissfully. She added suspiciously, 'I take it you have a hotel in mind? Not a back-street boarding house or a youth hostel?'

'No, not exactly,' Bill confessed, 'a railway carriage, aboard the Orient Express, en route to Venice, is what I had in mind.'

'The *Orient Express*?' The expression of joy on Gerry's face was something that Bill would never forget if he lived to be a hundred. 'Oh, Bill, how wonderful! How marvellous!' Her eyes sparkled. 'Venice: gondolas, St Mark's Square; gondoliers singing "O Sole Mio"; moonlight on the Grand Canal, and you – above all *you*! Being bossy and over-protective, I shouldn't wonder; speaking fluent Italian to the waiters. I've always wanted to sleep aboard a train. Can I have the upper bunk?' Then, 'Oh lord! What about Bruno?'

'Bruno?' Bill appeared startled. 'Who the hell's he? Now see here, darling, I'm a tolerant man as you well know, but if you're thinking in terms of a ménage à trois, forget it!' His lips twitched upwards in a smile. 'Of course Bruno could sleep in the lower bunk and I could spend the night standing in the corridor. Seems hardly fair, though, since he has twice as many legs as me!'

'Oh, Bill, you remembered! Poor Annie Scott loved that dog. He's been in custody, but he's ours if we want him. We *do* want him, don't we?'

'No home should be without a dog called Bruno.' Bill nodded sagely. 'I might ask him to be my best man. When shall we collect him? Tomorrow?'

'Yes *please*!' Gerry glowed. 'Course, he'll need a basket, bowls, Bonios, a bean-bag, blankets, a warm winter coat, lots of toys and tins of dog food, a new collar and lead. Oh lord!' Gerry's glow diminished, remembering that Annie had been strangled to death with the creature's last lead.

Bill said tenderly, 'I know what you're thinking, but try not to. Let's concentrate on the future, not the past, on giving Bruno a new home, lots of tender loving care of the kind Annie gave him. Carry on where she left off, so to speak. Agreed? The last thing I want is unhappy memories to come uppermost whenever you clip Bruno's new lead to his collar. In which case, I'd sooner he stayed where he is.'

'Fair enough,' Gerry conceded. 'It's just that the past *is* uppermost in my mind at the moment. Especially so today. Watching that search team, up to their ankles in wet earth, examining every inch of ground for a dead body, knocked the stuffing out of me. The reason why I came home. I just needed to be alone for a while, to get my thoughts in order. Then you turned up out of the blue, and I didn't want to be alone any more. You understand, Bill, don't you?'

Bill said, 'Look, darling, let's have supper, shall we, then finish the champagne in the drawing room? If you need to talk, I'm a pretty good listener, though I say so as shouldn't!' He added contritely, 'Sorry, love, I'm still a bit in the clouds about our forthcoming wedding.'

And so, later, in the drawing room, Gerry recounted the story of the case confronting Inspector Brambell, including the bizarre details of the faked death certificate, Dorothea Lazlo's disappearance, and the discovery of Lazlo's revolver in the gizzard of a fourteen-pound turkey.

'Ye gods,' Bill uttered, when she had finished speaking, 'no wonder you're upset, you poor kid! Talk about an Edgar Allen Poe scenario! Why the hell didn't you send for me? I'd have dropped Klaus Winterhalten like a hot potato!'

'I didn't want to worry you,' Gerry confessed. 'I know how much your business means to you; the kudos attached to netting a multimillionaire author as a client. Be honest, Bill, how would you have felt if I'd rung up begging you to come home? If I'd told you that someone had taken a potshot at me, and missed? After all, why make a mountain from a molehill? That's not my style, Bill, and you know it! Well, I'm not exactly the clinging vine type, am I?'

'No, I guess not,' Bill conceded thoughtfully, 'though I wouldn't mind being clung to once in a while.' He grinned wryly. 'The way you clung to me during the final stages of the "Antiques Murders", remember?'

189

'No. Did I really? What did I say? "Kiss me, Hardy"?'

'Nothing so romantic,' Bill reminded her. 'Your exact words, as I recall, were, "What the hell took you so long?".'

They talked until the early hours, about Bruno, the wedding, their honeymoon trip to Venice: the wedding reception, who and who not to invite. The fewer people the better, they agreed. Both wanted a quiet wedding. Exchanging ideas, Gerry said she'd really like organ music and lots of flowers, preferably roses and carnations. No hymns, just music; a touch of Tchaikovsky's theme for 'Romeo and Juliet'; Elgar's 'Chanson d'Amour'; Debussy's 'Claire de Lune'. And she'd love to invite Detective Inspector Brambell, Detective Sergeant Briggs, and their respective spouses, to the wedding.

'Sounds fine to me, love,' Bill responded happily. 'How about the reception?'

'Why not here?' Gerry supplied eagerly, conjuring up in her mind's eye a long, damask-covered table near the bay window, set with smoked-salmon sandwiches, chicken and mushroom vol-au-vents, fruit and green salads, a wedding cake, champagne and caviar. Ah, bliss!

'Shall you invite your mother and sister to the wedding?' Gerry asked. 'They'd be welcome to stay here, if so. There's room and to spare. And how about your best man, just in case Bruno turns down the offer?'

'Well, there's an old university chum of mine,' Bill mused. 'Not that we've seen much of each other lately, but we've kept in touch. A really nice guy, a nuclear physicist by profession. I'll contact him first thing tomorrow morning.'

'Bill darling, this *is* tomorrow morning,' Gerry reminded him.

Detective Chief Inspector Dancey of the York Constabulary had rung DCI Brambell, in his Scotland Yard office, at nine thirty that morning, to discuss developments in the Alex French murder inquiry.

Unfortunately, due to the lack of substantiative evidence linking Bretton and Carla Sandys to the murder, he had been bound by law to release them. In any case, he continued, Mrs June Scott had, albeit reluctantly, admitted that she and Carla Sandys had been together, on the night of the murder, at the